Nightingale

Nightingale

Susan May Warren

Summerside Press™
Minneapolis 55438
www.summersidepress.com
Nightingale

ISBN 978-1-60936-025-2

Scripture references are from the following sources:
The Holy Bible, King James Version (KJV).

All characters are fictional. Any resemblances to actual people are purely coincidental.

Cover design by Chris Gilbert | www.studiogearbox.com

Cover image of nurse: Steve Gardner/ShootPW.com
Cover Image of farm: 123rf.com

Interior design by Müllerhaus Publishing Group | www.mullerhaus.net

Summerside Press™ is an inspirational publisher offering fresh, irresistible books to uplift the heart and engage the mind.

Printed in USA.

EPIGRAPH

For your Glory, Lord.

DEDICATION

For my children who delight my heart,
and my husband, who knows me and loves me anyway.

ACKNOWLEDGMENTS

God blessed me with so many "Nightingales" for this story. My deepest gratitude goes to the following people for their assistance in creating this story.

Sarah May Warren, who wrote the song that is woven throughout the book. Your talent takes my breath away.

Susan Downs, dear friend and amazing editor. Thank you for believing in me.

Ellen Taver, another dear friend and amazing line editor. Thank you for knowing exactly how to tame my words.

Rachel Hauck, writing partner and best friend who is always on the other end of the phone with answers to, "what do I do next?" Thank you for your faithfulness and prayers.

Harry Kraus , M.D. Thank you for helping me sound like a medic.

Jeannette Kelly, who graciously gave me a tour of the Reedsburg Hospital and let me quiz her for two hours about life in WWII. Your insights were invaluable.

Donna Hoffman and her family at Parkview B&B in Reedsburg. Thank you for making Reedsburg (Roosevelt) come to life and for your wonderful hospitality and research!

The Library staff in Reedsburg, WI, for helping me gather information about the local hospital and POW camp."

PART 1

Good night my dear,
You must never fear—
For your love is here,
And she'll hide you from everything.

'cuz you, my dear,
You're my everything,
You're the song I sing
When my nights are starless.

CHAPTER 1

Given a different day, a different hour, she might have jumped with him. That thought, perhaps, shook Esther most of all.

Two hours before Charlie Fadden perched himself on the edge of the top floor of the Roosevelt Mercy Hospital, Esther Lange had fed him cookies and beat him soundly in a game of gin rummy.

He'd taken the cookies, smiled at her with eyes that appeared lucid, and declared that she couldn't possibly beat him in poker, if she dared to play, and what book was she reading to the patient in bed number six, because he had a few questions himself.

Thornton Wilder. *The Bridge of San Luis Rey.*

She understood his question. Why did unexplainable events happen to the innocent?

Perhaps that particular piece of conversation accounted for why she found him on the roof with the biting wind pasting his flimsy army-issue pajamas to his skeleton, staring out over the blanketed town of Roosevelt. Still, she should have seen the desperation rising in his eyes, right?

Another moment she longed to snatch back, replay.

Somehow she had to learn how to stop living with one eye over her shoulder. Or she'd end up on the roof, like Charlie.

A full moon and the splatter of stars along the Milky Way illuminated the GI, his hands whitened on his crutches, staring into the clear midnight. He glanced over his shoulder at her with a wild-eyed fury. "Get away."

Esther drew a breath from where she crouched near the chimney, her fingers digging into the brittle cement, the petroleum odor of the tar roof curdling her nose. Her bare legs prickled against the lick of the night air.

"I can't do that, you know. I'm here to help you."

"There ain't no help for me." He turned away, his shoulders rigid.

She glanced past him, measuring the distance to the ground below.

The blackout curtains washed the town into the milky darkness—the Queen Anne–style homes, the bungalow "box houses," purchased once upon a time from Sears Roebuck and Company, the stately colonials, the few Victorians with their steep-roofed towers and ornamented gables—like Caroline's boardinghouse, all nested between the budding oaks, maples, and elms, the balsam firs, and occasional cottonwoods, the sidewalks that cordoned off Locust, Park, and Walnut streets. A gentle town, filled with hardy German immigrants, the kind that sent their boys to war in the land of their ancestors.

Her gaze tripped over Judge and Mrs. Hahn's three-story French Empire monstrosity, with the mansard roof that sat like a cap upon the house, the round windows' eyes despising the peasantry along Pine Street. Above it all, the twin spires of the Lutheran church parted the night.

And as if it were a woman in repose, watching the doings of the Wisconsin hamlet, the dark shadow of the Baraboo range lounged along the horizon.

What it took for Charlie to drag his shattered body out of the second-story convalescent ward, down the hall to the roof access closet, up the ten-foot ladder, and out to the crisp, fluorescent night, well... Despair made a person lose herself sometimes.

Charlie, for sure, had left too much of himself on the beaches of Normandy.

Her feet scuffled as she stood, but Charlie didn't move, as if contemplating freedom.

Of course Esther should tell him not to jump.

Of course she should scream that life was worth living. Really.

Of course she should remind him that he couldn't fly, and a nearly three-story plunge wouldn't release him from his wounds.

But the words lodged in her throat.

Because PFC Charlie Fadden was right. Up here on top of Roosevelt Mercy Hospital, flying seemed downright congenial.

Even triumphant.

Especially with the stars swelling against the velvet black of midnight, so resplendent that she could probably pluck one from its mount. She'd tuck a jewel in the pocket of her apron and after her shift take it home to Sadie and save it for the dark, starless nights ahead.

Yes, plucked, not caught from the sky, but a gal in her position couldn't wait for providence. She had to create her own starlight.

Perhaps Charlie wrestled his way to the roof to wrangle his own pocketful of stars. For a breath, she clung to that hope, even glancing back at Caroline for confirmation.

Caroline's nightingale cap hung askew on the back of her head, her hay-spun hair vagrant in the wind as she perched on the ladder that led to the roof access, peering out over the rim of the opening.

Esther had lost her cap the moment she climbed onto the roof. She should have thought to bring a coat, but one didn't stop to consider such items as her nurse's cape when tracking down escaping GIs.

Charlie shuffled to the very edge of the brick border, his moaning twining with the wind even as he peered out over the edge.

Please, Charlie, don't…

He dropped his crutch. Spread his arms, as if to gather the wind to his breast.

"Charlie!"

He glanced again over his shoulder, and for a staggering moment, she thought she might have dislodged the voices that deformed Charlie from a boy who'd simply survived—while his buddies perished next to him—to a twenty-one-year-old battle-fatigued veteran with a lifetime of ache in his eyes.

"No one blames you…." No, not when he'd lain helpless, his leg shattered, his body scraped raw, soggy, and half-drowned in some sandy gully hedged with barbed wire while the groans of his compatriots bled into his mind. Until, of course, after two days, they'd simply died to silence, leaving only the growl of Panzers to drill into his bones, curdle his mind.

"I'm a coward." His voice turned to washboard, jerky and stiff against the wind, sharp-edged with the remnants of winter. He drew in a breath, turned away from her, and she lunged at the moment to inch farther across the roof, away from the chimney.

"Es—!" The wind snatched Caroline's hiss, tossing it into the night, away from Charlie's notice. Esther waved her friend away.

"Charlie, you're not a coward. You're hurt. Come back inside. This isn't the way to—"

"I don't understand why…" He turned again to her just as a spotlight from below—thank you, Chief Darren—rebuffed the darkness.

For a brutal second, Charlie stood in brilliance, the bath of light carving out his scars: the reddened gnarl of skin on his neck dragging down the left side of his face, the knotted hand, three fingers barely recognizable. And of course the stump that she'd just finished redressing, the residual portion of his leg right above his knee, now puckered and hot with an infection.

But only his eyes frightened her. No longer wild, they'd calmed to a deadly, smoldering gray, nearly sane.

As if he'd already weighed his options.

"Charlie, please don't move."

He narrowed his eyes. Then slowly, painfully, shook his head. "I can't live like this. I ain't got nobody. Them guys were my family." His jaw clenched then, only the heaving of his breast evidence of his battles.

She ran her hands up her goosefleshed arms. "That's not true, Charlie. You have family here. Me, and Caroline, and the rest of the staff at Mercy—"

"You ain't my family. You *have* a family. Your husband—your daughter. You have people who love you."

She didn't know where to start arguing. First, she hadn't actually married Linus Hahn yet, thanks to the war. And she could hardly call Linus's words a proposal. More of a decree, or an epitaph.

As for people who loved her…

"Charlie, I *am* your family—you aren't alone. And you're getting better, every day…" She dug deep and lied better than she thought she could. But then, after three years of practice, what did she expect? "You will recover—and you'll find someone—"

"I'm trapped! I'm trapped in this mangled body and there ain't no fixin' it." He turned away, cursed at the cadre of spectators below. "There ain't no fixin' this."

His words dug into soft flesh and caused Esther to abandon herself and simply walk out beside him. His bedridden, almost antiseptic odor poured over her, and she made the mistake of looking down, all three stories. The spotlight blinded her, blotted out the stars, and she had to close her eyes, lest she wobble forward.

She extended her hands, wide. Imagined herself instead—

"What are you doing?" Charlie's voice turned to a wisp of horror.

She inhaled the scent of the cedar, the breeze weighty with the birth of spring, the redolence of grass needling out of the winter thatch. Yes, up here she might exhale, might even find her footing.

Or…fly.

"You're scaring me."

She opened her eyes, smiled at him. "Then we're even, aren't we, soldier?"

He considered her a moment, a flicker of anger in his eyes. Good, a piece of sanity she could grasp. Tug, hold on to, make him again consider hope.

Although, from where she stood, with the stars winking from the sky, freedom on the wing, away from the cloistered odor of the dying, perhaps he wasn't the crazy one.

She shivered then. "There are people down there, watching. The guys from the ward are probably at the windows. You don't want them to see you jump." But her voice sounded thin, even tinny. "And no matter how much you wish it, private, you can't fly."

Swallowing her words, she found something honest. "Charlie, don't think for a moment that I—that those guys haven't stood on this edge and wished to fly away. To escape the moments that hold us captive, the people we see in the mirror. This war has stripped everyone down to the bone, and it's not pretty." She reached for his damaged hand, squeezed the cold, ridged flesh.

"I don't know why you're alive and your buddies aren't. I do know that we all gotta believe that there's something bigger ahead of us. Something better. That God isn't laughing at the way our lives turned out." The wind chapped her wet cheeks. "Maybe He's even crying."

Not for her, however. Never for her.

She drew in a breath. "You didn't come home in a box, Charlie, and that's not a sin."

Charlie drew in a long breath, his knurled grip tightening. "Is it a sin to wish I had? Because it feels like it."

Yes, it did, didn't it? The truth inside Charlie's words could tear her asunder.

The wind had fingers and tugged her hair from its netting, pushed her toward the edge. Perhaps…

No.

She had Sadie, after all.

"I hope not, Charlie. I hope God understands. But you can't find out this way. You have to believe that God spared you for a reason. Don't give up now."

Sunday school words, but she poured them out as if she believed them. Another sin, perhaps. But she allowed herself to taste them, to swallow them down despite the bitterness, and hoped Charlie did too.

He just stood in the limelight and held her hand.

She trolled her heart for something more, some pithy, poignant wisdom. But she starved on her own feeble encouragements and had nothing left for Charlie.

They should have sent beautiful Caroline out here to stand by him on the edge, but then again, Caroline might be even more bereft of words than she.

After all, Esther had a daughter. And, as long as she returned home every day without a telegram waiting on the bureau, Linus lived.

Linus lived.

If she looked down, the distance might just knot her stomach. She shuffled back, away from the lip of the roof. "C'mon, Charlie, let's go inside. It's cold out."

He didn't move. "I can still hear the German saws. The machine guns drill into my brain when I sleep,and the sound is shrapnel through my entire body." His voice emerged, aged. "I try to wake up, but I can't. And then there are the meemies. They drop with a whistle, and I know they're coming, my breath stiffening inside me. Then everything erupts and turns into a thousand needles in my skin, *under* my skin, lifting it from my bones."

He closed his eyes. "But that's nothing compared to the tanks. They rattle, the rumble chewing my insides. I want to move, but I'm paralyzed, so I hold my breath, waiting for them to mow over me. There's shouting, sometimes, but I can't open my mouth, and besides, they're too far away to hear me. So, I lie there. And it's—it's dark. Very dark. And...I lie there...."

She looked at him then through the water in her eyes and nodded. Nodded.

She meant to convey that she understood, that she, too, relived the sounds of her own demise, although hers had been whispers, laughter, and soft, lethal words. But she could understand how you could lie paralyzed, the sound of your voice trapped in your throat. Or the feeling of something bigger than yourself mowing over you, crushing you.

But perhaps Charlie didn't read her nod that way.

It happened so fast that later she couldn't piece out the movements in her mind. She wanted to believe that he'd been leaning out too far, that maybe he lost his balance.

Wanted to believe that he didn't jump but merely toppled forward over the edge of the hospital roof.

For one terrifying, quick moment, she fell to her stomach, her hand gripped to his.

And oh, she knew it, he gripped it back. She felt his stump fingers tighten in hers, a pulse of hope, of redemption.

She knew it because when their hold broke free, it snapped, like the ice breaking beneath her feet at the edge of winter, crisp and sharp and fatal.

Not at all like flying.

*****

Fort McCoy Army Base

Wisconsin

May 1945

To Miss Esther Lange,

I admit that I don't exactly know how to begin this letter. Perhaps with a description of myself, only that can't possibly matter in balance with the way we are meeting. I am not sure how to ease into the information of how I came upon the contents of this envelope, what details would be pertinent in this moment, or on the contrary, overwhelming. I suspect this letter is quite late, and fear it reopens wounds. For this, I apologize.

I've never been a man of eloquence, as comfortable

on the back of my uncle's Ford Ferguson, plowing up the soft, dark Iowa earth as I am trying to field dress the wounded, so I ask your forbearance as I unravel the events of our meeting.

Let me clarify, for by now, you must be thinking, get to the point! Of course. I am a medic, not a man of war, but I found myself in battle on the border of Germany, in a town called Beisdorf on the 10th of February, of this year. My task was simply to retrieve two fallen comrades pinned down for two days. I had no idea that your friend Linus would be with them.

I am sorry for your loss. I am sure he was a good man. Trusting. Honorable. I saw this in how he allowed me to tend to his wounds, and I admit they appeared significant. Without burdening you with painful images you might inaccurately conjure, let me say that he didn't suffer. He had adequate morphine on his person, and I used it for his comfort. He also offered it to the others—those I'd come to attend, and they benefited by his generosity.

We were unable to immediately evacuate our location, and thus, I spent a goodly amount of time with Linus. He talked of his family in Roosevelt, and of course mentioned you. As morning crested, I assessed his wounds further, and only then did he pass along this envelope to me. He pressed it into my hand, asking me to send it to you, fully trusting I would keep my word.

And, by God's grace, I promised I would.

Reinforcements came for him—for us—at dawn, yet

I suspect you already know his fate. Let me say that while I returned to America, I kept this letter upon my person at all times, waiting for the opportunity to send it, to do that one right thing in an age when everything else feels askew. I know, for me, the world has turned kilter for quite some time.

I again apologize for the delay in sending this. I pray the fulfillment of my promise and the contents of the letter might give you some comfort in the darkness of your hour.

Regards,
Peter Hess
Medic

CHAPTER 2

Listening to the oxygen, watching the yellow tubes, the IV over his bed feed life into his veins, Esther wasn't sure who to blame for the life of the man in bed sixteen.

Chief of Surgery Neil O'Grady…or God.

One of the two had kept Charlie alive. His heart continued to beat, despite the fact he'd shattered his good leg, crushed nearly all his ribs on one side, and cracked his skull. They'd had to drill it open to save his life.

She should be praying for him to live. Instead she found herself at the end of his bed, her hand blanched around the metal footboard, her heart choking off her breathing as she stared at his distorted, purple-ballooned face, his shattered eye socket, now Frankenstein grotesque, his leg, pieced together with spikes slung above the bed.

He'd just wanted to be free.

"You did good in there," Caroline said, brushing past her. She pressed her fingers to Charlie's wrist, counted the second-hand clicks on her watch. She checked his IV drip then reached for the BP cuff. "It's like you knew what the chief was thinking. You had the right instrument in his hand even before he said it. You're an amazing surgical nurse."

"There weren't enough nurses on duty. Someone should have been here, watching him. Where was Rosemary? She was due on at seven this morning."

"Probably spent the evening at the USO and overslept. Must be nice not to have to go home to an empty bed."

"Caroline!"

"Just because she doesn't have a man to write to doesn't mean she shouldn't be doing her part." Caroline glanced at her, added a lilt to her voice, Kate Smith on the radio, *"Can you pass a mailbox with a clear conscience?"*

"At least she's not pining for some soldier. She's the lucky one, to be single, to not have to worry every night, fight the darkness with prayers of desperation or grief."

At Esther's words, Caroline shot her a look, something in it Esther couldn't decipher. "Uh, that wasn't directed at you."

For a moment, grief pulsed between them, that empty place where words fall shallow. Then, Caroline turned back to Charlie.

Esther reached for something to erase her gaffe. When would she remember that Caroline had actually *loved* her fiancé? "Besides, maybe Rosemary was out spotting for enemy aircraft. Never can be too careful."

"Probably saw a blackbird and called it in as a Messerschmitt. Good grief, who's going to bomb Wisconsin?" Caroline hooked the BP cuff onto Charlie's arm, unwound her stethoscope from her neck. "You should rethink that application to the nursing management program."

"I have a daughter, Caroline. When would I attend classes? Who would take care of Sadie?"

Caroline finished listening to Charlie's vitals then removed her stethoscope and unhooked the BP cuff. "Maybe I would."

She didn't look at Esther when she said it.

Esther smoothed her hand along the metal bed frame. "Linus said he doesn't want me working. Once he comes home…"

"That's his father talking. Linus met you when you were working, and he certainly knows you have a job you love."

"Linus met me at a USO event. Everyone worked for the Red Cross. He couldn't distinguish me from a recreation worker. For all he knew, I served donuts and made coffee." She lowered her voice. "Linus took about as much time looking at me as I did him."

Caroline picked up Charlie's chart, made a notation. "So, you start over. He might not be as prosaic as his old man. Talk to him—how hard can that be?"

You trapped my son into marrying you. She shook the judge's words from her head. See, that's what fatigue did to her. Fatigue and watching a young man try to end his life. Despair seeped into the crannies she'd tried so hard to bind.

Except, maybe Linus *would* end up being nothing like his family. "How is Charlie?"

"He's holding on. I don't know how." Caroline hooked the chart back on the end of his bed. "I'm beat. I'm going straight home, to bed, and you'd better too. You're two hours into the next shift."

Esther picked up the dusky odor of cigarette smoke as Caroline moved past her. "Thank you, Caroline."

"Get some sleep." Caroline slid her arm over hers. Kissed her on the cheek. "And think about what I said."

Esther watched Charlie's oxygen breathe for him, his chest rising and falling with the forced air. Probably she should pray—a gasp of penitence swelled inside her. But she swallowed it down.

What could she say, really?

Instead, she walked to his bedside, touched his maimed hand. "I'm sorry, Charlie." Then she turned and walked the gauntlet of ten other men recuperating in the surgical ward, taking pulses, blood pressures, checking IV bottles. Her body buzzed with the residual adrenaline of the surgical theater, the smells of Betadine, and blood lodged in her senses.

She *had* kept up with Dr. O'Grady. Had anticipated his requests. Had been essential to saving Charlie's life, benefit or no.

She liked being needed. In charge.

It stirred inside the old ambition, and she tasted it for a moment, standing in the sunlight at the last bed. A dangerous sweetness that left in its residue only bitterness.

She hung the chart on the end of Lieutenant Nelson's bed. She couldn't wait to get home, climb into the lumpy double bed in the attic with Sadie, savor those last precious moments when her daughter's lips lay askew, moisture at the corner of her mouth, her chestnut hair tangled in curls, her pudgy body sweetly limp with sleep even as she burrowed into her mother's chest.

Only, with the sun already clearing the hips of the Baraboo mountain range, perhaps she'd join her daughter for some of Bertha's porridge.

Caroline appeared at the doorway, her topcoat over her blue uniform, gloves crushed into her boney hand, a flush on her face. She gestured to Esther.

Oh no, please let it not be a code—

"It's over!"

"What's over?" Esther strode past the beds.

Caroline met her, tucked her arm into Esther's. "The war—it's over!"

"What?" Esther spied a cluster of nurses at the desk down the hall, could hear a male voice cutting through the static of the radio.

"It's President Truman—Germany surrendered yesterday. The war is over."

"I can't believe the war's over!"

Esther recognized the voice of Ellen Savage, fresh out of nursing school, too young, it seemed, to even understand the significance of her words. Or perhaps not, because her brother was stationed on a ship somewhere in the Atlantic.

Over.

"It's over?" This voice from Lieutenant Simon, who appeared at the door of the fourth ward, his pajama arm floppy, his head bandaged from his last bout of skin grafts. She'd just begun to get used to seeing a man with so much of himself missing. "It's really over?"

"Back to bed with you," Esther said, catching him before his dizziness sent him to the linoleum floor.

"The Nazis surrendered?"

She draped his arm over her shoulder, turned him back to the twenty-bed ward, the long-term convalescents who waited for prostheses, more surgery, or even to simply remember their names.

She didn't look at bed sixteen.

"They must have."

"I heard yesterday that Berlin was burning. We got 'em on the run!" PFC Jimbo Harris used the t-bar to pull himself into a sitting position. His upper body had doubled in size since he'd begun PT in gym, and he'd become a traffic hazard in his wheelchair. Just two days ago, he'd caught up with Esther and pulled her onto his lap, nearly toppling the stack of linens in her arms, living proof that a guy didn't need legs to be a charmer.

She lowered the lieutenant back into his bed. Gave him a sturdy look and got him a drink of water. "As soon as we have more information, I'll send the nurse in, boys."

But, for a moment, she stood there, cataloguing the remains of the men who'd come home. They'd all left too much of themselves across the ocean. They deserved people who honored them.

Loved them.

Longed for them with open arms.

She pressed her hand against the swell of acid in her chest.

The war had ended. Which meant hers had too.

She brushed past the celebration at the nurses' station and headed to the locker room, where she retrieved her coat, her hat. Her hands shook as she tried to pin it to her head, skewering herself twice.

The pin dropped to the floor, bounced under the long bench.

Maybe she didn't need a hat.

She'd just abandon her hair to the wind. After all, the war was over.

Flags flapped in the wind, the sun hot upon her cheeks as she walked down Park, turned right on Third, passed the church, and then turned again on Pine.

She waved to the Walkers, dodged Ernie Olson as he pedaled to school, his lunch pail swinging over the handlebar. Probably school would be dismissed, but she didn't call after him.

She found Sadie waiting for her on the front step, dressed in her Sunday sailor dress with white trim, her hair in high pigtails.

"Mama!" Sadie leaped to her feet, threw herself down the front steps and into Esther's arms. "We're going to church!"

Esther tucked the little girl close, inhaled the Camay embedded in her skin. So Mrs. Hahn had bathed her too. "Why?"

"The war is over. We need to thank God, of course." Arlene Hahn worked on her gloves as she descended the front steps. Dressed in a light blue wool suit and a pair of contraband hosiery, prim in a pillbox hat and veil as if she might be going to luncheon at the Rotary, she appeared to have already recovered from the four years of rationing, the sleepless nights.

The shame of her illegitimate granddaughter.

She stopped in front of Esther. "No hat?"

"Not today."

Mrs. Hahn nodded, her lips in a knot of disapproval. Esther supposed they might someday just solidify putty that way. "I don't suppose you'll be joining us."

Esther swallowed, kissed her daughter's creamy cheek. "No." She put her down. "Mind your grandmother."

Mrs. Hahn held out her hand for Sadie.

The toddler skipped alongside her grandmother, down the sidewalk, as if on her way to a party, nothing to weigh her steps.

Esther watched her. Last time she remembered skipping may have been the day she'd met her sister Hedy at the train, that last time Hedy visited the Lange farm in Ames, fresh from the big city of Chicago. The memory rose so crisp, so vivid, Esther could smell the green corn in the fields, the earthy redolence of her uncle's pig farm as they rode in the back of her father's 1925 pickup, taste the crisp August air, the tang of her mother's apple pie waiting on the windowsill. She couldn't tear her eyes away from her beautiful sister, with her painted red lips and that funny accent and the mysterious way she called her "dahling."

It took nearly a decade for her eight-year-old brain to comprehend why Hedy didn't want to ride up front with her parents. Or why, after giving Esther a white-as-snow rabbit stole, Hedy fought with her parents over it.

And why, two days later, Hedy left, never to return.

Esther climbed the step, noticed the V-Home sticker in the window—probably they could take that down—and opened the front door. The house still bore the chill of the Wisconsin winter, the coal furnace having been shut down for the season, the windows opened at Easter, during cleaning. From the kitchen at the end of the hallway, the remnants of cinnamon, the tinge of nutmeg beckoned her.

Maybe Bertha had left her some porridge on the stove.

Esther shucked off her coat, hanging it on the mirrored rack, pausing too long to sweep her blond hair back into place. After today's shift, she felt eighty, rather than twenty-six, and the etchings around her eyes didn't offer any solace.

Oh yes, Linus would be thrilled to see her. Maybe he wouldn't recall what she looked like. She might not have remembered that little scar on his jaw, the nearly pitch darkness of his eyes, except for his photographs on the living room wall. Mrs. Hahn had assigned her to Linus's bedroom after she'd arrived, outcast from the Red Cross and destitute on her doorstep, armed with Linus's letter, three months pregnant and desperate, and there she'd also lived with Linus's face, in boyhood, staring at her from the corner shelf.

She endured being an interloper in their lives until three months before Sadie's birth, when she'd begged to be allowed to clean out a place of habitation in the attic. Where, perhaps, she might see the stars and sing her child to sleep without Mrs. Hahn's puttering presence.

Oh, sure, she could hardly wait for wedded bliss.

That wasn't fair. Linus would be a perfectly adequate husband. He would provide for her and Sadie, and perhaps they would come to love each other.

What choice did she have, really?

Sometimes, the moment—the one where he asked her if she was sure, if she knew what her yes meant—rushed at her, gulped her whole. Oh, how had she let her independence, her overseas assignment with the Red Cross, the fact she and Linus were shipping out to war, cajole her into departure from her senses?

No, actually, it was her senses that took over in that sultry, alluring moment. The way Linus danced with her, as if he needed her, the musky allure of his cologne, Benny Goodman in her ears, the taste of his kisses.

Indeed, her senses had betrayed her, and she'd departed from the woman she'd wanted to be, the places she wanted to visit, the love she had pledged to wait for.

That starless night outside Fort Dix, in Atlantic City, she'd lost herself.

And three years later, she still couldn't seem to find the Esther she'd left behind in the front seat of his Ford.

With the war over perhaps she'd never find her.

Esther treaded down the hallway to the kitchen. Yes, there on the stove, in the aluminum pot, a batch of milky porridge and covered in a towel, fresh bread.

She lit a match, turned on the heat to the stove, poured herself a glass of milk from the icebox, and then cut herself a piece of bread, standing at the counter to tear it into pieces, watching a squirrel contemplate its way up the cottonwood outside.

"Oh, Esther, you're back." Bertha came into the kitchen carrying a fresh stack of starched table linens. In her midfifties, dark-haired and solid, the woman had long ago mastered English, although her native German still spiced her words. She routinely refused to speak about the family—a mother and two sisters—she'd left behind in Germany when she'd immigrated at the age of seventeen. "Did you see the letter I left for you on the bureau?"

Esther stopped chewing, the bread caught in her throat. She reached for her glass, washed the bread down, meeting Bertha's eyes. "Letter? Is it a..."

"Och! No!" Bertha caught her hand. "Nothing like that. It's just a letter."

Just a letter. "I haven't heard from Linus in almost two years." No, he'd sent her to his parents and forgotten her. Not to mention Sadie.

"It's not from Linus." Bertha picked up the linens.

Not from Linus? Perhaps her mother... But she hadn't written to her since Esther informed them, as succinctly and gently as she could, that she'd defied everything they'd ever taught her, and God too, and given herself away.

She turned off the heat to the bubbling porridge, finished the milk, and returned to the hallway.

There it lay in the center of the bureau, white and bold, with red and blue striping on the sides—an aerogram. She'd walked right past it as if she were blind. She picked it up, studied the handwriting. Crisp, neat, the addresser clearly possessed an education.

The return address read Fort McCoy, the base just thirty miles north of Roosevelt.

A soldier.

The envelope felt bulky, as if it contained something else.

She opened the flap, probably too fast, for the paper ripped, and out dropped another letter. It hiccupped on the floor, twice folded and grimy, a plain brown envelope. She stared at it, her heart jammed into her ribs, climbing up her throat.

No.

She just…wouldn't pick up it up.

Just leave it on the floor. Just put her foot over it. Just… But she bent down and scooped it up, her breath turning to razors. Fingerprints on the outside, brown and ruddy, and a smell, the faintest tang of blood—or perhaps sweat—rose from the paper.

She held both letters in her hand, not sure, unable…

Oh, God, please—no…

She dropped the aerogram on the bureau and unfolded the brown envelope. Read the words scrawled on the front.

To Esther, upon my death.

*****

Esther stood outside the door to Linus's room, the door closed, her hand palming the smooth walnut.

Downstairs, Bertha fried cabbage and onions for lunch, a dish she'd brought over from Dusseldorf, back when the Hahns paid her way across the ocean. The tangy enticement of onions frying in butter nearly detoured Esther back downstairs.

She touched the letters—Linus's still unopened—curled together in the pocket of her apron. She'd read the letter from the soldier, the one who'd been with Linus during his last hours.

Linus's letter, however, remained sealed.

What if he'd poured out his heart to her? Told her that only she kept him alive? His silence over the past two years had actually loosened the stranglehold of guilt around her heart. Until today.

What if he truly had loved her?

Perhaps that, more than anything, made her a harlot.

Are you sure?

Oh, she should have said no. Why didn't she say no?

She gripped the brass door handle. Closing her eyes, she willed herself to hear Linus's voice. Soft and low, with an edge of husk, and luring her into dark places, it had sent a forbidden thrill through her when he bent close on the dance floor. *There isn't another as beautiful as you, Esther Lange.*

Ah, there he was, lurking on the outskirts of her heart. She grabbed at him, clinging, hoping for the appropriate fist around her heart. She turned the handle, the moment ripe, and entered his past.

His mother made Bertha dust his room once a week, and Esther had barely moved the books from his desk, never removed the clothing from his closet, or even peered into his dresser drawers. No, for three months she'd lived out of her tattered suitcase, reading Linus's vast collection of Hardy Boys, listening to *Fibber McGee and Molly*, Benny Goodman and Bing Crosby, *The Adventures of Ellery Queen* on his Emerson—anything, really, to fill the hours.

Finally, six months pregnant, she'd gone to the hospital and begged Dr. O'Grady for a job. And she'd moved into the attic.

Now she stood in Linus's room and drew in his scent—Old Spice, only now stewed with the boyhood smells of leather footballs and starched cotton. His letterman's sweater hung in the closet, and on the floor, side by side, his polished loafers.

Linus never seemed more of a mystery than the day she first sat on his patchwork quilt and ran her hand over his child inside her.

Pennants from Notre Dame and more locally, the University of Wisconsin, hung on the wall over his bed, and on the shelf beneath the night table lay copies of *Argosy Weekly*, with a picture of Zorro swashbuckling in a green Spanish conquistador's outfit and a red matador's cape gracing the top cover.

She lowered herself again to the quilted bedspread—the springs squealed—oh, how she'd frozen in horror the first night, realizing every movement squawked her unwelcome presence down the hallway and into his parents' bedroom.

She picked up the boys' magazine, paged through it.

"He sprawled right there, the first Tuesday of every month, when that came in the mail, and read it cover to cover." Bertha stood in the doorway. "And then I'd find him in the backyard, the next day, acting it out. Zorro, or the Lone Ranger. He had such an imagination, that Linus." She came in, closed his closet door. "Already I see so much of him in Sadie."

Bertha saw Linus in Sadie? To Esther, Sadie seemed her own unique, perfect imprint in the world. She put the magazine back and turned to find Bertha handing her a picture.

"One of my favorites. He was two. Same as Sadie."

Esther stared at the picture, traced her finger along the pudgy cheeks, the twinkle in his eyes, the high and tight crew cut. She cupped her hand around the face. Yes, there, of course.

Sadie.

The fist tightened. Yes. Linus had deserved a woman who loved his fascination with comic book heroes and teenage sleuths. Had deserved a woman whose letters contained not the trivial, but passionate petitions to return home to her arms.

Had deserved to watch his daughter grow up in his likeness.

The pain came swift, sharp, grabbed her by the throat, burned tears in her eyes.

There, *finally*. She closed her eyes, surrendering to it.

"What is it?" Bertha said quietly, removing the picture.

Esther wiped a tear from her cheek. Shook her head.

Bertha pressed her hand to the glass of the picture. "I know. I pray every day for his safe return. And now that the war is over, perhaps my prayers have been answered."

I suspect this letter is quite late...

No. In fact, it had clearly preceded the army's cruel telegram, or even a visit from Reverend Myers. At least now she had a warning, could plot her words, her exit from their lives.

And, until then, she would say nothing. She had no right to destroy their world, having already unraveled it enough.

Esther turned away, looked out the window. Overhead, the sky celebrated victory with a glorious blue, not a hint of cirrus, the sun triumphant upon the day.

Of all days, she longed for rain, tears upon the windowpane, a chill that might embed her bones and cause her to steal the quilt from his bed, inhale his scent, and let his loss hollow her.

And, for Sadie's sake, it could.

She drew a breath, wiped her tears, turned to Bertha. "How long have you worked for the judge and Mrs. Hahn?"

"They paid my passage over when I was sixteen. Mr. Hahn's father is my father's second cousin."

She saw her then, the black hair, dusted with gray, pulled tight into a bun, the sinewy, strong arms, the day dress protected by a gray apron, sensible black shoes, a woman in shadow. "You've worked for them since you were seventeen, haven't you?"

"I worked for Judge Hahn's parents first, but when Mr. and Mrs.

Hahn married, they asked if I could come and work for them. Of course I did. I practically raised Linus."

Something about the way she said it, with a downy fondness in her voice, made Esther pause....

Linus's death would rip a gash through Mrs. Hahn, through the judge, through even Bertha that nothing could repair. Their only son, lost on the battlefield.

Only Sadie left to balm the wound.

Bertha set the picture back on the shelf, pressed her fingers to it, as if leaving behind her affection, and Esther's breath lodged in her lungs.

Sadie belonged to the Hahns.

Even if Esther left, the judge and Mrs. Hahn would never allow her to take Sadie away. Judge Hahn would see to that—whatever it took.

"Are you all right, Esther? You look pale."

Esther rocked up from the bed, steadying herself on the side table, finding her voice, the one she used in the ward when talking to the soldiers. "Everything's fine. I—I just had a long shift, and I'm rather hungry."

"Your porridge is downstairs. I dished it up for you to cool."

Esther turned to the window, her eyes blurry again. She couldn't decide why. "Thank you."

Sadie and Mrs. Hahn skipped up the walk, their hands swinging between them.

"Are you sure there is nothing wrong?"

Esther's fist curled around the letters in her pocket. Maybe he wasn't dead. After all, they hadn't received a telegram. Not even an MIA...

She closed her eyes, hearing the door squeal downstairs.

"Mama!"

No one had to know. Until they received an official telegram, no one needed to know.

There'd been enough desperation for one day.

CHAPTER 3

May 1945

Green Lake, Wisconsin

Dear Miss Lange,

I am not sure how to answer your question. Obviously, I could begin with the facts. I believe he may have shattered all the bones in his leg, including the thigh bone or femur and both bones below the knee, the fibula and tibia. I worried about the blood flow to his foot, due to the cyanotic color. I also feared that he might have at numerous broken ribs, due to the instability of his chest. He also had an open wound that extended into the chest cavity. I did my best to seal it. Because of the darkness, I was unable to determine further bruising or swelling on his body. I also believe he may have had a concussion, because at points he lost coherency and reverted to his childhood as I talked with him.

As to how his injuries occurred, I cannot accurately ascertain. As I mentioned in my previous letter, I came upon him quite unexpectedly, assigned instead to assist two other solders in the same location. When I discovered his wounds, of course I attended them after determining the other two solders under my care had been sufficiently tended. I can only guess at the circumstances that wounded him.

The German army had fortified the Seigfried Line, the southern flank of Field Marshall von Rundstedt's stronghold. Admittedly, it seemed an impregnable defense, located beyond the Our and Sauer Rivers, now torrent with the spring thaw. I remember the night of February tenth, when the attack commenced, an icy rain dripped through the coniferous forest and down the back of my coat. I worried my medic pack might be saturated.

Then, the German line exploded. The 80th Infantry coordinated their attack to light up the pillboxes that fortified the steep incline from the rivers, and in the eerie glow of the flames, I could see the infantry charging up through the rocks, hitting the dirt as screaming meemies, tore open the forest, churned up the ground. Assault boats swamped in the river, and the German line littered the onslaught with artillery and machine gun fire. The world turned to fire, despite the hounding drizzle.

My world, then, became a blur of dodging bullets, pulling the wounded to safety, assessing them through triage, dressing their wounds, only to repeat this, hour upon hour.

The 80th broke through the Seigfried line sometime that night and pressed forward through Wallendorf, in house-to-house, hand-to-hand combat. It was in the middle of this desperate hour that I found myself in Linus's company.

To be sure, I didn't care for his nationality. Only knew that, after hours of dodging mines and mortars, chewing dirt, the rain and blood seeping through to my skin, my ears numb with the thunder of artillery and the moans of my compatriots, I hated this war.

I still hate it. With everything inside me, I long for the hot Iowa sun on my face, the earthy lure of freshly turned soil. The melody of the breeze over the fields.

As to your other question—did Linus speak of you in his fading hours? You must know that talking with such injuries as I detailed was difficult. However, he did talk of Roosevelt and his love for his family, how he missed fishing in the Baraboo River. He mentioned someone named Bertha, for whom I believe he holds great affection. He spoke of her in his delirium, those incoherent moments when he believed himself a child. And, when he cried—perhaps you shouldn't know his weakness, but the truth is, too many men cry when peering at their final hours—he called out for her. He spoke of others, although their names began to blur as the night progressed.

I can also assure you of the great depth of emotion in his tone when he asked me to give you his note. I can only imagine you are a childhood sweetheart, one perhaps whom he had forgotten until the war. Or maybe you are a cousin. I myself have fond affection for my cousin Shelby in Mason, Iowa, with whom I once accidentally burned down my uncle's hay barn.

I wish I could deliver a happier account to you.

I know your friend must be greatly missed, and I am happy to answer any further inquiries, although I confess, I try to revisit that night as rarely as possible.

Best,
Peter Hess
Medic

*****

Glenn Miller's "Little Brown Jug" bee-bopped into the night as Esther opened the doors to the Germania building-turned USO Hall off Main Street. A Red Cross VICTORY! banner hung across the back of the hall, over the community band ensemble—a trombone, drums, trumpeter, and bass player—including, much to her surprise, Dr. O'Grady on the saxophone. Ladies dressed in v-necked swing dresses, a few with real stockings instead of the line drawn up the back of their legs, and men in uniforms lindy-hopped around the wooden dance floor.

The room pulsed with a cheer that no longer felt manufactured. Indeed, the entire country seemed to be rejoicing, the Ladies' Auxiliary wild with planning the Fourth of July pie social and parade. Mrs. Hahn nearly wore a hole in the kitchen floor linoleum next to her telephone.

Esther hung her trench coat on the racks by the door then, glancing into the mirror, fixed her hair back into its snood and pressed her hands to her cheeks. Her bones seemed to protrude even more and shadows hung, traitorous under her eyes.

"There you are!" Caroline bumped up next to her, rolled out a shade of siren red lipstick, smoothed it over her lips. She seemed brighter than usual tonight, her creamy brown hair parted Veronica-Lake style, pin-curled into waves, and she wore a floral wrap dress that restored what remained of her figure, as bombshell as she could manage.

Caroline drew in a long breath. "Tonight, I'm going to dance."

"Indeed. Where did all these service men come from?" The soldiers milled around the punch table, some seated at tables, most of them gaunt, wounds in their eyes. But they tapped their feet, eyeing the women who'd dressed their best for their heroes.

"It's a victory party." Caroline stepped back, surveyed Esther. "Why are you wearing your uniform?"

"I have a shift at eleven and I didn't want to go home to change."

"Horsefeathers. You don't want the judge and the Mrs. to know you're here."

Esther pressed her lips together.

Caroline turned her to the dance floor, hooked her arm around Esther's. "You have to tell them, you know. You can't keep Linus's letter a secret. It's been two weeks."

"I'm waiting for a telegram."

"What if he's lost—what if they never find his body?"

It seemed a betrayal to speak of him without so much as a spark of warmth. She lowered her voice. "Then they'll eventually declare him dead."

Caroline rounded on her. "Are you kidding me? That could take years. They're still trying to locate missing soldiers from the Great War. You'll wait for decades in limbo, locked in their attic, waiting for Linus to be declared dead!"

"Keep your voice down. I don't think the entire town heard you."

Caroline narrowed her eyes. "You don't want to tell them."

Esther met her narrowed eyes with her own. Then looked away.

"Why not?"

"Because as soon as they find out that Linus is gone, they'll throw me out. I need time."

"Come and live with me. There's room in the boardinghouse."

"I need to go farther than that. If they find me, they'll come after Sadie." She said it softly, but the words still made Caroline clamp her mouth shut, as good as a slap.

"They wouldn't."

"They would. How many times have you told me you wished you and Wayne hadn't waited, that you'd gotten pregnant with Wayne's child so you'd have something of him? Sadie is all they have of Linus. Of course they'd keep her. And why not, I hardly blame them."

"She's your daughter."

"Yes. And she's Linus's daughter. And their granddaughter."

"Which means you're going to spend the rest of your life locked up in their attic?"

Esther closed her eyes. "I didn't come here to fight with you. I wanted to show you this."

She reached into her jacket, pulled out the aerogram then handed it over to Caroline.

She took it, read the address. "It's from him."

"I just got it." Esther ran her slick hands down her hips, drying them. "Today. I got it today."

Caroline had already opened it and was scanning it. "I can't believe you wrote to this GI."

"I just thought that maybe if I knew what Linus was thinking… Maybe he didn't love me either. Maybe…"

Caroline held up her hand, cutting off Esther's words, her eyes glued to the page.

Over Caroline's shoulder, Esther noticed two wide-shouldered servicemen eyeballing them from their café table. "Uh, I think I'll have some punch."

She shuffled Caroline—still caught up in the letter—to the punch table. Rosemary poured her punch, handed her the cup, her smile stiffening, not even bothering to hide her resentment. And why not? Rosemary had more hours, more seniority, and yet, more often than not the doctors chose Esther as their surgical nurse.

Still, something about her—perhaps her too-bright smile—moved a place inside Esther. She would have liked to have made friends with the redheaded nurse.

Now, Esther ignored Rosemary and guided Caroline to a table.

The men had turned away, perhaps watching them in their periphery. The band started in on "Don't Sit under the Apple Tree."

"He doesn't even mention Sadie. What kind of man doesn't mention his daughter on his—" Thankfully she cut off the rest of her words, although Esther could guess "deathbed." Caroline put the letter down, shook her head, those brown eyes so wide that Esther wanted to hug her. "And who are you?"

"I don't know. The friend. The *cousin*. You tell me." She leaned forward, taking Caroline's hand in hers, crushing the letter. "But don't you see—maybe he didn't love me! Maybe he thought back to that night and cringed too. I don't know, I guess I was thinking that if I show this to the judge, he'll understand the entire thing was a big mistake, and that Linus and I just…"

"Sinned?"

Esther jerked. Took her hands away. "Yes. Sinned. But I can only ask their forgiveness so many times before it feels futile."

Caroline shook her head and folded the letter. "That's not what I mean, Es. I know you're sorry. And frankly, I understand." She handed her back the letter, not meeting her eyes. "Wayne and I were terribly tempted before—well, that's why we wanted to push up our wedding date and get married at the base."

"Sadie is my entire life. I won't lose her."

Caroline smiled, waved to a huddle of nurses who walked in the front door. "Then show the judge the letter. You're right, if Linus didn't love you, then maybe they'll stop holding on so tight." She turned back to her. "What did his letter say?"

"I haven't opened it yet."

Caroline stared at her, words on her face that Esther had no trouble reading.

"I—I can't. I keep thinking... Well, what if he *did* love me? What if his last words were of adoration, and longing, and..."

Or, what if he knew, had guessed from her veiled letters that she hadn't loved him back? "I can't bear that, Caroline. I already stare at the rafters every night and ask what kind of woman hopes the war won't end? What kind of woman hopes with everything inside her that her fiancé doesn't come home?"

The kind of woman who deserved Caroline's expression.

"See?" She shook her head. "If he loved me... Oh, Caroline, that makes me even more of a scarlet woman, don't you see it?"

"A scarlet woman to whom?"

"To...myself." Esther's voice shook and she lowered it, looked away. "Myself."

Caroline stood there, saying nothing.

The music changed, slowed, and the band leader added romance with the bittersweet crooning of "At Last."

At last, my love has come along...

From the open window the fragrance of spring, a lilac heavy with bud, perfumed the night.

The men at the café table rose.

"I need to get to work."

"Stay for one song, Es."

"Not this one." She got up, backing away just as the two men approached. One, she recognized as having spent a month in the ward. He seemed to be walking well, his fractured leg healing.

I believe he may have shattered all the bones in his leg, including the thigh bone or femur and both bones below the knee, the fibula and tibia.

What if Linus didn't die, but came home without a leg? Or a face like Charlie's? Could she love him then, if she didn't love him now, her memories of him still whole?

She imagined him, lying in the darkness, the medic, Peter, beside him, packing his wounds, shivering. At least he hadn't been alone.

"Would you like to dance?" the soldier she'd seen in the ward asked. Esther shook her head, hating the disappointment on his face.

"I have to get to work."

That tempered his expression, and she cast a look at the girls around the punch table. The GI followed her gaze—and her hint.

On the floor, Caroline danced well in the arms of her partner, her smile fixed, her feet light. In truth, Esther missed dancing.

She wrapped her arms around her waist, smiling into the music, the memory of the USO club, the American flag turning the club patriotic, the room packed with the servicemen with chili-bowl haircuts, their youthful arrogance creating a wartime magic, the air rich with summer recklessness.

Can I have this dance, ma'am? In her memory, Linus swaggered up, leaned against the pole beside her.

Me?

"No, the hairy ape behind you. Of course you."

Yet, the slightest hue of hesitancy in his voice, even the texture of fear in his eyes caught her, more than this attempt to be suave. Snappy in his pressed green-gray army jacket, the knotted tie, the shiny gold buttons—even his shoes gleamed. *Yes.* She let the soldier cajole her to the floor, let herself wrap her arms around his shoulders, let herself ease into his arms.

"You know how to dance," she said with a smile as she caught his lead.

"Years of lessons." Linus moved her out into a lindy circle, back in, back out, then into a closed jitterbug hold. "My mother told me she didn't want me to embarrass her at the community socials."

"Your mother seems like a smart woman."

"That or just calculated." He smiled, twirled her out, back in. She laughed, and even in her memory, the twinkle in his eyes charmed her stomach into a swirl.

She placed him a couple years younger than herself, although they all seemed too young. But he made her laugh with stories about basic training and the other yanks on his squad. And after the dance, walked her back to the Red Cross dormitory, properly, without a kiss.

The scoundrel.

He showed up every Friday and Saturday night for a month.

Kissed her on week three, and the night he got his orders, showed up in a borrowed, shiny 1942 Ford Coupe and whisked her away to the Flamingo Ballroom.

The band played "At Last," a song she had yet to dislodge from her head.

At last, my love has come along. My lonely days are over. And life is like a song...

The fact she'd received her own orders from the Red Cross that afternoon contrived their undoing.

Are you sure?

I don't know—

"Can I have this dance?" The question jerked her from the past. Another soldier stood before her, his hand extended. She stared at it, the lines of his palm, then back up to his face. He seemed a gentleman.

Didn't they all.

The band hooted out "Chattanooga Choo Choo" and she froze.

Linus had leaned close, sung the words into her ear during this song.

You leave the Pennsylvania station 'bout a quarter to four...

"No—no, I'm sorry. No." She brushed past the poor man, beelined for her coat.

Caroline met her there. "Where are you going?"

"I think—" She shook her head, picked up her coat. "I need to get to the hospital. Check on Charlie."

"Charlie's fine. Stay and dance. I saw that GI ask—"

"I can't dance!" She rounded on Caroline, cut her voice low, affixed a smile. "I can't dance. What if the Hahns found out?"

"How?"

Esther scanned the room, the dancers swinging to the beat. Her suitors had found other partners. Perhaps no one would care—after all, they were celebrating, right? She began to unbutton her jacket, but then she caught Rosemary, now standing on the sidelines, watching her from across the room.

Esther had always thought Rosemary had such dark, poignant eyes. Now, they seemed to bear something else, something Esther couldn't quite name.

"I can't stay."

But Caroline wrapped her fingers around her wrist. "The longer you wait to tell the Hahns the truth, the tighter the noose around your neck. Linus is gone, and you're free to dance."

Esther stared at her, the too-red lipstick, her sunken, painted eyes. "I'll never be free, Caroline. Not really."

She hugged her friend then stepped out into the night.

A thumbnail moon hung above, the Milky Way blurry with the cover of clouds. She shoved her hands into her pockets, moving out of the nook of the dance hall.

Out of Linus's disastrous embrace.

The hospital always seemed most despairing in the last hours of the day, when visitors had returned to the living and only the skeleton staff remained to endure the long vigil of the night. She hung her coat in her locker and slipped the deck of cards from the top shelf. If Mrs. Hahn caught her with a deck at home…

Well, even her own mother would cringe at the way Esther knew how to shuffle and deal out a deck of cards. But she'd learned for the troops. For Charlie.

Esther closed her locker, checked her watch. An hour until her shift started. She had time for a quick game with Charlie.

They'd moved him to a semi-private room two days ago, needing the beds in the surgical unit. Her shoes clipped down the hallway, and she ducked her head as she passed the nurses' station.

Vacant. She tried not to let her mind wander to where the night nurse might be. With the advent of V-E day, people had begun to forget their priorities.

Yesterday she'd found a group of nurses in the break room, pining over two of the soldiers in the convalescent ward.

Someone had opened the curtains in Charlie's room, let the wan light of the moon wax the floor, turn the metal bed to ice. Charlie lay, his head still bandaged, his leg still in traction. He'd begun to breathe on his own, but his gaunt form now turned him into a teenager. In the shadows his scars seemed less brutal, and she could make out the features that had once made him handsome. She had the crazy urge to run her thumb down his cheek. He needed a shave—another neglected duty from today.

She turned on the light next to the bed, filled a chin basin with water from the sink, set it on the table, then went in search of a shaving kit.

Pulling up a stool, she fitted a new blade into the razor and set it on a towel on the table. Then she dipped her brush in the water and worked the soap in the shaving mug into a lather. She wet his face then coated it.

"I promise not to nick you," she said quietly. Charlie, of course, didn't move. She shaved one cheek, cleaned the blade, then shaved the other cheek.

"You know, all the girls have been asking about you. They miss your crazy jokes." She lifted his chin, ran the blade up his neck, avoiding his scars.

She washed the blade. "I went to a dance tonight. But I didn't dance." She finished up along his jaw.

"Why? Because I shouldn't—you know that. I mean, Linus hasn't even been declared dead. At least not by the army. And—well, what if he's not even dead? Oh, I don't know."

She doused the razor again. "No, I don't think I'm overreacting. Listen, I've already brought enough shame to his family." She picked up the towel, wiped his neck. "Of course, it was his fault too. But it doesn't exactly feel that way." She leaned back. "Oh, Charlie, see, this is why you're such a lady killer."

She took the razor and bowl to the sink, dumped out the water, rinsed the razor, emptied the blade into the trash. "And no, Mr. Nosy, I haven't told them. I mean, I don't know anything yet, so it would just hurt them."

Returning to the bench, she closed the shaving kit. "I don't know what I'll do. Caroline suggested the management program. But, well, that would mean more studying, and I'm already away from Sadie too much."

She pulled out the pack of cards, unwrapped the rubber band. "Best two out of three?" She shuffled then dealt out his hand. Hers fanned out to a flush of hearts, a pair of tens, with the jack of clubs odd man out. "You open."

She picked up his hand. Two useless flushes with a ten of diamonds. She discarded it. "I don't know, Charlie, your hand's a mess."

She drew a queen and tucked it next to the jack, discarding a four of clubs. "You know, I wrote to that soldier, Peter. He was with Linus when he died. He's a medic. I think he must be home on leave, although he's stationed at Fort McCoy."

She picked up the four, added it to his flush of clubs, and discarded a two of hearts.

"I keep thinking, he didn't mention any injuries, but maybe he's up there in the VA hospital, just like you."

She added the two of hearts to her hand, moved the ten of clubs to join the jack and queen, and discarded the ten of hearts.

"I mean, what if he doesn't have family either? What if he's—well, not as handsome as you, of course, but maybe..." *I confess, I try to revisit that night as rarely as possible.* "Well, it's difficult. You know." She retrieved his hand, rearranged it. "I just keep thinking about what you said on the roof, about being alone, and of course, you're not, but what if he feels the same way?"

She picked up the ten, added it to his hand. "Oh my goodness, you have a straight flush here. I'm in trouble." She discarded his king of hearts.

She stared out the window to where the clouds moved over the cut-out moon.

"I was thinking I might write him back. See if he needed anything. Maybe a care package. We have those extras in the Red Cross closet."

She picked up her hand. Oops. "I'm honestly not trying to win here, but you're going to have to learn to be more cagey." She picked up the king and placed it between her ace and queen. "Gin. Better luck next time."

She gathered up the cards. "I'm just getting better, you have to admit it." She sighed, shuffling. "Okay, fine. I'll write him one more letter, and just ask him straight out, so we know for sure—did he watch Linus die?"

"Linus died? Linus is *dead*?"

The voice, the shrill of it, rocked Esther off the chair. She turned.

Rosemary, still dressed in her red siren's dress, her hair tied up in a snood, wearing a flower at her lapel, stood in the doorway. Her painted lips trembled. "Is he… When? When did you find out?"

"Rosemary, what are you doing here?"

"I followed you from the dance. I knew there was something wrong. You…" She advanced into the room, her dark eyes lit. "You *tramp.* You took him and now he's gone. And he's never coming back—and…" She closed her eyes, shook her head.

"Rosemary… Listen, I don't know what's going on—"

"Sadie should have been my child!"

Oh.

"I—oh, I'm so sorry—"

"Just stay away from me, just… You came here, and you destroyed everything. He was supposed to come home to *me* when he was on furlough before he shipped out. But he didn't come home. He stayed in Atlantic City. With you. And now—"

"He's not dead!"

Esther didn't know exactly from where the words issued—or why—but they spat out of her, a wave of desperation rather than assurance. "He's—I don't know if he's dead, okay? I got a letter from this soldier who said he…. Well, he thought he died, but we've never received a telegram, okay? Nothing. Not even an MIA. So, *I don't know.*"

Rosemary stared at her, unblinking, as if trying to comprehend her words.

"I–I'll find out, okay? Just don't say…anything. Please. I don't know, and I don't want anyone to be upset. To jump to conclusions. You can understand that, right? Think of the judge and Mrs. Hahn. Think of their grief if it isn't true."

Rosemary continued to stare at her, or through her, her eyes fixed.

"I promise you, I never meant to hurt anyone."

That shook the woman back to herself, and for a second: the words seemed to find a soft place, because her breathing hiccupped, as she held her hand to her mouth. Then she closed her eyes...

Took a breath.

Opened them.

"You might not have, but you did. And if Linus is dead—" Her breath caught, her hand behind it. But her jaw tightened, her voice lethally quiet. "I promise to make you pay for what you stole from me."

CHAPTER 4

June 1945
Ripon, Wisconsin

Dear Miss Lange,

It was with great horror that I read of your confusion over your friend's passing. I cannot believe the gross neglect of the United States military, and I deeply apologize for the crudeness of the information I conveyed. I know it could only have caused deeper pain as your confusion increased.

As to a direct answer to your question. No. I did not see your friend Linus pass from this life to the next. I do know that by the time more medics arrived, he'd lapsed into a non-communicative state, and his pulse had turned thready and weak. His constitution began to fail, and in my estimation as a doctor I cannot see how he survived long enough to reach an aid station.

Yet, the silence as to his fate, from all parties including himself, makes me question whether the medics even reached their field destination. You must remember, we were in the middle of a siege, the artillery and mortar stirring a fog so thick that a man could barely see his weapon, let alone where to point it. It is possible the medics who carried him fell, alongside Linus.

I am so sorry. I truly understand the biting ache of not knowing the fate of the ones you love. I myself left family in a precarious situation when I went to war, and I pray for them daily. I can only hope that my dedication to my task has made them proud, and that in the end, it will benefit them. I miss my family greatly, and without information as to their health, the wound festers.

My father is a doctor, much beloved in our city. I grew up watching him tend the wounds of Iowa farmers, sturdy stock that they are. I even assisted him as he turned to veterinary medicine one day and delivered a breeched calf. I sat in the straw, holding the birth-slick animal as it struggled in my arms, and a piece of light burned in me, so fresh, so vivid I could taste the heat in my mouth. I knew then I would be a healer, someone who comforts. Alas, I barely passed my exams before the government pressed me to war.

Enough of those brutal memories. You asked me if you could contact my family. Thank you for your kind offer, but I fear they have moved, the war demanding that they find relatives that might harbor them. I cling to a fragile hope they are safely moored on my uncle's farm just south of the border, in Iowa. You may write to my cousin, Dorothy Hess, there, and ask her, perhaps. Unfortunately, I don't have their address, having left it in my supplies on the battlefield. I dream, however, of returning home, to my mother's kitchen, savory with the scent of onions and fried cabbage. She makes a kuchen that could call me from distant lands.

I had forgotten how beautiful Wisconsin is, the rolling hills, like waves upon the horizon falling over sandstone ravines. I stood in a field of peas today, agog with the color of oaks and cedar against a cerulean sky. Black Angus lounged like boulders, and I wished, for a moment, the world might stop and breathe in the peace of the unblemished morning. The other man inside of me could have been a farmer.

Do you live on a farm, perhaps? I am sadly ignorant of the cities in Wisconsin. Is Roosevelt large?

Finally, you asked about my health. I am uninjured, in the basic sense of the word. Of course, can one endure the loss of comrades without bearing wounds? And I fear I will never again lay my head on my pillow without hearing the thunder of shelling or the brutal staccato of machine gun fire. Perhaps, indeed, I shouldn't.

I will admit that your letter surprised me. And selfishly, I hope you will write again. But more, I pray that your friend Linus returns safely home to you, and that all of your grief will be for naught.

Regards,

Peter

*****

"'Peter never stopped running or looked behind him till he got home to the big fir tree. He was so tired that he flopped down upon the nice soft sand on the floor of the rabbit-hole and shut his eyes.'"

Sadie placed her hand over the page before Esther could turn it. "I want to live in a rabbit hole, mama!"

"But you're not a rabbit, silly. And we have a pretty bed, with your pretty daisy quilt Grandmother made you."

Sadie looked up at her and wrinkled her nose. Again. Then she took her pudgy fingers and mashed them to her nose, pushing it around.

"What are you doing?"

"I'm being a rabbit."

Esther kissed her on her nose, then her cheek, inhaling her fresh-washed scent. Her tawny ringlets sprang from her head as they dried. Esther could stay right here, Sadie pocketed in her lap, forever. Just she and Sadie, chasing Beatrix Potter's Peter Rabbit and eating bread and milk and blackberries with Flopsy, Mopsy, and Cottontail.

Dusk had already settled upon the town, a haze of gray laden with the drizzle of a somnolent storm. She didn't relish her walk to work. Perhaps she should drag her bicycle out of the shed. One of these days, they might loosen the rations and she would borrow Linus's roadster.

Or perhaps not.

"You're a very pretty rabbit." Esther tapped Sadie on her nose then poked a finger in her tummy. Sadie doubled over with giggles.

She finished the story then scooped Sadie up and set her on one side of the double bed, rolling back the covers and then tucking her in, down one side, then the other.

"Why do you tuck me in like a sammich, Mama?"

"It's what my mama did for me. So you'll be warm and toasty all night." She kissed Sadie on the forehead, grabbed Peter, and snuggled the flop-eared rabbit next to her pillow.

She hated leaving Sadie in the attic every night, but with Bertha's room at the foot of the stairs, at least the housekeeper could hear her daughter's cries, should she awaken. Esther had made the attic as homey as possible—a bouquet of lilacs in a milk-glass vase on the bedside table, a throw carpet with a basket of dolls for Sadie when the judge demanded quiet in the rooms outside his den, and an old rocking chair where Esther had spent her most cherished hours, Sadie at her breast, believing in redemption.

"Sweet dreams, Peanut. I'll be here when you wake up."

She got up, but Sadie reached out of her cocoon and fisted her sleeve. "Mama? Is my daddy coming back?"

Esther sat back on the side of the bed. Pressed her daughter's curls from her cherub face, running them through her fingers. Oh, to have such curls, not have to wear rags to bed. "Why?" See, she managed to keep her voice soft, without the blemish of fear.

"Grandmother said so. That he would come home soon, and that Bertha will make bread pudding."

"Of course she will. You love Bertha's bread pudding, don't you?"

Sadie grinned, her baby teeth rickrack in her mouth. Nodded.

"I hope so, Sadie." Except her throat burned when she said it. She swallowed it back, found her truth in Sadie's blue eyes. "I hope he comes home real soon."

"Me too." Sadie grabbed Peter and pulled the rabbit to her chest. "Leave the light on."

Esther pressed another kiss to Sadie's forehead, lingering for a moment, longing to crawl in beside her, spoon her tiny, sweet body against her own. *I hope he comes home real soon*. For a moment, one she savored, those words didn't burn. Yes, she could imagine Linus here, beside her, tucking in Sadie, perhaps capturing her hand, smiling down at her.

Sadie should have been my child.

Rosemary's serrated voice tore through her.

Of course. The minute the words spat from Rosemary's mouth, the barbs and shadowed glances made sense.

Rosemary had been Linus's girl. In truth, Linus had probably never intended more with Esther than his conquest in the backseat of the coupe.

Are you sure?

And if she'd said no?

She blew a kiss to her daughter then picked up her pocketbook and tiptoed down the stairs.

As she gathered her trench coat near the door, the judge looked up from where he sat under the glow of light in the living room, reading the newspaper. A summer fire flickered in the hearth, the pine popping with the drippings of sap. "Esther, a word?"

From the moment she met the man, she tried to imagine him as an older version of Linus. But Judge Hahn bore none of Linus's humor—the way his blue eyes twinkled, the husky, dark tones that made his charm lethal. Yes, at fifty, Judge Hahn still struck her as handsome—dark, Brylcreemed hair, salty at the temples, a build that bespoke his German ancestry—solid and strong. If only his eyes didn't render her mute, turn her to stone.

She forced herself into the family room, summoned to the bench of the judge.

He closed the paper, folded it across his lap. Considered her a long moment before he reached into his pocket. "This came for you today." He held out a letter. An aerogram.

She stared at it, her body stiffening. "I—he's a medic..."

"I understand that it's part of your nursing duty to correspond with soldiers, but I would ask that you refrain from having these come to our home." He continued to hold the letter, now raised a brow.

Why did her hand shake? She had committed no sin in writing to Peter. None. She found her breath as she took the letter. "Sorry. Of course."

He picked up his paper. "I know waiting is difficult. And of course, this is hardly the ideal situation. But soon Linus will be home, and everything will be put right." He sighed as he opened the pages. "You may consider going to church and thanking God he wasn't lost in battle."

She stared at the letter, the neat, crisp handwriting.

Were you with Linus when he died? She had formed the sentence in her head, churning it over, letting the question press through her before carving it into the paper.

And he had written his answer—at least she dared hoped he had—in his precise, detailed, even poetic words. What kind of a man described war or delivered the news of the death of a man he barely knew with such compassion?

The judge's dark eyes lingered on her. She looked up and met them, and for a second the saliva left her mouth, her heart becoming granite in her chest.

"Because, you know, Arlene couldn't bear to lose both Linus and Sadie."

He held her gaze, probably wanting his words to impel her to liquid. Indeed, she had no strength to tear away from him—or better, to leap upon him and claw at his eyes, tear his callous arrogance from his face.

"Have a good shift," he finally said.

She willed herself to shuffle away yet stood in the hall, scrabbling for the pieces of herself.

"Esther." The voice emerged so softly, she barely heard it over the torrent inside.

Bertha filled the doorway at the end of the hallway, in the gray swath of the unlit kitchen. She met Esther's eyes then backed into the shadows.

Esther didn't hazard a glance at the judge, just tucked her coat over her arm and followed her.

Bertha closed the swinging door. Dressed in her dark blue house-coat, the one that buttoned to the neck, her black hair down her back and tucked into a scarf, she appeared eerily young, a teenage desperation in her posture, the way she swallowed then wrapped her strong fingers around Esther's wrist.

"Listen to me. Do not think for one moment that the judge won't put you out on the street, lock you out of Sadie's life." Her gaze panned to the letter in Esther's hand.

"This is nothing." The words tasted inexplicably acrid on her tongue.

"Perhaps. But you must remember, you are nothing to them."

"I'm Sadie's mother." But her protest emerged terribly feeble.

"Yes. But Linus is her father."

"I'm her *mother*."

"It doesn't matter! It has never mattered to them! Oh!" Bertha's eyes sparked as she cupped her hand to her mouth. She shook her head, her eyes shiny.

"What—"

Bertha turned away, swiped up a flour cloth, pressed it to her face.

Esther stood, lost.

Finally, "Why did you come here, to us? Why didn't you go home to your own parents, Esther?"

Surely Bertha had been beautiful as a young woman, with her satin black hair, those crisp blue eyes, so fervent in hers. A woman who might spellbind a man.

"I wrote to my parents when I found out I was pregnant. They telegrammed back that I'd have to make my own way, just like my sister Hedy did when she started to live a life they didn't approve of."

Bertha drew in a long breath, something on her face that felt like compassion.

"I didn't know what to do. I had to tell the Red Cross, and of course they discharged me, and I—I didn't know what to do. I telegrammed Linus, who was already on the way to Germany, and he telegrammed back that I should come here. He must have written to the judge, because they were waiting—"

"Yes. I remember when they received his letter. Mrs. Hahn locked herself in her room for two days. Called Linus a man after his father." She pressed her reddened fingers against her lips. "Perhaps."

Outside, the rain had begun to spit upon the house, the growl of thunder rumbling the leaded panes.

"What are you trying to tell me? Is Sadie in danger?"

"No."

"Am I?"

Bertha's hand closed around Esther's wrist again. "You just heed my words. It may be different elsewhere, but in Roosevelt, the judge is always right. Mind yourself..." Her gaze drifted down to the letter in Esther's hand. "You don't have the luxury of a choice. You traded that away."

"But what if—what if Linus... What if he doesn't come back?"

Bertha closed her eyes. Breathed. "He must. For us all, he must."

He must.

She dropped her grip on Esther, who rubbed the hot spot.

"You'll be there if Sadie cries?" Esther said softly.

"Of course. Where would I go?"

The judge didn't move when Esther tucked the letter into her pocket, buttoned up her trench coat, and retrieved her umbrella. Nor did he look up as she let herself out into the night.

The umbrella required two hands, and by the time she reached the hospital, her leather shoes squealed, weak and soggy. They protested upon the linoleum floor as she deposited her coat in her locker, set her umbrella to dry on the radiator.

"I had a date last night," Caroline said in greeting as Esther entered the break room. She stood at the mirror, pinning her cap to her head. "With a soldier from the dance. His name is Teddy, and he works for the brewery."

Esther sat down, smoothed the aerogram on the table.

"Is that...?" Caroline turned.

"It's from the medic. I asked him straight out..."

"Open it."

Esther drew in a breath. "I had the strangest conversation with Bertha. I think—I think she knows something about Linus and his family."

Caroline reached out for a chair.

Esther rolled the words around her head before she let them tumble out, slowly, one boulder at a time. "Could Bertha be—no." She held up her hand. "I'm just..."

"What?"

Esther smoothed the letter, the heat from Bertha's grip still upon her skin. "I don't mean to offend, but I've always seen more of Linus in Bertha than his mother—Mrs. Hahn's shorter, and her coloring is lighter, but Bertha is tall, and dark, and—she has Linus's eyes." She ran her finger around the edge of the letter. "She said she worked for the judge's family. I can imagine the judge then, handsome and bold. He probably whispered things into her ear, probably made her feel beautiful."

Caroline reached out, took the aerogram.

"What if he got her pregnant?" She spoke almost to herself. "I'll bet when she had the baby, the Judge told her that he would take him. Maybe her only choice had been to stay behind. To raise him. To continue working as their housekeeper."

She raised her gaze to Caroline. Who stared at her. "I'm going to end up imprisoned in that house. As their *housekeeper*."

"Don't be overdramatic. Linus is not Bertha's child—"

"I'm serious. Unless I can find a way to tear Sadie away from them, I can't leave. Bertha practically said that I'd be out on the street if they thought I was betraying Linus. And how would I support us, anyway? The shift here barely covers our expenses. I hand my entire check over to the Hahns every week for rent, not to mention my ration coupons."

"They demand that?"

"I demand that."

Caroline handed her the letter. "Open it. See if he's really dead."

Sadie took the letter. "And if he's not?"

"Then you open Linus's letter and learn the truth. It's the only thing that's going to set you free. Either way, you'll have an answer. You'll know what to do."

"What is Esther going to do?"

The voice startled her nearly off her chair. She turned.

Dr. O'Grady stood in the doorway, his stethoscope in his hand. "Excuse me, ladies. I am in search of coffee."

She'd always considered Dr. O'Grady kind, probably because of the texture in his hazel eyes, but also the way he treated the nurses as more than servants, knowing their names, speaking to them with a hue of respect. That and the compassion in his voice the day she showed up, two and a half years ago, six months pregnant in his office, desperation in her voice.

Back then, he didn't ask questions, didn't glance at her empty finger. Just folded his long fingers together on his wooden desk and listened to the mostly truth.

He always seemed younger than his forty years, with his dark hair slicked back, and a flash of memory of him with the saxophone at the victory dance made her smile. Now, standing in the doorway, he looked at her with those same kind eyes. "The war is over. It's a question for all of us."

Caroline got up. "I'll make a fresh pot."

Esther took the letter from the table, crumpled it into her pocket. "How is Charlie?"

"I just checked in on him. He's in God's hands now. We just have to wait. And pray."

Pray. Yes, well, she could hardly expect favors from a God she'd betrayed.

"And talk to him. I believe Charlie can hear us. Knows we care." Dr. O'Grady winked at her. "He might even know when someone cheats at gin."

Oh. She allowed another smile, though.

Caroline lit the burner on the stove, started a pot of coffee perking.

O'Grady sat down at the table. Set his empty cup on it, ran his long surgeon's finger around the rim.

"I sit on the grading committee for the nursing superintendent program from my alma mater at the University of Madison. We offer a fellowship at the hospital for a one-year program, and I believe you'd be perfect for it."

She froze.

"You'd have to take the graduate exam, of course. But if you pass, I'll write you a letter of recommendation, and… Well, like I said, I am on the board." He looked up at her, smiled.

Yes, he had kind eyes. So kind they whisked tears into her own. She glanced at Caroline, who turned away, her back to them. "I…"

"I know the war is over, and that your husband—I'm sorry, *fiancé*—will return and you'll probably want to think about your family, and Sadie, of course. But with all the injured soldiers returning every day, we need nursing superintendents to help manage the staff, to assist our boys as they get back to their lives. Think about it, Esther. You already make an excellent scrub nurse, and you display great calm in an emergency. Madison is only a few hours by train—you might be able to return here on weekends, occasionally. Mercy Hospital could certainly use your skills."

She opened her mouth, not sure what she might say. But he picked up his cup, glanced at Caroline. "I have rounds. I'll be back."

"Yes, doctor."

Esther watched him leave, unable to look at Caroline.

"Open the letter, Esther."

CHAPTER 5

June 1945

Markesan, Wisconsin

Dear Miss Esther,

I should have guessed that you were a nurse, proved by the compassion of writing this poor sot, who too much had hoped you'd receive my not-so-subtle hint. With joy I stepped forward during mail call, and your letter became the light in a sunless, rainy day. Indeed, for a week now, the sky has refused to cooperate, and I drag back to camp each night, soaked to my pores, anxious for a cup of joe, and today, to reply to your kind note.

As to what I look like? Better to ask my bunkmates, although they would probably reply that you are better off not knowing. My ego would like to suggest that I resemble the dashing Errol Flynn, although I'm not nearly as good-hearted as Robin Hood. Perhaps a biography would serve best. I am around six feet tall. Have unremarkable muddy blond hair, blue eyes, and a scar on my chin where my cousin once tried to spear me with a pitchfork. He has a similar scar on his upper arm. If I were at a dance, I fear you might rebuff me for some other chap, and worse, I am cursed with two feet that seem to have their own minds. I am a fan of literature rather than sports, although I played point guard for our basketball team in Conroy, Iowa until my junior year.

I will admit some envy that you are pressing forward with your studies to become a nursing superintendent. I remember standing at my own crossroads, my commitments behind me, my future before me. I sat in a café beside the Elbe, drinking a bracer of espresso, the scent of marigolds in the air, watching ferries and excursion boats parting the undulating shadows of the opera house in the *theaterplatz.* At that moment I could taste the wideness of my future as surely as if I were lying in the middle of a cornfield. Or as Huck Finn might say, *It's lovely to live on a raft. We had the sky up there, all speckled with stars, and we used to lay on our backs and look up at them, and discuss about whether they was made or only just happened.*

It is the wideness that I miss the most, perhaps.

Unfortunately, duty called me, and while I couldn't deny the peace in it, the road left untraveled in my life haunts me. I wonder, perhaps, if I would be here today if I had stayed the course of my studies. Perhaps.

Second chances are rare, and I applaud your courage to leap out and grasp yours. I am praying for my own second chance. Regrets are not easily digested when one lies in his bunk at night, only the chill and old porridge in his gut for comfort.

I am returning this note to the hospital, as you requested. I hope it finds you studying, and well. And although you did not mention it, I hope your efforts to find your friend's fate resulted in happy news. He is in my prayers daily, as are you.

With warm regard,
Peter

* * * * *

"It's from him, isn't it?" Caroline sat at the round pine table, setting a bowl of freshly washed strawberries between them.

Esther slid the letter into the chapter entitled "Sterilization and Care of Common Supplies" and closed the *Textbook of Surgical Nursing.*

"Let me read the letter."

"No. Shh, don't wake Sadie." She cast a look at her sleeping daughter on Caroline's bed, her little mouth open, drooling into her rabbit.

Caroline's expression softened and she cut her voice to a whisper. "I love her curly hair." She touched her own, tied into silky brown rag curls around her head.

"She can already read. I'm telling you, I gave birth to a genius."

"Of course you did. Now—let me see the letter."

Esther made a face.

"It's only fair—I tell you about my dates with Teddy."

"I can assure you, your dates are far more exciting. It says nothing, just an encouragement to continue my studies, and a quote from *Huckleberry Finn.*"

"A quote from *Huckleberry Finn*? Are you sure he's a doctor?"

"He's also a farm boy from Iowa. One who seems to have seen the world."

Caroline raised an eyebrow.

"Okay, fine. Here you go." She slid out the aerogram then got up to pour herself a cup of sludge from the coffeepot on the stove. The afternoon sun pressed through the window, creeping across the wooden floor, the rag rug. The July breeze tickled the eyelet curtains, tangy with the smells of fresh-cut grass and summer roses.

"Thank you, by the way, for letting me study in your room." She stood at the window of Caroline's second-story boardinghouse and bit into a strawberry, captured by the sparkle of the sun on the limey grass, the way the peonies in the front yard exploded in pink and white, the daylilies, tall and sleek, the bleeding heart and its fragile pink blossoms weeping in the front lawn. And right outside her window, a yellow climbing rose, its heady scent meandering into the room. "No more victory gardens?"

"Are you kidding me? Mrs. Delano spent last week planting a late crop of potatoes. And I weeded the strawberry bed for an hour to earn this paltry basket. She's downstairs, sweat caught in the cracks in her neck, fanning herself as she stirs up strawberry jam. I fear victory gardens are here to stay." Caroline began to untie the rags from her hair, the sun sweet on her face. "I hope the curls stay. My hair is taking forever to dry." The hair fell out, one spiral curl at a time. "Your Peter sounds handsome. Just the way he describes himself."

"I simply said that I wanted to picture him as he sat in the dark next to Linus, in my mind, and he assumed I wanted a description. Who knows what he must think of me."

"I think he's grateful for your letters. Why do you write to him?"

She ran her fingers through her curls. "Do you like him?"

Esther shot her a look. "Of course not." Except, yes, maybe something stirred inside her this morning when she discovered his letter in her box, neat and crisp, like a gift.

But probably, simply the sense of someone wanting to know more about her dulled the blade of loneliness inside. At least for the few minutes it took for her to read—no, savor his letter.

Caroline held up her hand. "Calm down, it's me. He seems smart—like you. And what does he mean by the Elbe? Where is that? Ohio?"

"I don't know. Maybe it's a place in the South. Or maybe in Europe. He did say theaterplatz—what's that? Funny, his quote—I actually remember that passage, 'We said there warn't no home like a raft, after all. Other places do seem so cramped up and smothery, but a raft don't. You feel mighty free and easy and comfortable on a raft.'"

She looked over her shoulder to catch Caroline's smirk. "I don't do a Mississippi accent very well."

"No, you don't. But it's sort of strange that you can both quote the same book."

"Maybe it's because we both grew up in Iowa. The prairie can feel like a river, constantly moving. And maybe, like me, he wanted to see the world."

From the bed, Sadie stirred. "You did, didn't you?"

Esther cut her voice low, her words almost for herself. "I was going to Europe. I was just waiting for my official orders when I met Linus." She blew into her coffee. "Did you know that Linus has the complete collection of Hardy Boys mysteries? And a stack of about a million comic books. But not one copy of *Tom Sawyer* or *Huckleberry Finn* or even something bolder, Hemingway, or Fitzgerald."

Caroline turned over the letter. "This Peter moves around a lot. This is the third location he's written you from."

"I noticed that too. I wonder if he's not with one of those army units, you know, the ones with the German prisoners of war?"

"Prisoners of war? In Wisconsin?"

"I read an article in the newspaper. I can't believe you missed it—we had a crew of prisoners pass through here a few weeks ago, on their way to Fort McCoy. They hire the prisoners out to pick peas and work in processing plants." She helped herself to another strawberry. "He's probably making sure they all stay healthy—a traveling medic."

"I don't know how I feel about having Nazis in our backyard."

"Not all the POWs are Nazis. I read a letter to the editor from a woman who said she heard some of them singing 'Amazing Grace,' and that they held regular church services at their camps."

"Germans, singing hymns?"

"Half our town is German, Caroline. You might be Dutch, or whatever, but I would bet that your neighbors still have relatives in Germany. Even Bertha—she hasn't said anything, but I suspect her family was fighting for the other side."

"I don't know. If I saw a Nazi, I'd spit on him where he stood." Caroline bit into another strawberry, catching the bloody juice as it ran down her chin. She slurped it up. "I just hope they don't come to Roosevelt. We might have the Battle of the Bulge right in the middle of the convalescent ward." Caroline finished off the strawberry then opened Esther's book. "I'll quiz you."

"I'm not ready."

"Sure you are. You've been at this every waking hour. Do the Hahns know?"

Sadie whimpered in her sleep. Esther got up, settled next to her on the bed, peeled her sweaty hair from her face. "No. I think a part of me is hoping I get this scholarship and then I can leave—be on my own."

"What, escape with Sadie in the middle of the night?"

"Shh!"

"But you're going to sneak out of town?"

"And, I was hoping you might come with me."

Caroline blinked, swallowed, her gaze falling to Sadie, then back. Slowly, she nodded.

Esther took her hand. A smile pulsed between them.

"What if Linus is alive?" Caroline said quietly.

"He's not."

"Did you get a telegram?"

"No. But he must be dead. He has to be. He hasn't written." She cut her voice to just above a whisper. "He's not coming back, and I have to be ready when the Hahns find out."

Caroline drew a deep breath. "When is the exam?"

Sadie drew her thumb up to her mouth. Sighed, her body shuddering before she settled back into slumber.

"In two weeks. I'll be ready." Esther got up, sat down again at the table. Opened the book. "Did you know that Rosemary was in love with Linus? He was supposed to come home during his last furlough—the one he spent with me."

"How do you know that?"

"She heard me talking to Charlie—"

"One of these days, he's going to wake up and spill your secrets—"

"And when she found out that he might be dead—she was nearly hysterical. I—I told her that we weren't sure he was dead."

Caroline stood up, walked over to the fan, its blades whirring in front of the window. She bent down, let it dice her words. "Oh, that's swell, Esther."

"I didn't know what else to do! I could see her running to the Hahns, telling them Linus is dead."

Caroline's mouth tightened, pursing at the corners. Then, "What if his letter mentions her?" Caroline cut a look at Sadie, back at her, and leaned close. "What if he was writing to tell you that he loved her?"

"He wouldn't be that cruel."

"Really? He made love to you in the back seat of a borrowed Ford coupe. *Those* are manners."

Esther's face burned.

"I'm just saying, you knew you didn't love him within days of his leaving. Maybe he figured out the same." Caroline went to her closet. "You need to open his letter."

"I can't."

"Why not? You know he didn't love you, right? So, open it, like ripping off a scab, and then deal with the blood. Eventually time will heal…" She picked out a floral swing dress, white with giant splashes of red flowers. It reminded Esther of one Hedy used to own. Caroline hung the hanger over her neck, the dress flapping like an apron in front of her. "I wore this on my second date with Wayne. I'm trying not to duplicate anything with Teddy."

Esther opened the book, didn't look at her friend. "Sometimes, I try to lie to myself, to go back to that moment on the dance floor when he whispered in my ear, when he made me believe that yes, two fools could fall in love in a month's time. It would have been nice if the fairytale came true."

Caroline pulled the dress from around her head. "I know. I sometimes let myself linger in Wayne's arms that night that he proposed. I'll never forget the smell of the water as it lapped the beach, salty and mysterious, the way he got down on one knee, his sailor's uniform shiny like the stars. I just stop my mind right there, and don't move until morning."

Yes, to pluck life's happy moments and pocket them next to her stars.

"My date arrives in one hour." Caroline picked up her bathrobe, a basket of toiletries. She turned to Esther. "The longer you wait to tell everyone the truth, the more you're going to bleed when you finally do." She bent down and kissed Sadie's cheek. "And, next time you write to Peter, send him your picture."

"There won't be a next time."

"Mmm-hmm."

*****

June 1945
Galesville

Dear Esther,

I have no doubt that you will pass your test, but you will be in my prayers for that day! Remember the difference between the Pitkin method of spinal anesthesia and the Stout method is that the second dissolves the Novocain crystals in the aspirated spinal fluid. The other injects spinocain right into the canal. I confused these two during my own graduate school exams.

You guessed correctly. I am with a traveling prisoner of war group. We are a tanned lot, the Wisconsin sun greedy for our winter skin. Every night, I go to bed with the zest of the summer licked upon my skin, the creak of hard work in my bones. Reminds me of when I was eight, mowing hay for my uncle, except I miss the hay chaff in my hair and sprinkling my skin, as well as the lick of a cool pond at the end of the day.

You asked if my uncle raised pigs. Yes, and corn too. We rented a small plot of land, and my father set up an exam room in our front parlor. I tended my uncle's hogs, corn, and hay fields. As to the other question, no, I am not married, and never have been, although I was probably sweet on my cousin Dorothy until I was twelve. After that, Mary Jane Allsworth caught my eye, with her blond curls and the way she blushed when I waved to her from the half-court line after making a basket. I mentioned to you my wretched dancing, and unfortunately, she can attest to the truth of it. I asked her to the junior prom then proceeded to park us both at a corner table, drown her in punch, and bring her home early, mortified. We moved away before I had an opportunity to redeem myself.

But what about you? Have you ever had a great love? Or perhaps just a sweet folly of youth? I know you dream of being a superintendent—why that, and not a home or family, may I ask? I can imagine it must be in your nature to attend to the needs of others, because your letters are a drink of fresh water on a parched day. Thank you for your kindness in writing.

Fondly,

Peter

*****

The patter of the rain woke her. Yet, in the earthy, almost moldy smell of the straw bed, Esther recognized the dream—or perhaps the memory, something from her childhood. No, not awake, even as she opened her eyes, the prickly straw upon her hands, the odor of ammonia and animal waste telling her she'd dreamed herself into the swine barn, again.

More accurately—yes, she recognized it now—their assigned stall at the Iowa State Fair. Indeed, scattered hay, woodchips, and straw littered the dirt floor, pockets of pungent moisture where hoofs had punctured the mud then collected the debris. A cool mist hung in the air, and she stumbled out of the stall to see water running off the doorpost, down the pipe to piddle into a rain barrel.

Then it came to her—the silence. No cows lowing, no dogs barking, no children crying from the pressing, grainy heat of the past five days. She turned back to the stall. Empty, except for the straw mattress where she'd awoken, only her crumbled cotton blanket evidence that anyone, let alone she and Hedy and their parents—had spent a week showing—and selling—their prize hogs at the fair.

"Hello?" The immensity of the swine pavilion sucked her feeble voice. She pulled her canvas jacket around her, shuffled down the rows of empty, smelly stalls. "Hedy?"

When had they left? She stood at the open doors of the pavilion, staring out onto the littered fairground. Ice-cream cups and wooden spoons, corn dog sticks, and the paper tubes for cotton candy, and popcorn—so much popcorn, it embedded the dirt like the pox. She watched a dog, its accordion bones protruding through its skin, dig at a kernel then abandon it for a morsel of hotdog bun marinating in a puddle.

The sky stopped weeping and Esther pulled up her jacket, ventured out of the barn. "Mama?"

Behind the concession stands she spied a row of Ferris wheels, giant tractor wheels churning the gray sky, their tinny music twining through the murky air. Beyond that she knew were the campgrounds—she remembered lying in the back of the flatbed Ford, watching the twinkling lights, wondering if Hedy might be riding on one of the metal buggies with a handsome carny. She'd promised to shake Esther awake when she climbed in next to her, to whisper the stories of her night on the midway.

Someday, Esther might be just as beautiful as Hedy, with her hair—not as golden blond as Hedy's, no, but a color Hedy said reminded her of wheat in September, pinned into waves, and boys turning to admire her as she walked by, giggling with Marge Parker.

Maybe, someday too, Mama would let *her* ride the Ferris wheel.

Esther took off in a run, past the ice-cream stands, the abandoned mini-donut machines, the sale pavilion where daddy had sold Nancy, their prize hog. She cut through the park, where she'd watched a vaudeville show and real live Indians wearing shaggy headdresses. Hunger pressed into her spine and she slowed, her breath sour in her lungs. How she longed for some of her mother's honey—on display in the horticulture building, or maybe some of the applesauce that had won a blue ribbon. But Mama would be waiting at camp with some cheese and maybe honey and bread.

She ran down the deserted midway. The carnys had packed up, taking their stuffed animals, their giant lollipops, their beads and necklaces, posters of Greta Garbo. The silence seemed eerie without the music of the carousel, laughter from the haunted house, the roar from the auto races.

The Ferris wheel's melody lured her, but she cut past the "guess your weight" stand and left the midway, jogging now through the entrance to the camp.

Empty.

Where once stood a sea of canvas tents and flatbed trucks, now a field, churned to near mud, nothing but the forgotten remained—an old shoe, a roll of brown toilet paper, an empty laundry line—

"Mama? Hedy?"

Daddy?

She stood in the field, the sky again spitting upon her, and trembled.

Why would they leave her?

The Ferris wheel music whined behind her. Perhaps she'd climb aboard, let it take her high—Hedy told her she could see clear through to Chicago from the top. She'd find her family, call to them…

The Ferris wheel whined in an endless, migrating circle, slow enough for her to dash up the ramp, climb aboard one of the dangling buggy seats.

No one stepped from the booth to collect a ticket, to stop her.

She sat in a puddle, the water saturating her jeans. It took her backwards, the world dropping away until she began to crest the top.

Her breath caught in her chest and she tightened her hold around the slick, cold security bar. She could see—maybe to Chicago, yes. The rows of dilapidated carny stands, the muddy rivers of pathways to the pavilion, the horticulture and dairy buildings, the curved roof of the swine barn. The grassy park of the entertainment pavilion, now a yawning, dark mouth, lay like a glistening carpet in the center of the destruction. Beyond that, the tall fair entrance gates, and in the far-off distance, the shiny dome of the Iowa capitol building, like a castle among the trees.

For a moment, she hung at the top of the world.

Then she descended, the world shrinking, back to the mud of the midway, the whine of the machinery, the dark cables snaking through matted grass. Water dropped from the gears and trickled down the back of her jacket. She shivered, and in a moment, the platform passed beside her. She made to move, to get off, but it slipped away too quickly.

She held on as the wheel slid her up towards the sky again. This time, she searched for Daddy's Ford pickup, blood red. Maybe Hedy sitting on the back in her white dress, printed with the big orange flowers, holding a new hat to her head.

At the top, the vast estate of the fairgrounds again scooped her out. And right behind it…

Not a soul remained.

Nothing but the melancholy drizzle, an occasional feral cat, the rank remains of too many animals confined in one space.

"Mama?" She didn't exactly shout it, but to fall back to the ground without so much as a cry seemed derelict. "Hedy?"

The platform again slid by, and she watched it drop away from her, take her stomach with it.

She closed her eyes as the wheel cranked her up again to the sky, bit her lip as it lurched her forward to plunge again to the earth. Gathering her breath, she inched toward the edge of the buggy, put her foot out to leap to the platform. But it moved out from her foot, and she yanked herself back, her breath hiccupping out, her fists squeezing the bar.

She heard the sob, choked it back, refusing to let it take hold, but by the time she reached the pinnacle, her body began to rack with them. She closed her eyes, letting her tears mix with the rain, her body shivering, surrendering to her cries, muffled as they were beneath the grinding of the Ferris wheel gears.

"Esther!"

Her eyes opened with the voice, and there, on the platform, her arms outstretched, Hedy stood, dress plastered to her curves, hair stringy against her face. "Grab my hand!"

She reached and missed it, her heart in her throat as the ride took her away from Hedy's hand. "Hedy!"

"Don't panic! Just jump off the next time it comes around. I'll catch you, I promise!"

She ground her jaw, closed her eyes again at the top, but peeked them open when she felt her stomach tip into her throat. She looked down, found Hedy nodding, arms outstretched. The moment the bucket reached the lip of the platform, Hedy caught her hand.

She scrabbled out, launching herself at Hedy, arms around her skinny waist, sobbing into her breasts.

"Oh, Esther." Hedy smoothed her hair, and Esther just breathed in her sister's scent, the softness of her touch. "You're okay, kid."

"I was lost. Hedy, I was lost." Her sob caught in her throat.

Hedy shook her head, pressed a kiss to Esther's forehead. "Kid, you weren't lost. We knew where you were. You just weren't found yet. You didn't think I'd let you stay lost, did you?"

Esther pressed her gaze up, her heroine blurry. "I couldn't get off."

Hedy smiled at her, a gentleness in her eyes. "All you had to do was reach out and let me catch you." Then she pulled her tight, and Esther burrowed into the curve of her embrace, listening to her hum, letting her sister's heat warm her as the rain pattered down upon them.

"Mama!"

The word jerked her forward, out of Hedy's embrace, into the murky dawn of the attic. Sadie lay against her, holding her rabbit by the ear, her little body a furnace against the cradle of Esther's breast. "Mama, I hungry."

Esther yawned, rolled over, her gaze falling across the clock. "Just a moment, honey. Let Mama—"

No. She blinked, launched over Sadie, grabbed the alarm clock. No! "Sadie, get up, right now. We need to go."

"I hungry, Mama!"

"I'll feed you at Caroline's—hurry!" She nearly fell out of bed, over her daughter, swept her up, smelling now the ammonia, remembering the sogginess of her jeans in the dream. Perfect. But she didn't have time to give Sadie a bath.

Not when her exam started ten minutes ago.

CHAPTER 6

July
Fort McCoy

Dear Esther,

I am sure you passed your exam, with high marks. I picture Dr. O'Grady in my mind as someone much like my father. I dare say he may have even allowed you to take it had you shown up a year late. I know I would have. I look forward to a celebratory letter, perhaps, when you receive your high marks and entrance into your graduate program.

Your letter contained a strange sentence: "Rosemary sat at the end table, her eyes upon me. I suspect that she took the exam precisely to keep her promise to make me suffer for my crimes against her." What crimes? I conjured up a few answers of my own, but as I thought them, attempting to be humorous, it occurred to me that you may be serious. I do not understand why someone with your compassionate heart might think they'd committed a crime, but I can only give to you the same words my father delivered to me on the advent of my enlistment. *May your God, whom you serve continually, rescue you!*

Yes, I do remember, by the way, the Ferris wheel at the Iowa State Fair. Perhaps you were the girl in blond braids with pretty red bows at the end, waving to her parents as she took flight over the midway? I remember standing in the middle of the grounds, the cotton candy dissolving in my mouth, watching her raise her hands above her as the wheel reached its zenith, as if she might fly.

You asked me why we moved. My parents longed for life back with their family, in a city that knew their name, in their own home, their own niche. I am their only child, so of course, I accompanied them. However, I remember the day we pulled from the station in the train, waving to Dorothy, I left a piece of myself—and probably plenty of my youthful blood!—embedded in the soil. I will always belong, most, to the people I left behind.

It is not fair for you to have a mental conjuring of me, and leave me bereft. What do you look like? What will you do for the Fourth of July celebration? I look forward to a day of rest, and perhaps even the sound of the national anthem playing over the loudspeakers. It will be such a day!

Let me know as soon as you receive your marks. I am waiting with great belief in your abilities.

With great affection,
Peter

*****

"With great affection?" Caroline uncrossed her legs, stood up from the bed. "With *great* affection." She added a singsong tone. "Great *affection*!"

"Stop. He's a lonely GI who's confused my letters with something more."

Caroline came over to where Esther stood at the mirror and plopped her chin on her shoulder. "And he wants to know what you look like. What will you tell him?"

"That I am boring and drab, without a face that could launch ships. That it is has been so long since my skin has seen the sun—what with hours cooped up studying, and so in need of a trip to the hairdresser that I fear I have become a jungle girl." She finished applying her lipstick, glancing at Sadie at play with a paper doll that Caroline and Esther had spent the better part of an hour cutting out clothing for.

"I think I'll write that part." Caroline sat down at the table, grabbed the pencil, tucked it into her mouth, as if she might be a gal Friday. "I am fair, for sure, with pale blond hair and red lips, and my friend Caroline believes that if I weren't so shy, perhaps I might even label myself beautiful—"

"I'm not writing that."

"Although I am way too stubborn and cross to ever allow myself a romance—"

"Caroline!" Esther glanced at Sadie. "The last thing I need in my life is romance, thank you. How about simply a friendship."

With great belief in your abilities. She *had* let those words sink into her, balm her, tear from her the fear even as she endured Rosemary's cruel smirks.

She should have known that Rosemary wanted to pursue a new

life. Because, even if Linus had survived, well, Rosemary had her own future to consider. One outside Linus's promise, if he'd even made her one. Yet, honestly, if Esther had to choose a nurse to serve with in a trauma, or under the glare of surgical lights, Rosemary would be the first she chose. She could think on her feet, keep a cool head, had great instincts. Rosemary could save lives.

"It's been nearly two months since you received Linus's letter. He's gone, Esther, and you best take a good look at your heart, because I think you're sweet on Petey."

"Peter." Esther drew in a breath, glanced at Caroline, then sat behind Sadie to brush out her hair, catch it into two piglet tails. Sadie made a face at her, and Esther held up her pointer finger, raised an eyebrow. How her daughter managed to knot her hair in an hour baffled her. "I am not sweet on him. I don't have that luxury."

"Not as long as Linus's letter stays unopened. It's time to say goodbye, Esther."

Esther tied one of Sadie's pigtails with a red bow. She'd used blue for the other. "Okay, Sadie, go get your shoes."

The little girl got up, toddling to the door.

Esther returned to the sofa. "I want to, Caroline. I really do. But I can't help but feel it's just another, a final betrayal…"

"Seriously? First you don't want to open it because you're afraid that he really loved you. Then you discover that he left a brokenhearted girlfriend behind, that he cheated on, and that no, he probably didn't love you when he, um, *celebrated* with you in the back of his Ford—"

"Sadie's in the room, you know."

"She's three."

"I no tree. Ina *two*." Sadie held her red buckle shoes to her chest, balancing them as she held up her hand, tried to form two fingers.

"Of course you are, sweetie," Caroline said, catching her onto her lap. She picked up one of her shoes, began to fit it on Sadie's foot. "My point simply is that he's had a hold on your life too long. You don't owe him anything beyond what you've already given him. Sadie is a beautiful little girl—give me your other foot, honey—the proof that miracles and joy can come out of dark mistakes. But, most of all, you don't have to live with sackcloth and ashes for the rest of your life. You're forgiven, if I read my Bible story of Mary Magdalene correctly, so open the letter, say good-bye, and move on." She kissed Sadie on the top of her head, set her on the floor. "Go give your mama a kiss."

Sadie ran into her mother's arms, gave her a sloppy kiss on her cheek. Esther smiled over the top of Sadie's head at Caroline. "Okay. I'll do it tonight."

"Perfect. And then, I want you to go and see him."

"See who?"

"Him. Petey."

"I can't go see him!"

"Sure you can. Take the bus to Fort McCoy. Get off, walk to the army base, and ask for him. I just wish I could be there."

"I can't... No. Go see him? I mean—what if...?"

"No one is going to find out. I can watch Sadie for you, and frankly, I see the way you smile when you read his letters. You should meet him. Just see what happens."

"I don't know..."

"Let's see, how did you put it? Oh yeah, 'I do know that we all gotta believe that there's something bigger ahead of us. Something better. That God isn't laughing at the way our lives turned out.'"

Where...?

"You said that to Charlie. On the roof. I was listening. And that's what made me have the courage to start dating Teddy. Now, guess what—it's time for you to believe it too."

Esther drew in the words, tried to let them nourish her.

"You didn't come home in a box either, Esther. And *that's* not a sin." Caroline stood, held out her hand for Sadie, picked up a blanket, and draped it over her arm. "Sadie and I are going to go to the Fourth of July parade. The day we celebrate our freedom. Are you coming?"

The main street of Roosevelt heralded the day with patriotic banners hanging from the florist, the appliance store, the barber, the pharmacy, the bank, the auto shop, the dentist, and even the local pub. The entire town seemed gift wrapped for the day.

Children ran with sizzling sparklers along the blocked-off street. At one end the band warmed up, cracking the air with the bangs of a bass drum, the thunder of a tuba. Sadie clapped her hands, bouncing on the curb.

"There's Teddy," Caroline said, pointing out a soldier dressed in army greens. Esther waited for the familiar flash of memory, of Linus in his own army greens, but nothing came.

So maybe she should lean into Caroline's words, embrace them.

And yes, the thought of surprising Peter pushed a smile onto her face. Maybe today he marched in his own parade, in the Fort McCoy celebration. It sounded like he didn't have leave—but someone needed to guard the prisoners. If she could, she'd save him a piece of cake from the picnic at the community church. Except, well, she couldn't really go see him.

No.

Really, *no.*

Three hours later, with Sadie asleep on her lap, she listened to President Truman's address on the radio speakers in the former Germania hall.

"In this year of 1945, we have pride in the combined might of this nation which has contributed significantly to the defeat of the enemy in Europe."

Across the room, in her periphery, she watched Arlene Hahn dab a handkerchief to her eyes.

"We have confidence that, under Providence, we soon may crush the enemy in the Pacific."

What if Linus had been transferred—wasn't even in Europe? She'd already heard of soldiers being relocated. Sometimes she forgot that the war in the Pacific still raged.

"We have humility for the guidance that has been given us of God in serving His will as a leader of freedom for the world."

May your God, whom you serve continually, rescue you!

Peter's words pulsed inside her. She didn't deserve rescue, not really. And frankly, it simply didn't seem prudent to put her dreams into the hands of a God who owed her no favors.

Sadie stirred in her arms. Esther leaned over to Caroline, who twined fingers with Teddy. "I'm going to take her home. I'm afraid we're headed for a long night, between the candy, the sun, and all this excitement."

Caroline caught her hand, squeezed it. "Open the letter."

Esther relished the vacant house, the rarity of moments when she could be alone, uncensored with her thoughts. She closed the door and began to climb the stairs, but Sadie awoke on the creak of the fourth step. "I no feel good."

"I'll draw you a bath." She pressed a kiss to her daughter's sweaty head.

As the tub filled, she brought Sadie to the attic, wrapped her in a towel, then changed into her housecoat.

She tucked Linus's letter into her pocket then carried Sadie downstairs, adjusted her bath, and let her daughter splash in the lukewarm water.

Sliding onto the closed toilet, she pulled out the letter.

Under her fingers, the brown envelope crinkled, stained with sweat and blood then dried to a crispy shell. She stared at the script—and didn't mean to compare it to Peter's, but it seemed wide and loopy, even uneven.

Are you sure?

She turned it over and ran her thumb under the flap.

Opened it.

Out dropped her necklace, the one she'd given him in the car, with the windows fogged, right after she'd given him the secrets of herself.

I need you to remember me.

He'd laughed, twined his fingers into her hair. Sweat pricked his sideburns. "Of course I'll remember you, Esther. Don't be silly."

"No, I..." She'd reached then for her coat, drew it over herself. Somewhere, deep inside, she had the strangest urge to cry. "Take this, please." She unhooked the chain—the one with her baptism cross on it.

"I can't wear this into battle."

"Yes you can. Please. Maybe it'll keep you safe."

"Oh, Esther. I'll be just fine, I promise." He laughed and let her drop the chain into his palm. "And you take care of yourself too."

You take care of yourself too.

She'd gone the next day to see him off at the station, but he'd already boarded the train.

The necklace lay in a tangled ball in the well of her hand.

She tucked it into her pocket.

"Look at me, Mama!" Sadie lay on her stomach, put her face into the water, blew bubbles.

Esther found a smile.

She tugged out the letter and opened it.

Dear Esther,

If you are reading this, then I have not kept my promise, and your hopes for my safe return are not to be.

She took a breath, the blade through her heart so swift it pricked tears into her eyes. Blinked them away. Didn't she know this already? But yes, it felt final.

Not to be...

There's no way to talk about this without hurting your feelings. And perhaps you don't want to know, but I have been unable to escape the hold that the last night in Atlantic City has on me. The guilt has dug fingers into my soul, and if I hope to enter heaven I must try and wrestle free of it.

Esther, I am sorry you wasted your wedding night on me.

I was pledged to someone else, perhaps not formally, but in my heart, and I dishonored two people that night. Of course, at the time I gave no thought to the consequences, and in that I know I was young and stupid. There *are* consequences, and I am sorry that you have had to bear them alone. I know that sending you to my parents' home was probably cowardly at best, but I didn't know what else to do. I fear I only made the situation worse.

I have to be brutally frank. I feel nothing for Sadie. I don't mean this to be cruel, but I want to free you from guilt or any obligations you may feel to my family.

I have no idea what I might say to my parents, and I have to confess that in my heart I am a coward in that sense. I wish we could erase the moment in the back of the Ford. To put it in a box and bury it, as if it never happened.

I hope with this letter, you can.

Sincerely,
Linus

*****

She stopped at the Catholic church first. Or, probably, she'd term it as *last*, because entering Sacred Heart, breathing in the sweet, incensed air, redolent with age and so much desperation, her visit seemed more of a eulogy. *Good-bye, Linus.* Along the altar, hundreds of candles in blood-red glass holders flickered their petitions toward heaven.

She knew no one here. And perhaps God might not notice, either, her slink to the altar.

"Sadie, wait for Mommy in the pew, and don't move."

She went to the front, picked up a long match, and lit a candle for Linus.

Put that night in a box and bury it. How did she begin to collect the fragments of that night? To package the forbidden pleasures, the longing that, for that brief hour, he'd healed. How to capture the hollow places that only seemed to echo louder the more she realized what she'd betrayed. *Who* she'd betrayed.

Put that night in a box and bury it.

In truth, his letter gave her a way to begin. It allowed her to confess their foolishness—not just hers, but for the first time allowed her to put the mantle upon his shoulders too. Now, how to forgive herself—forgive him—and forget?

She crossed herself and knelt before the altar.

She expected perhaps a rush of penitence, perhaps shame to lay her prostrate. Instead, just a wound, finally scarring over, followed by a dull throb deep inside.

I'm sorry. I'm...

Esther, do you love me?

The question pulsed in her head, like it might be her own thoughts, except, well, perhaps they were.

She opened her eyes. The church, with the crimson carpet leading to the altar, the high stained glass windows melting the daylight over the pews. Sadie sat on her knees on the pew, trotting Peter Rabbit across the polished back.

Esther turned back to the figure of Christ, twisted on the cross, an ornament in the front of the altar.

Yes. Yes, Lord. I want to...

She pushed herself up from the rail.

"Are you all right, child?"

The priest stood behind her, dressed in the solemn visage of his calling. She stopped, looked up at him as she held out her hand for Sadie. "Yes, Father, I—I think I am." At least part of her might be.

"You're not staying for Saturday morning mass?"

She hustled past him.

Outside, the day bolstered her—fresh and clear and smelling of freedom. She walked under the attention of the golden sun, swinging Sadie's hand then breaking out in a skip together.

Thank you, Linus.

Caroline met her at the door, wearing jeans and a white blouse tied at the waist. "Ready to play with Aunt Caroline?" she said as she knelt before Sadie. Sadie popped a kiss on her nose.

"Are you sure?"

"What, sure that you should meet him? Absolutely. Sure I want to spend the day with the princess here? Again, absolutely. Sure that I want to go with you?" She grinned at her. "Absolutely."

Esther kissed her on the cheek. "I need to catch the bus."

"Yes, you do."

Esther had taken the train from New Jersey three months pregnant with Sadie, crammed close to other army or navy wives, most of them with handkerchiefs pressed to their faces, many with rounded bellies. She'd wanted to cry too, but couldn't bear to allow tears for herself.

Now, again, as she sat on the bus, third seat from the front, dressed in her church dress—the light blue one with the tiny daisies and cuffed sleeves, the one that brought out her eyes—she fought the strangest urge to cry, again. Her insides climbed over one another, and her hands slicked against her vinyl pocketbook.

What if he… Oh, she should get off this bus this moment, hike back to Roosevelt where she'd discarded her sanity.

"Are you going to visit your soldier?"

She turned to the voice, an elderly woman across the row, her knitting needles clicking as she looked at Esther. She reminded her of Mrs. Hahn, with rounder edges perhaps, in a brown cotton dress, matching sensible shoes. She wore a blue hat, fraying at the brim, as if it had made this trip a few times. "You sure do look pretty."

"I—um—yes, I guess I am." Esther turned back to the window, watched the ground as it pitched and rolled across the horizon, as if God had simply laid grass over the ocean. Creeks and rivers ran in the rivulets between sandstone cliffs, and oak and pine scrubbed the horizon against a sapphire sky.

I was pledged to someone else, perhaps not formally, but in my heart, and I dishonored two people that night.

She didn't know why those, of Linus's words, kept returning to her. When she read them, she'd simply brushed over them, like a hand over a flame, the other elements of his letter so much sharper. The other wounds she'd endured, accepted. But this wound seemed more tenacious, even unexpected. It bubbled up under her skin like a blister, festering. Not enough to warrant true pain, but a stinging perhaps, as she'd realized that he came to her, his heart already reserved for another.

Linus had loved Rosemary. And while he'd given Esther a piece of himself—probably one that he didn't share with Rosemary—he had wanted to give Rosemary his future.

His children.

Yes, Sadie should have been Rosemary's child.

More, what did that feel like, to be truly loved by handsome, dancing, brash Linus? The one who could turn her to sweet syrup with a look across the dance floor, make the music stop, call her beautiful with a smile?

What if that smile could have been for her, alone?

She closed her eyes. *Put it in a box. In the ground.*

The bus turned west and in the distance she could make out tall towers—like guard towers—and cyclone fencing around the perimeter at the far end of the camp.

"Every time I come here, it makes me want to cry for our boys overseas, the ones in camps like this in Germany."

"Like this?"

"POW camps. The entire north side of Fort McCoy is a prisoner of war camp—a few Japs, but mostly Germans."

She had seen the pictures of POWs from the newsreels at the cinema—emaciated soldiers being liberated from concentration camps, their bones protruding like clubs from their bodies. Surely America took better care of its prisoners.

If I saw a Nazi, I'd spit on him where he stood.

The bus stopped at the end of a dirt road, at the Fort McCoy sign. The woman next to her gathered her bags, backed out of her seat.

Esther waited for her to pass. She relieved her of one of her bags once they disembarked. "Who are you visiting?"

"My son, Carl. I brought him a fresh kuchen. I come up every Saturday from Madison."

"It's nice the army stationed him so close to home."

The woman looked her over, gave her a slight frown.

They stopped at the front gate, gave their names, and the guard ushered them into a visitors' room. The woman gave her son's name and then exited out the side door to a picnic table.

"Name?"

The soldier at the desk looked up, raised an eyebrow.

"Peter Hess. He's a medic." Esther smiled, glanced again at the picnic tables outside. The woman had taken out the kuchen, wrapped in cloth, and set it in front of her. Esther's stomach had begun to knot—maybe she should have brought something.

The guard nodded and gestured to the picnic area. She passed through the doors, outside, and noted the barbed wire fencing in the area.

She sat down at the table. "I feel like I'm in a prison."

The woman glanced at her. "Of course you do."

Esther knitted her fingers together, placed them on the table, took a breath, and tried to remember how Peter had described himself. Errol Flynn. She'd seen the movie *Robin Hood*, yes, and Errol Flynn, with his sandy blond hair and square jaw, could be considered handsome, perhaps. She'd forgotten to ask Peter his rank—probably lieutenant, but she supposed, as a doctor, he would possibly be a captain.

Oh, what was she doing here? She should just get up and run, and…

The gate squealed open. A scarecrow of a boy, probably no more than nineteen, with a half-beard and a thatch of haymow hair, wearing green pants and a work shirt, entered the gated area. His mother found her feet, grasped his hands. "Carl!"

Esther stared at his outfit, blood pooling in her feet. She braced her hands on the table. No. It couldn't… The boy wore a large P painted on one leg, a W on the other. And on his arm, a band. PW.

Prisoner of War.

Oh. No. She turned, untangling herself from the bench—

"It's…you."

Flattened Midwestern tones. A tone of surprise that caught her heart. She froze, swallowed.

Turned.

If she'd had time to conjure up her visions of a POW, she may have expected an emaciated man, the sort found in the reels from Europe, with sunken, battled eyes, defeat in his voice, his bones like knobs in his puppet body.

Not this man. Tall, with wide, ropy shoulders, he had the ruddy strength of a farm boy, tanned, with dark blond hair streaked by the

July sun. And his eyes—blue, so blue that she might have been seeing the ocean for the tumult in it, the way it tugged at her, hungry. He wore the same outfit as the boy—green army pants, the work shirt, the emblems of war on his legs and arms. But he'd rolled up his sleeves, revealing tanned forearms, and she recalled his words, *Another man inside of me could have been a farmer.* His hands, however, the long, lean fingers that reached out to her, were that of a surgeon.

No. "Peter Hess?"

He nodded, a smile on his face that bespoke disbelief—a sweet disbelief perhaps, because his blue eyes glistened. "Yes. I am… Peter." His voice ruckled out of him, as if he'd had to pry it from somewhere deep inside. "You—you came to see me."

And then he wiped his cheek, and she knew.

"Oh no." She got up, backed away, her hands around her waist. "No, I didn't…"

"Esther?"

She shook her head.

"Please—Esther—"

But she banged through the doors—"Esther!"—and through the visitor's room, out into the hot glaring sun, now burning heat down the back of her soggy dress.

She held in her hiccupping breath, the edge of tears, all the way down to the end of the driveway. She didn't look back once, not at the webbing of fence or at the voice that called after her, again, then again.

No, she stumbled until she found the shadow of the sign for Camp Fort McCoy, sat down in the feeble shade…and wept.

CHAPTER 7

July 1945

Markesan, Wisconsin

Dear Esther,

Please.

I stood there, my eyes disbelieving that you stood before me—you were more beautiful than I imagined with your blond hair in waves, the blue pillbox hat and dress that only matched your eyes. For a long moment I couldn't breathe, my hopes—and of course worst fears—pressing from my lungs any words that might soften the blow of my reality.

I wanted to reach out, to touch your hand, the one that spent so many hours cheering my darkening heart. And then—

Your face cracked, and with the look of horror in your eyes, my own horror rose up to choke me.

Please.

Then you turned, backed away, your hand pressed to your mouth, as if you might be ill, and although I tried to think of a thousand words that might convince you to stop, to listen, nothing came to me, except... Please.

I stood there in the hot dust of the gated cell, watching you disappear—and then rush down the dirt road, the sun running fingers of sweat down my back even as I fled from the pen and out into the yard, only your name in my mind, hoping to stop you. With everything inside me I hated my cruel fate, longing for the first time since my capture to wrestle the Thompson from the guard—a friend, really—and escape the barbed wire suffocating me. I imagined myself running after you, down the road, dropping to my knees. And then, finally, the right words spit out of me. A whisper at first, and then a cry.

Perhaps you didn't hear it—gone as you were, over the lip of the sizzling horizon.

Please, forgive me!

I stood at the fence, my jaw set against my grief, willing you to return. But as the sun melted into the horizon, the dusk devoured my hope and I knew.

I am a wretched man.

Please know I wasn't trying to deceive you. Not really. I simply avoided mentioning the truth, hoping you might read my clues. I told myself that a tactful omission didn't constitute lying. I deceived us both in that. But, please know, never did I intend to hurt you.

I know now what a cruel, desperate sap I was to continue to write to you.

Please, Esther, can you forgive me?

I know I cannot possibly retract the trauma of your discovery. I can imagine you were expecting a man with a uniform you could honor. And, while I wish I could be that man, I beg you to understand that I am not the man you might suspect when you look at a German soldier.

I did not lie to you when I said I grew up in Iowa. My parents moved to America during the reconstruction of Germany after the Great War. I was six years old, and while we had left a grand two-story flat in the beautiful city of Dresden, I fell in love with my uncle's simple farm. I thrived with hard work under my nails, the sun bronzing my skin, and learned English within a year. And I did play basketball for the Conroy team.

But while I prospered, my father struggled to put food on our table. My uncle's farm turned to a fine powder that dissolved in the prairie winds, and he exacted high rent for our home, despite the hours I tended his animals or worked the cornfields. I well remember the day my father returned from a house call with nothing but a doughy turnip for payment. He set it on our bare kitchen table, dirty and white, and my mother stared at it without words, the tears cutting her face. I stood in the doorway, just behind the curtain of my room—no more than a closet, really, and watched as my father walked out of the house, got on our only horse, and rode away. He walked back hours later with a bag of food and train tickets to New York City.

He paid for our passage back to Dresden the same way he afforded the ones to America—through the kindness of relatives. The year was 1934, and President Hindenburg had just died. We had no idea the power that Adolf Hitler would gather over the next four years. My grandparents welcomed us back to their home, where my father set up his practice. What could I do but join them? A seventeen-year-old immigrant, I had nothing but dirt in my pockets, no way to make a life, except with my hands. My father began to teach at university, and it paid my tuition to medical school.

We had no idea the consequences of our decision. Indeed, I fought conscription into the *Wehrmacht*. My degree allowed me the luxury of postponing my enlistment. I know now that the SS watched our movements and waited for my graduation as a part of their purposes. Most definitely, none of my family joined the Nazi party, which in the end, became our demise. It's an event I still cannot bear to recollect without wanting to wail. Esther, in truth, if I had the means, I would have secreted us all on an early transport out of Germany, back to Iowa, and would have gladly joined up with the GIs against the tyranny of Hitler.

To be pressed into a life where every breath is as if you are inhaling poisonous gasses...this is what it is like to betray yourself. Every day I served the fuhrer, the poison crept through me, until I felt charred, even hollow inside. But, I had also taken an oath to save lives and this I did. The night I sat beside your friend Linus, talking to him of home, I somehow found myself again.

Then, like a gift I met you. You were the pieces of

light that sprinkled from the heavens into my dark life. I breathed again fresh air with your every letter. Every note from you reminded me of the life I saw again on my landscape. Indeed, I dream that this war will end, and that I will be released into the freedoms I fought against. Stupidly, I even began to wonder if I might persuade you to wait outside these rickety gates. Clearly the hallucinations of a man easily detoured from his realities.

Now I find myself suffocating, once again, poison in my throat.

Esther, can you possibly forgive me? I can offer you nothing but my deepest respect for your kindness. And while I would understand if you returned this letter without opening it, my hope is that you have read it, and that you might see more of me than you did.

That you might, in fact, forebear to offer me a second chance.

You were more lovely than my feeble imagination, yet even now, the image of your pain makes me ache.

Please, Esther.
Peter

* * * * *

Esther had turned into her sister, Hedy. No, she'd never be as beautiful as Hedy, with her blond hair, those siren lips, the voice and moves that could turn a man—too many men—to butter.

No, she had none of the qualities that might draw men to her—but somehow, she managed to lure men—the wrong men. Or perhaps Esther had simply—always been—the wrong woman.

What kind of woman gave her heart away for a smile across the dance floor, for a few sugar words scripted on paper? What kind of woman allowed herself to be cajoled into the backseat of a car, who handed herself over without a moment's pause?

Are you sure?

She'd barely spoken, but she remembered nodding in the soft folds of the back seat.

And no one had forced her onto that bus to Fort McCoy, had they?

She sat on the roof of the hospital, Peter's letter folded in her hand under the glitter of night, the stars cruel in their scrutiny. A thousand eyes to watch her read his words, over and over, although she'd long ago memorized them.

Never did I intend to hurt you.

I know now what a cruel, desperate sap I was to continue to write to you.

Please, Esther, can you forgive me?

Please, Esther.

She bit the inside of her lip. Is this what Hedy's boyfriend, the Greek shyster who had stolen her from her family, whispered to her when he soured her from Iowa farm girl into a floozy, singing in the gin joints of Chicago? *Please, Hedy.*

Clearly, yes, she'd turned out just like her sister. Possessed the same foolish heart, so easily bartered for words of affection.

Please, Esther.

No. She folded the letter in half, then again.

No, she would not hear his desperation. Would not imagine him standing next to the gate in the hot sun, waiting for her to return.

Would not hear his voice, a wretched echo in her head. *Esther!*

No.

She ripped the letter into tiny squares and tossed it out into the wind. It scattered into the sky, melting into the stars, lost on the breeze. Good-bye, Peter Hess.

She took a breath of cool, summer air, tinged with pine, the tang of cut grass. She missed the prairie smells—the husky wheat, earthy hint of angus lounging in the field, the river's brisk freshness.

Good-bye, Peter Hess.

His letter scattered to the wind, no one ever had to know how close she'd come to betraying…

"What are you doing up here?"

Caroline's face appeared in the crack where Esther had propped open the roof door. She shoved it open and climbed out, protecting her white hosiery even as she wedged the block of wood back into the door and came over to stand beside Esther. "Are you crazy? I don't think sitting on the side of the building is such a good idea. They'll think you're going to pull a Charlie! Do you want them to call the fire department or storm up here and put you in a white jacket?"

"I'm not Charlie." Although, yes, she'd caved in on herself as she'd ridden home in the sweltering bus, behind the woman who had visited her POW son.

As the night fell around the bus, she saw her own reflection in the window, ruddy and swollen, and hated the woman who stared back.

She couldn't meet her eyes in her mirror since. Still, her voice sounded detached as she dredged it up, cool and sane for Caroline. "I'm not going to jump. I just—like it up here. It's quiet."

Caroline pulled a pack of cigarettes from her pocket. Lit one. Handed it to Esther. She stared at the red char on the end, considered it, then shook her head. Caroline shrugged then sat on the roof, despite the tar, her back to the wall.

"It didn't go well, did it? What happened—is he *married*?"

Esther shot her a look. Winced. Then shook her head. She might actually be able to blame him, then. But she'd looked at his letters and discovered that yes, he had dropped clues.

She'd simply ignored them. Because she had turned into Hedy.

"Then what's eating you? You looked a mess when you showed up. He wasn't glad to see you? And please, will you at least scoot away from the edge?"

Esther leaned back on her hands. "Did I ever tell you how my sister died?"

Caroline took another pull on her cigarette. Esther watched the smoke spiral into the night.

"No."

"She was shot in a speakeasy by Capone's gang. Fifteen years ago. I was ten years old, and I'll never forget how my parents found out. They picked up the *Chicago Times*, and her obituary made the inside front page."

"Oh no."

"She sang in a cabaret. I wouldn't have even known her—she'd changed her last name to Brooks, but they'd printed her picture. She was so beautiful, she could have done anything. But she became a flugie for one of the local gangsters. She came home a year before she died. I remember her talking about this real swell daddy she'd met. She and my folks got into a real humdinger of an argument, and she left the next day. I didn't know what she meant until the obituary listed her as the girlfriend of a local mobster. My mother just crushed the paper to herself, bent over in her chair, keening as if she'd been torn asunder." Esther pressed one hand to her ear, closed one eye, the scream somehow not as distant as it had been a week ago.

"I'm sorry." Caroline flicked out her ashes.

"Thing is, Hedy loved this local boy—Francis Mulligan. His family owned the hardware shop in town, and he loved her back something fierce. He'd come over every Sunday, sit on our porch, ask her to take a walk. I remember watching her fix herself up for him. She had long golden corn blond hair, and she'd braid it down her back, put on a hat. I remember thinking that even without her makeup—she didn't start wearing it until Chicago—Hedy could make any boy fall hard for her. She always came back after dark, the wind in her hair, her eyes shining. I thought for sure they'd get married. Then one day, he stopped coming over. She sat by the window three Sundays in a row until her face was all puckered and red. He never showed. I saw him in the hardware store after that, and he ducked behind the feed aisle. Then one day Hedy came home from school and said she decided to answer an ad for secretaries, even though she hadn't a lick of secretarial experience. She was seventeen when she hopped on a train to Chicago. I didn't see her for a year, when she returned, all gussied up, full of stories of gin mills, hep-cats, rum runners, and her jakey. I had a feeling her 'daddy' wasn't the only one, even then."

"What happened with Francis?"

"I don't know. But Hedy had a thirsty heart, and I think she might have…" She lifted a shoulder, glanced at Caroline.

"Given him too much of herself in the back seat of a coupe?" Caroline blew out the smoke.

Esther watched it dissipate into the night. "I figure that Hedy decided that she had already given away the biggest parts of herself, so there was nothing left but pieces. And those she gave away like penny candy. A desperation for someone to taste enough of her to want more."

I'm lost, Hedy. I'm lost.

Caroline rolled out the end of her cigarette. "What happened at Fort McCoy, Esther?"

Esther shook her head.

Caroline didn't reply, the wind shifting her question between them. Below, Esther saw Rosemary exit the building, her trench coat over her arm, the milky sky turning her red hair to mahogany. She'd already changed into a red swing dress, probably on her way to the Saturday night USO dance.

Maybe they were all destined to give away bits of themselves, piece by piece.

Rosemary walked out of the halo of light spilling from the clinic and into the darkness.

"By the way, you didn't pick up your test score. I saw the letter in your box." Caroline pulled a folded envelope out of her apron pocket, smiled at her. "Rosemary got a 90 percent."

"How do you know that?"

"I might have stolen a peek while she went on rounds with Dr. O'Grady. She left the open envelope in her box."

Ninety percent.

"Open it."

Esther took it. Ran her thumb along the smooth surface. Ninety percent. *I will make you pay for what you stole from me.*

Please, Esther.

She cut Peter's voice from her mind.

She wasn't lost. And she most definitely wouldn't be giving pieces of herself away like Hedy.

Turning over the envelope, she ran her finger along the inside lip. The paper tore, and she sawed open the envelope, finally wrestling out the paper.

The envelope slipped from her grasp, flew out into the wind, sailing on the breeze until the night swallowed it.

She took a breath and opened the letter. Her body turned hot. "I got a 98 percent."

"That's wonderful!" Caroline grabbed her hand. "Esther, that is wonderful! You beat Rosemary!"

"I still need Dr. O'Grady's recommendation."

"Oh, I have no doubt you'll get it. Especially with Linus's death."

"What—What are you talking about?"

"You don't know Dr. O'Grady's story?" Caroline got up, dusted off her uniform. "He was in the Great War. Married his high school sweetheart the day after they graduated. She got pregnant right away, but she and the baby died in childbirth while he was off fighting the Germans."

So that was why he showed her such compassion when she walked into his office, six months pregnant.

Caroline ran her hands up her arms, as if cold. "He understands what it is to lose someone you love because of war. He hates the Germans nearly as much as we do."

Esther's throat thickened, her breath grating through it. She nodded, managed a smile.

"I'm going inside, and you'd better hurry up before they come looking for you and call the psych ward."

"I'll be right in. I have to beat Charlie at a game of gin rummy."

"Seems to me there's something not right about the way you keep winning." Caroline smiled at her, then opened the roof door and disappeared.

He hates the Germans nearly as much as we do.

Except, that was the problem, wasn't it?

She didn't.

Let me know as soon as you receive your marks. I am waiting with great belief in your abilities.

I got a 98 percent, Peter.

She put a hand to her mouth, and it trembled.

Peter had believed in her, saw her without her scars. Peter knew what it felt like to betray oneself. *The poison crept through me, until I felt charred, even hollow inside.*

And yet, he'd seen the woman she wanted to be.

I am waiting with great belief in your abilities.

With great affection,

Peter

Why had she torn up his letter?

Please, Esther.

She closed her eyes, but they burned against her lids, longing to reach out, gather the pieces, to repair his words, draw them into herself.

No, she didn't hate him at all.

* * * * *

"Sadie, don't kick Teddy, and please stop blowing bubbles into your malt."

Esther removed the candy cane straw from her daughter's mouth, wiped her gooey chin. Then she placed a hand on Sadie's knee to keep her foot from whacking Caroline's beau in the knee, again. She hoped she could get the chocolate stain out of the bib of Sadie's sailor dress.

"It's all right, Esther." Teddy held Caroline's hand atop the café table, his long fingers woven through hers.

They matched well, with Caroline's deep chestnut brown hair, chocolate eyes, and Teddy's Swedish heritage—golden-blond hair, pale blue eyes. They would have beautiful children.

"I can't believe the army is sending the POWs here. Here. Right here to Roosevelt. And worse, the hospital is making me assist in their exams this weekend at the POW camp—did you know that we actually provide monthly exams to the patients?" Caroline stabbed her straw through her own chocolate malt. "Who's taking care of our prisoners of war, I'd like to know?"

"Shh, Caroline." Teddy tightened his hand in hers. "We need them. The pea crop needs to be harvested, and with our men still away at war, we need workers. Trust me, they'll get the worst jobs in the cannery, and most of them will work out in the fields. Besides, it's not about what others are doing—but what *we* do."

She withdrew her hand. "If anyone should be throwing a fit, it should be you. You nearly lost your leg because of those Germans! What if you hadn't been found by the medics—you might have bled out on that beach—"

"Caroline. I can't keep fighting the war. The war in Europe is over, and hopefully the one in the Pacific will be too. It's time to start living our lives, right?" He leaned over, kissed her cheek.

Esther looked away. But the news hadn't left her brain since she'd heard it at the hospital.

The army had already begun to erect canvas tents, haul in snow fencing.

Snow fencing?

At the counter, two navy men, home on leave and seated at the round counter stools, flirted with the waitress while she washed ice cream dishes. Behind them, a group of teenagers jockeyed for control of the jukebox where a twangy Billie Holiday voice crooned out "Good Night My Dear."

Good night my dear,
You must never fear—
For your love is here,

"And the worst part is that Teddy and I were planning on visiting his parents this weekend in Milwaukee."

"We can go next weekend," Teddy said softly, but Caroline met Esther's eyes.

Oh. This was *that* kind of weekend—the one where she might be getting his parents' approval. Well, like Teddy said, time to live their lives.

"I'll work in your place, Caroline." Esther wasn't sure how or why the words bubbled from her mouth. Maybe because she needed to get away from the cauldron of lies at the Hahn household. Any day now, Linus's telegram might arrive.

Then what?

She tossed most of her nights away, recalling the pain in Peter's eyes, the rough edge of desperation in his voice, both real and imagined. She managed to pound her pillow into a concrete block.

And, in the wan light of dawn, with Sadie curled against her, she'd even scratched out the beginning of a few letters.

~~Peter,~~

~~I don't know why I didn't see the truth —~~

~~Dear Peter,~~

~~Seeing you, like that, behind barbed wire —~~

~~Dear Peter,~~

~~I don't blame you for not telling me —~~

~~Peter,~~

~~I wish I could write, that I could see you again. But I... don't think~~

The crumpled attempts lay in the bottom of the wicker basket in her room.

Oh, who was she kidding.

"Really, you'd do that?"

Esther found a cool smile. "Yes. You're my friend, right?"

Caroline looked at Teddy. "Could we still get bus tickets?"

"Of course."

The look he gave her made something hot and sharp curl inside Esther.

The voice sang on.

'Cuz you, my dear,
You're my everything,
You're the song I sing
When my nights are starless.

Caroline touched her hand. "Thank you, Esther. Dr. Sullivan is leading the team—normally Dr. O'Grady goes, which is a shame, because it would be the perfect opportunity for you to impress him. Have you talked to him yet?"

"I can't—not unless he talks to me first. Stupid hospital rules. I'm hoping he'll keep his word. I did put in my application for—"

"There you are, you little tramp."

Esther froze.

She turned and had no words for the woman standing there dressed like domestic help, with her hair in a white handkerchief, wearing a pair of jeans and one of the judge's old dress shirts. Mrs. Hahn gripped crumpled, now flattened discarded letters, written on Esther's lavender stationery.

Sadie sucked the last of her malt. "Grandmother!"

"Who are these to?" Mrs. Hahn ignored Sadie.

It seemed that even Billie Holiday had silenced at her tone.

"They're to a soldier." Even as Esther said it, the words clawed her chest tight.

"A soldier." Mrs. Hahn's voice shrilled. "You're writing—and according to this—*visiting* another man while my Linus is fighting across the ocean, for your freedom, your life—"

"No! It's not..." She gulped in a breath, shot a look at Caroline. "Arlene—Mrs. Hahn—I can exp—"

"Not only do you trick my son into marriage, but now, already, you are *cheating* on him."

"No I'm not."

"Then what do you call this?" She shoved the letters at Esther, who let them drop to the ground like leaflets.

"He's already dead!"

Oh. No. She hadn't.

Except, she had, because Mrs. Hahn stopped moving, her mouth working but her eyes fixed. Then, lethally quiet, her words so sharp they slid up between Esther's ribs and serrated her heart, "*Who's already dead?*"

Who. Oh, for a second she wanted to point at the ground, to the letters—because, in a way, wasn't he, to her?

No. And Linus's mother clearly saw the truth on Esther's face, because she began to tremble.

Sadie began to cry, flung herself at her mother, her legs vised around Esther's waist.

Caroline came around the table. "Sadie, come with me."

Sadie clamped her arms around her mother's neck.

Esther schooled her voice, added something gentle. "Mrs. Hahn, maybe we should just go home—"

"You tell me what you're talking about *right now*!"

Esther pried Sadie's arms from her neck, shoved her into Caroline's grasp. "Listen, we don't even know if it's true—I mean, it could be, but—"

"*What* are you talking about?"

Teddy moved to stand beside them. "Ma'am—"

"I got his letter." Esther drew a breath. "I got…the letter."

Mrs. Hahn's eyes widened. She clamped a hand over her mouth. Shook her head. "No you didn't."

"I did. Before..." Oh why hadn't she told them? "On V-E day. Or just before. Peter sent it."

The name didn't register with Mrs. Hahn, and Esther didn't bother to explain.

"Linus didn't love me, Mrs. Hahn. He—it was all a terrible mistake. We were foolish and only thinking of the war, and what could happen, and—he didn't love me. And he didn't love Sadie—"

"That's a *lie.*" Her voice dropped so low it tremored through Esther. "That's a *vicious lie.* Of course he did—*does!* He sent you here, to us, so that we could—well, clearly, watch over you, keep you from your whoring ways—"

From behind the counter, the waitress wrapped her arms around her waist.

But probably Esther deserved that.

"He wrote it in his letter—he even apologized for sending me here."

"You're a filthy liar."

No, for the first time, a dam had burst inside her, the truth came rushing out of her, filling her with the taste of something fresh and alive.

"I'm *not* a liar. But I have been for three years. Lied to everyone. I don't love Linus either—probably never did. And unfortunately, you and the judge and Sadie paid for our—"

Mrs. Hahn's hand connected with her face, a stinging slap that jerked her head back, split her face into flames.

"Ma'am—" Teddy took a step towards them.

Mrs. Hahn's eyes filled, her finger pressed into Esther's face, her voice so low it must have been dug out of the darkest places inside. "You came into our lives to steal from us. Did you think you were going to live off our money, on the dole and my son's inheritance for your bastard child? Linus isn't even the father, is he?"

"Of course he is."

But oh, how she wished he wasn't. And she hated that, yes, in that brief moment, she hoped it all might be true. Awfully, finally true, that Linus had died on the battlefields of Germany.

Because she simply couldn't bear to be married to a man who felt nothing for his daughter, and possibly despised her. Married into a family who hated her.

Are you sure?

No. *Never!*

"I don't believe you. I don't believe any of it. You're just trying to justify your own promiscuity!"

"I haven't—" She shook her head, cut her voice low and polite. "I'll prove it to you. I'll show you Linus's letter. It's back at the house. I swear it's true. He didn't love me, Mrs. Hahn."

Linus's mother took a step back, her foot grinding Esther's crumpled letters to Peter into the linoleum. "You do realize that if you are telling me the truth, then I want you out of our house tonight. *Tonight*!"

Then she turned, and the silence parted for her as she stalked out.

CHAPTER 8

"Get out. Get *out*!"

Mrs. Hahn's words, on the fraying end of her sanity after she read Linus's letter, clawed their way into Esther's brain, finding her in the night. Sadie fitted herself into the embrace of Esther's body on Caroline's narrow sofa, the heat slicking them together. The blades of the fan whirred, stirring the tepid air, and she would have liked to blame her insomnia on the way summer lay over Roosevelt like a washcloth.

You *tramp*!

She didn't know what she would have done without Bertha.

With Esther's clothing, her books, her shoes, even Sadie's rabbit cast into the yard, and dusk closing in, Bertha stepped off the porch and began to gather the debris into the battered case Esther had—not soon enough—hauled out from under her bed in the attic.

The woman spoke nothing, however, and if it hadn't been for the glisten in her eyes, Esther might have suspected her of simply attending to one of her daily housekeeping tasks.

But something must have moved her, because the next day Bertha waited for Esther outside the hospital and offered to help babysit, anytime.

But of course the housekeeper cared more for Sadie than her own grandparents. Because, well, why pretend any longer? If only Esther had the words to confront—or perhaps comfort—her.

At least the Hahns weren't trying to wrest Sadie from her. This, perhaps, Esther could look upon as providence.

And, Bertha's offer allowed her the means to serve in Caroline's place at the POW camp set up on the hill above the brewery.

Maybe he wouldn't be here. She'd spent most of the last week forcing him from her mind.

Heidi Swan carried a box of candy from the truck toward the canvas tent set up as the PX. "My brother and his buddy were on bikes, and they watched them pull up at the station. They said the men rode in Pullmans and had little red and white flags with the swastika on them on the outside of the car. My brother waved, but he said they didn't wave back."

The entire camp consisted of no more than a dozen canvas tents with a hasty mess hall set up in the middle, all penned in by a rickety perimeter of knee-high snow fencing. Even a half-hearted insurrection would overrun the few lazy guards at the gate before they woke from their Saturday afternoon naps.

"We live just across the street, and sometimes at night we can hear them singing hymns. And they play with a ball, kicking it with their feet. Sometimes it goes over the fence and Albert fetches it."

She and Heidi walked into the canvas tent, and the smell nearly knocked Esther to her knees. Sweat, and the rank odor of old milk and cigarette smoke, all marinating under the July sun. She set her box of socks on the table. Behind it, Dr. Sullivan, an elderly man with silver-gray hair and wide hands, sat on a stool, readying his equipment to meet with the POWs who were lining up at the door. Most had their hair slicked back, wet, as if they'd just showered.

"My father says they're working for the Roosevelt Food company, shelling peas." Heidi brushed away the hair from her face. Esther had piled her hair into a bun at the back of her head. At least they didn't have to wear their uniforms. No, instead she had on a pair of jeans and a sleeveless shirt.

"And some of them are working at the cannery—right beside the other workers! Shirley says they're as polite as can be—letting her go first to get a drink. She says they're hard workers too. She made them popcorn to put in their lunches."

Esther picked up a box from the back of the truck, checked it—bandages and antiseptic.

"Have you ever met a German?" Heidi said, retrieving a box of penicillin.

"Heidi, half the town is German," Esther said, returning through the gate, nodding to the two guards she knew eyed her long after she passed by.

"You know what I mean." She cut her voice low, like she might be a French conspirator. "*Nazis.* Have you ever met a Nazi?"

"Not all these prisoners are Nazis, Heidi. It's—well, not everyone in Germany was a Nazi. Some were just forced to fight."

Most definitely, none of my family joined the Nazi party, which in the end became our demise....

She wouldn't look for him. She'd already determined it. No. The last thing she needed was scandal heaped upon the town's mutterings, thank you, Mrs. Hahn.

No. She would not look. Besides, there were over eighty branch POW camps in Wisconsin alone.

He wouldn't come here.

Stepping inside the canvas tent, she set the box down on the table. Wiped her forehead.

Heard an intake of breath.

She looked up as Dr. Sullivan pressed his stethoscope to the bare chest of a patient seated across from him. Wide-shouldered, with strung muscles and the hue of hard work on his skin, the patient stared at her, his burnished blond hair tousled by the heat, wearing a rugged husk of reddish blond whiskers on his face. His blue eyes fixed on her like he might be seeing the sunrise for the first time.

Oh no.

"Esther." He mouthed it, but she could nearly hear his voice, dark and soft, slipping in under her skin, like a whisper, or a sweet breeze. It caught her breath, ran a fine thrill under her skin.

Peter.

Of course he would be here—hadn't he been working in pea fields all over the state?

Of course he would be here—because she'd lain in bed, hands clasped around Sadie, and wished it with a sort of aching dread that she couldn't deny.

Of course he'd be here, because God wanted to her to suffer for her crimes.

Peter.

"Nurse, I'll need you to take his blood pressure. And it looks like his wound is getting infected, so he'll need it redressed. And make sure to give him a shot of penicillin."

Perhaps she needed the shot of penicillin for the way he looked at her. His eyes seemed to spear right through her, opening fresh wounds, and she nearly cried out with the sweet pain of it.

Oh, in the deepest pockets of her heart, how she'd thirsted for this moment.

Except, what did the doctor mean about *his wound*? As Peter picked up his shirt and slid off the stool, she saw the puckered flesh, the needle marks, the catgut stitches across his ribs. She met his eyes and he caught her gaze, shook his head.

It looked like a knife wound—or perhaps something from the fields.

Picking up a box of penicillin, she led him to an area curtained off from the room. Behind it, cotton swabs, bandages, iodine, and a jar of needles on a wooden table suggested a makeshift clinic. She patted the metal examination table behind her, her eyes away from him, her heart in her throat. Her entire body, even her head, buzzed with the closeness of him.

Yes, he'd showered. She could smell the Ivory soap on his skin.

She didn't hear him move.

"Esther."

He barely spoke, but she heard it now, and turned. He stood over her, so close she could smell the finest layer of sweat on him, despite the shower. He lifted his hand, as if to touch her cheek—

"Put your arm behind your head." She couldn't meet his eyes.

He did, and she tried not to inhale, tried not to wish for his hand curled around the back of her neck, pulling her close as she examined the wound, the stitches. She even managed a cool voice as she asked, "What happened?"

"Did you get my letter?" he asked quietly.

She couldn't—no. She said nothing as she probed the infection for signs of discharge. One of his eyes closed, his jaw tightening. "What happened, soldier?"

"Esther." The way he said it, so softly, like a caress—she had to step back, turn away.

He followed. "I thought I'd never see you again. This is like a miracle."

She closed her eyes, shook her head. The iodine spilled out over her hand as she tried to moisten the cotton to clean his wound.

He reached around her, took the iodine from her hand. Set it down. "Tell me you didn't come to see me."

I didn't come to see you. But she couldn't, her hopes in the night filling her chest.

She pressed her hands against the counter, took a breath. "Peter, I..."

He backed up, slid onto the table. "Tell me you got my letter." He lifted his arm as she turned.

She picked up the cotton, swabbed it over his wound, hating the way he flinched, the quick intake of breath. "I got your letter."

"Tell me you don't despise me."

She applied antibiotic. Lowered her voice to a whisper, wishing it didn't come out as if dragged through a dusty road. "I don't, ever, despise you." She met his eyes a quick moment before she turned away, grabbed a fresh dressing.

"Tell me why you came to visit me."

She pressed the cotton mesh to his wound, ignored his wince, then let him hold it in place as she unrolled the bandage around his body, her arms spanning his torso. Why? She gritted her jaw, blinking back the heat in her eyes. "You—you know why."

"I do."

Then he reached out and pressed his hand to her check. She closed her eyes, allowing herself the touch of him, the strength in his wide, work-hewn hands. He ran his thumb down her face. "You are like the stars in my dark night."

She cradled her hand over his on her face. And finally, finally met his eyes.

They could look through her, probably, right down to the jagged, angry pieces of her heart. Blue eyes, with the slightest flecks of gold, and she saw the healer in them, a compassion that made her bite her lip, press her hand to her mouth.

"Please don't cry, Esther." He touched his forehead to hers. "Please."

She swallowed, shook her head. "I just—when you look at me, I —my world stops spinning. I feel like I can find my feet. Like maybe I'm not quite so lost."

The slightest smile tugged at his mouth.

Then, before she could find herself, return to the woman who had a child and sins pressing against her, she let him touch his lips to hers.

His hand cupped her chin, an invitation rather than a hunger. And for a second, she just stood there, tasting something—root beer—probably candy—on his lips. More of a whisper, perhaps, because the kiss ended too soon and left her standing there, wondering if she had imagined it.

"Give me a shot before I do something dangerous."

She opened her eyes, found him smiling at her. "I know I shouldn't have done that, but..." He gave a shake of his head. "Sorry."

"You don't look sorry." She smiled back. "Turn around."

He slid off the table, leaned over, hooked the waistband of his pants with his thumb, pulled them down just enough to reveal his hip.

She popped him fast with the penicillin shot. He held the cotton swab in place as he tugged himself back together.

His smile had vanished by the time she deposited the needle and turned to meet his gaze.

"Are you going to be okay?"

"That's my question for you." Her eyes went to the wound. "You're not going to tell me how that happened, are you?"

"Nope."

Oh, how she wanted to raise herself on her toes, press another kiss to his lips, maybe fling her arms around his neck. For a short, glorious moment, she saw him sweeping her into his arms, charging out through the POW ward into the yard, kicking his way past the guards and out into freedom.

Better, she saw them sitting under the winking stars, hands twined together.

Yes, she'd become a thirsty woman.

She wiped the wetness from under her eyes. "I passed my test—98 percent."

"Atta girl. I knew you would." Gathering his shirt, he ground his jaw as he tucked his arm into the sleeve. She helped him draw it up over his shoulder. "May I write to you?"

She averted her eyes from him. "Yes, please. I—I enjoy hearing from you."

He reached up, directed her chin to him, and wiped another gathering of moisture from her eye. "You're not lost, Esther Lange. Not anymore."

* * * * *

The dark, cool night dropped around her as she left camp, a thousand eyes winking from the sky, harboring her secret. *You're not lost.*

No, for the first time in three years, yes, she felt…perhaps not so much as if she'd left herself behind, no longer wandering around looking for the woman who'd once believed in herself.

Peter Hess made her feel found.

She pressed her fingers to her lips, still feeling his whisper kiss there, still tasting the sweet root beer candy on his lips, husky, with a licorice tang.

He'd stood in the yard, away from the fence, his hands in his pockets, while the other prisoners played soccer, or smoked cigarettes, or even played cards. Just stood there, the evening draping over his shoulders, smiling as she walked away.

She'd glanced over her shoulder. Still he stood there.

She didn't lift a hand, didn't turn completely. But she felt his eyes on her all the way down the hill as she dropped out of sight.

Atta girl. His simple, easy encouragement filled her chest—she could nearly taste the texture of his words, rich and tangy, and she let them seep into her.

The wind nestled the oak and maple leaves, dark fingers reaching out to her, to wave her home.

She'd finish her training and wait for him. How long before the troops started returning home—and soon the army would grow tired of holding prisoners and send them back to Germany. He would return home, fetch his parents, and then…

Then.

She stopped on the sidewalk. Then.

Then they'd find each other.

She knew it, like she knew her heart would beat, that breath would fill her lungs. She would find him—or he would find her, or…

Then. If she hung on, and believed it, they would have a then. After the war, after the rubble, after the ache. Then.

She could love him through her letters until then.

She hummed the tune she'd heard earlier, the husky tones nourishing her steps back to Caroline's.

'Cuz you, my dear,
You're my everything,
You're the song I sing
When my nights are starless.

Although, suddenly they didn't seem quite so starless.

The light to the boardinghouse spilled out over the porch, onto the groomed, cool lawn. Crickets seesawed into the night, and the door creaked as she opened it.

The lamp's glow from the parlor pressed into the hallway. She moved through it then stopped.

Bertha sat in the rocking chair, Sadie curled asleep in her arms. Her fawny hair lay like a halo around her chubby face.

Bertha hummed softly and looked up at Esther's step.

Esther stopped at her expression. She'd been crying—the skin on her cheeks angry and red. But Bertha's eyes—they were lit from within, and a smile unlike any she'd seen before emanated, as if, after barely flickering for three years, a flame had stirred to life.

"What is it? Is Sadie okay?"

"She's fine." Bertha got up, gathered the child close, then trundled her over to Esther. "But—you have to come home."

Esther took her daughter, pressed a kiss to her forehead. She smelled of bubble bath, her skin powdery soft. "I am home."

"No, I mean, back to the Hahns'."

Esther met her eyes. "No. Mrs. Hahn made me leave. I don't… No, Bertha. That life is over. I'm on my own now."

You're not lost.

Bertha reached out, and in a gesture that stopped Esther's heart, touched Sadie's cheek, running her finger down it. "Sadie needs her father."

Esther didn't move.

Bertha then sighed, a smile at the end. "He's come home, Esther. Linus has come home."

PART 2

Lullaby,
I'll be your lullaby,
And your sweet moonlight,
And you'll never have to fear again.

CHAPTER 9

One look could change his entire life.

Peter let the image of Esther leaving the camp, the twilight behind her, turning her hair to gold, a light in her blue eyes as she smiled at him through the barbed wire, melt into him, strengthen him.

Stir his hope.

I enjoy hearing from you.

Her soft voice, the touch of her lips, the softest hum she gave as he brushed his lips over hers—yes, he let that soak into him too. Quench the parched places inside.

"Hess!"

Peter lowered the canteen, wiped his mouth with his bare arm. The touch left a sting where he'd begun to burn. He handed the water back to Arne then rolled the cuffs of his shirt down. He had about ten cords of wood to finish chopping, then he could tuck himself into the long shadows of the barn and rest before the trucks came to haul the POW crew back to the Roosevelt camp.

Where maybe—he could barely breathe with the hope of it—Esther might come and visit him.

Arne splashed water over his bare shoulders, down his chest. The kid had filled out with the hard work, the nurture of the sun, the pale hue of the long German winter flushed out of him. One might even say that prison camp had saved his life.

And, days like this one, with the sun pouring life into their bones, the air fresh with the oats in the field, the tang of the white pine that ringed land, Peter touched freedom.

"Stop hogging it—" Fritz grabbed the canteen with his beefy hands. He poured the remainder of its contents over his oily black hair, wetting his gray undershirt, the back of his canvas pants.

"We can fill up it up at the pump. Mrs. Janzen said—"

Fritz shot him a shut-up look and Arne shrank into himself. Their guard probably couldn't understand their German, but after spending six months with them, he may have picked up the meaning of a few words, if not Fritz's tone.

"Now I'll have to go fill it." Fritz's eyes flicked over to Peter, a smirk up one side of his face.

Oh no. And his wound had just begun to heal. "Just leave it, Fritz."

"You saw how those farmers' daughters were looking at me." He shucked his hair—much longer than when they'd been hauled out of Germany six months ago—back from his face.

"This is a good gig, Fritz. The Janzens like us—"

"Hurry up, krauts." Their lone guard, a doughy man named Bert, who had been aboard a boat in the Pacific, came toward them, his uniform sleeves rolled up, sweat caught in the creases of his neck. "The Janzens offered to feed you lunch."

Fritz tucked in his T-shirt but didn't bother to put on the green POW-designated shirt. It hung over the rail of a corral fence, flapping in the hot July breeze.

"I told you that blond one was sweet on me." Fritz grinned, a wolfish look that pushed a thumb into Peter's gut.

"Behave yourself."

"What, you think you're the only one who can find a little fraulein to pass the time? I saw you standing out by the fence yesterday, watching her. Everyone knows if you could, you'd march right over Bert and the rest of the guards, track her down, and disappear with her over the border."

Peter glanced at Bert, his Winchester he'd left propped against a water barrel while he washed the grime of the day from his face. More than once he'd laid the shotgun down in the fields, helping them haul out boulders or load trucks. Yes, Bert would be easy to walk over.

Then, yes, he'd find Esther and…disappear.

A guy like him, without an accent, looking like an Iowa farm boy… He'd blend right in to the Wisconsin horizon.

"You're thinking about it, I knew it. You want to escape." Fritz jolted him from his thoughts, back to the rude heat of reality.

He shaved his voice to low. "And get shot?"

"Bert couldn't hit the side of this barn." Fritz held the door open for the guard, smiling at him real nice as he entered the house. He glanced at Peter, smile still sweetly glued to his face. "You'd be to the border of Canada before they even knew you were gone. Free."

Free.

Arne and Fritz followed Bert into the house, scraping off their boots at the door. Mrs. Janzen waved to Peter as he pumped the handle to wash his hands.

Free.

Yesterday Mrs. Janzen had handed him a plate of crispy, oil-fried kuchen, sizzling from the cast iron pot. Then, she'd asked him about her son. Had any of them seen a skinny redhead who'd been conscripted while visiting his grandparents in Germany? It happened more than Peter wanted to admit—immigrant boys sent back to the homeland for university or to visit family, swept into the Nazi war machine, forced to fight for the führer. Too many boys fighting on the wrong side of the war, too many skinny redheads, their bodies crushed by the advance of Sherman's armies, wearing the wrong uniform.

Just like him.

"No, ma'am," he said in English, even though she'd asked in German.

With all the Germans living in America, and especially here in Wisconsin, the line between sides seemed, at best, gauzy. Any one of the farmers he'd worked for over the past three months could have been a neighbor down the street in Dresden. His father's cohort at the pub.

His cousin or uncle or best friend.

Peter had watched her brown eyes skim over them, the texture of desperation so palpable it fisted his chest. He'd wanted to give her an answer. *Yes, I've seen him. He's alive.*

He understood the nearly rabid hope for that answer. *Yes, I've seen him. He's alive.*

If he could, he'd ask the same question about his family.

He held his hands under the flow of water, cleaning the woodchips from his hands. He'd developed a blister at the base of his thumb from the smooth axe handle, and the icy nip soothed the burn.

"Sir?"

He turned and found the little Janzen boy—he placed him at eight or nine perhaps—standing in the sunlight. "Is that where you got shot?"

He pointed to the wound on Peter's side. In the last day, since Esther gave him penicillin, the festering had lessened. He could nearly swing the axe over his head without wincing.

"I wasn't shot."

The kid was probably a younger version of the boy's skinny redheaded brother fighting the "krauts" overseas.

"What happened, then?"

He pulled his hand out of the water, shook it. "Some wars aren't fought with guns, kid." He tousled the boy's hair and went into the house.

Fritz, Arne, and Bert sat at the farm table, devouring potato pancakes and milk. Mrs. Janzen stood at the stove, another batch of pancakes complaining in her cast iron pan.

"Sit down now and dig in," she said without a smile.

He pulled out a chair. Mrs. Janzen slapped two still angry pancakes onto his plate, the smell turning him inside out. He poured fresh sour cream over them. The milk balmed his parched throat, the potato pancakes sweet and crispy. He tried not to let the taste of them pull him back to his mother's kitchen, but—

Peter, you need to eat. To study.

In his memory, she bent over him, whisked a kiss onto his cheek, the smell of her perfume—English lavender—drifting into his thoughts. *Join us for dinner this Sunday, after church?*

Yes, Mutter.

His mother would like Esther, he knew it in his bones. Someday—

A thump on the stairs made them look up, and of course Mrs. Janzen's daughter, the one with corn braids and a too easy smile, appeared from the attic. Maybe a day over sixteen, she flushed when her gaze traveled over them.

He glanced at Fritz, who'd put down his fork. At least this time he didn't have a knife.

Still, Peter's wound ached.

Fritz rose, pulled out a chair for the girl. "Fraulein," he said quietly.

She giggled.

Peter's chest clenched. Run. But he'd already warned the guards—Bert especially—of the last time he found Fritz in a barn with a farm girl. He'd had his hands in places that made Peter hot inside, and the girl had gone from giggles to whimpers by the time Peter pulled Fritz away.

Fritz—a warning breeched his tongue but never made it out because, as if he could read his mind, Fritz glanced at him. His gaze flicked to Peter's wound, back to his eyes.

Peter left his gaze hard in Fritz's. He didn't care what kind of tableware Fritz put into his pocket, the Janzen girl wasn't going to get trapped in the barn with Fritz. Besides, if Peter recalled correctly, he'd been the one with the axe this morning.

Fritz's mouth tightened around the edges before he turned back to the girl and practiced his broken English.

She giggled again.

Peter finished the pancake, despite the sour in his stomach. Oh, to take men like Fritz and his gang of Nazis back at the camp and throw them into a hole where they belonged. But, well, according to the locals, he belonged there too.

And, if he kept getting in Fritz's way, he might just get there first.

"Would you like more, Peter?" Mrs. Janzen stood over him with a pancake turner stacked with mini cakes. He shook his head. "Then perhaps you'll play the piano for us again?"

She nodded to the upright in the parlor.

Bert layered another pancake onto his plate. Arne, too, reached for another.

Peter stood up, wiped off his hands, then took his place at the round stool, still turned to his height.

He ran his fingers up and down the keys in a couple scales then let himself remember the chords to "A Mighty Fortress Is Our God."

A mighty fortress is our God, a bulwark never failing;
Our helper He amid the flood of mortal ills prevailing:
For still our ancient foe doth seek to work us woe;
His craft and power are great, and, armed with cruel hate,
On earth is not his equal.

On earth is not his equal. He forgot that sometimes. Like when he'd tried to staunch the blood of Linus Hahn from seeping into the dirt, to the rancor of explosions around them. Or when, at night, he heard Fritz and his Nazi pals take their fists to one of the new prisoners, just to remind him that he hadn't escaped the Third Reich, even in Wisconsin. Or even, as he'd stood in the dirt, the barbed wire cutting through his vision as he watched Esther return to her life, the one to which he couldn't belong.

Yet.

Did we in our own strength confide, our striving would be losing;

No, not yet. And mowing down Bert and running with Esther to the far-off horizon wouldn't make any of them free. He just had to keep reminding himself of that.

Mrs. Janzen stepped up behind him, and he didn't know what jolted him more—her farm-worked hand on his shoulder, or her taking up the verse in her vibrato German.

Es steit't für uns der rechte Mann, Den Gott hat selbst erkoren.

Fragst du, wer der ist? Er heisst Jesu Christ,
Der Herr Zebaoth, Und ist kein andrer Gott,
Das Feld muss er behalten.

At the table, Arne had stopped chewing, now looked up at Peter.

And though this world, with devils filled, should threaten to undo us,
We will not fear, for God hath willed His truth to triumph through us:

Arne smiled.

Yes, God had willed His truth to triumph. Sometimes Peter forgot that too. Truth *would* triumph. He had believed that the day he'd watched the SS wrestle his father from his bed, throw him onto the street, haul him off to the Gestapo offices.

Truth would triumph. He'd believed that when he'd bailed his father from jail and bartered his medical service to the Third Reich for his parents' freedom.

He'd forgotten that watching too many boys die in the frozen mud, on either side of the battlefield.

But he needed truth to triumph now. Needed to believe that, if he kept pursuing faithfulness, he might have a happy ending. Don't pick any fights, don't try to escape, just keep his head down and trust in God's deliverance for him, and his family.

He played the rest of the song, humming out the words, hearing Mrs. Janzen pour them out in a tongue he'd often hated. Now, he let it seep into him, not caring what language the hymn ministered in.

Let goods and kindred go, this mortal life also;

The body they may kill: God's truth abideth still,
His kingdom is forever.

He rolled the final chord, letting the sound fill the farmhouse, resonate through his fingers to resound inside. *His kingdom is forever.*

That, he wouldn't forget.

"Thank you, Peter," Mrs. Janzen said softly. She ran a finger under her eye.

He got up and then, because something inside him told him to, he bent down and softly kissed her floury cheek.

She let him, not making a move even as he went out of the house and into the hot sunlight.

Fritz followed him out. But when he glanced over at Peter, something dark lurked in his eyes.

And Peter knew that yes, indeed, one look could change his life.

*****

But Linus had said he didn't want her.

Esther stood more than an arm's length from the knot of people—Mrs. Hahn, Bertha, even two of the patients who must have attended grammar school with Linus—as he regaled them with the tale of how he cheated death on the grimy operating tables of a field hospital, how they took his leg, and how he nearly choked on his own blood. She could imagine with him how he clung to life during those gray days of recovery, clawing through the pain. She could even understand his nearly frantic longing to return home to his family, to his life.

But he'd said he didn't want her.

And that he felt *nothing* for Sadie.

Esther ran her hands up her bare arms, her eyelet sundress hot against her skin. He'd waited for her on the portico of the hospital this morning, where the roses and hydrangeas bloomed as if contemplating something romantic.

However, nothing but relief lifted to his eyes when he turned in his wheelchair and found her, unable to hide the question in her eyes.

She had, however, hidden away Sadie with Caroline. She wouldn't give him Sadie—not yet. Not until she understood.

Mrs. Hahn barely allowed them a moment of terse greeting before she thundered in. Now she moved back from the storytelling to stand beside Esther.

She appeared re-birthed in a resurrection white suit, a pink scarf at her throat, a white pillbox hat atop her dark hair. She didn't look at Esther. "He asked you to move home."

Esther stared at the ground, where the cracks ran through the flagstone.

"Of course, Linus will have his old room until the wedding, but you're used to the attic."

"I think he'll be at the hospital, recuperating for some time." Esther's voice melted in the summer heat.

"He'll want you with us. Sadie with us. Preparing for his return."

Esther's gaze ran to Bertha, who stood back from the group, her expression granite, ensconced in a pained relief. Still, Esther could see emotion moving behind it. Now and again the housekeeper adjusted the blanket on Linus's legs.

Her voice dropped from her, more mumble than protest. "He said he didn't love me. He didn't want Sadie." She turned her face away as she said it, her gaze on the far end of the grounds, the pine that rimmed the hill. The heat of the day dripped moisture down her back. Where was Peter today? Working at the cannery? Perhaps in a field?

"Linus was confused. Ill."

"He wrote it before he was injured."

"Things are different now. He needs you."

He didn't need her. He needed his mother. He needed Bertha. He needed…Rosemary. Esther tightened her arms over her stomach, pressing down against a bubble of ache. She'd seen Rosemary this morning, lurking down the hall, peeking out a window to the portico where Linus sat in the sun. Esther pressed herself down the hall and to the double French doors.

By the time she opened them, Rosemary had vanished.

"You told me to leave." She let her voice carry an edge.

"Now I'm inviting you back." Mrs. Hahn smiled to one of Linus's friends, pressing a kiss to his cheek as he walked past, back inside the hospital. "Thank you for coming, Ricky."

"Don't you think it would be best if we didn't pretend—"

Mrs. Hahn's hand snaked out, vised Esther's arm right above her elbow, turned her slightly. Esther didn't wince or betray the pain that shot up to her neck.

Mrs. Hahn took a breath. "None of us is pretending, dear. Return home, where you're needed. We have a wedding to plan." She released her.

"I have a job. And I've applied to the nursing management program—"

"No."

She turned to the crowd. "Linus is back, and he needs his wife to take care of him. You'll quit—"

"I'm not quitting—"

"It doesn't matter. I will ask Dr. O'Grady to let you go." She looked over at her. "Or perhaps I should tell the judge about your friend at the POW camp. See what he says about women who betray their country."

She swallowed down the blade lodged in her throat. "I haven't betrayed my country."

"He's an enemy. And you've been writing to him."

"He's a man. A German, yes, but he loves America. He grew up here."

Bertha raised her head, looked at them.

"He's on the wrong side of the barbed wire for that."

Esther tightened her jaw. "This isn't about… It doesn't matter. Linus doesn't have the right to change his mind."

Mrs. Hahn took a breath, her chest moving up and down. Then she turned, and with a smile that didn't reach her eyes, "He's a Hahn. So, yes, my dear Esther, he does."

She patted her on the arm then moved back to the group as Linus turned his wheelchair around. His eyes—she barely remembered them, and certainly never that dark—landed on her, and something in them rushed a chill down her spine.

Then it vanished, and the smallest smile tipped his lips. He held out his hand and what could she do? She found her nightingale smile and walked over to him.

"Are you tired? I can take you back to your room."

He nodded, and something about it churned real pity in her chest. Yes, maybe he did have a right, after everything he'd sacrificed, to want someone waiting for him at home.

Just not her.

She moved behind his wheelchair and pushed it away from his fans. "Visiting hours are over. See you troublemakers tomorrow." She winked at Private Johansson, glad she didn't know he and Linus had been playmates the last time she gave him a sponge bath.

She moved past Mrs. Hahn without looking at her.

The judge had secured his son a semi-private room, although the other bed remained empty. She wheeled him to the side of his bed. Leaned over to help him in.

"I can do it." His voice contained an edge, but she recognized the frustration of so many wounded men who came home with half—or less—of themselves. She held the wheelchair steady as he worked his way, not without the kind of grunts that she felt to her bones, into his bed. He used the trapeze bar for leverage and tucked his empty pajama leg under the covers as she pulled them up.

Then he leaned back, just breathing.

In. Out. The second hand of the clock over the door ticked behind them. Already, the sun dropped gray across the hospital grounds.

"I have to start my shift soon."

He continued to stare at the ceiling. She'd forgotten so much of him—the dark, ebony hair that fell over his face, the eyes that before could turn her to liquid. Or perhaps that had been a different girl on which they'd had that effect. So different. She recognized the dimple in his chin, but for the first time she realized how young he seemed. A boy, really, one who'd tried to grow up too fast.

Scars carved the history of his wounds into his neck, his arm also knotted, with serpentine scars running the length of it. How he'd lived attested, probably, to Peter's expertise.

His name nearly broached her lips.

She swallowed it back down.

Still—did Linus remember the letter, remember the man to whom he'd given it for delivery? Remember what he'd written inside it?

"I'm sorry, Linus, but—"

"Don't go."

Linus looked at her, his mouth tight, his eyes glistening.

"Are you in pain? Would you like some med—"

He grabbed her arm, right above the wrist. "Please, Esther. Don't go."

She covered his hand. "No, of course not. I can sit with you awhile after I clock in and do rounds."

"No, I mean—" He swallowed and met her eyes. She couldn't read them—or perhaps didn't want to. But she couldn't ignore the tug on her wrist, the urgency as he pulled her toward him.

He slid his good hand up her other arm, his hand cold and soft. "I remember your skin."

"Linus—I—"

His hand wove behind her neck. He tugged.

Oh no. "Linus, I don't think—"

He leaned up to meet his hold on her and before she could stop him, he pressed his mouth against hers, hard, gulping her in.

She stilled, not sure what to do. Trapped in his grip—his hand on her wrist, around her neck, Linus bruising her lips—No! Please—"No! Linus!"

She pushed him away, and the force of it made him grunt. But he loosened his grip, enough for her to step away, to hold up her hands. "Not. Yet." But her voice shook and she turned away, closing her eyes against their burn.

He said nothing, and she only heard his long thick breaths. Then, finally, "I guess I don't blame you."

What? She turned, her hand on her cheek. "What?"

"I'm a freak." He wouldn't look at her. "I even disgust myself." He wound his arm over his eyes.

And then to her horror, his body began to shake. Deep wrenching sobs tunneled out of him, wracking his body.

Oh, Linus.

She moved toward him, her hands out, not sure how to comfort him—not sure she should.

No, of course she should.

She put her hands on his arm, drew it away. Ran her hand down his wet cheek even as he turned away from her. "Please, Linus… I'm sorry. Don't… Cry. Don't cry."

He opened his eyes then, and the way his expression reached for her, she didn't know how to defend herself. So she let him swallow her in.

"You're going to stay with me, right? Don't leave, Esther. Please don't leave me. You're all I have left."

She sank down on the leather seat of the wheelchair. Pushed that dark hair from his face, pressed her palm against his cheek. He needed a shave.

"No, Linus. I'm not going anywhere."

CHAPTER 10

Papa, you're just going to get us all killed.

The memory visited Peter in the darkest hours of the night, when exhaustion pressed him into his cot, when only his heartbeat reminded him he still survived.

"Keep your voice down." His father turned to him, as vivid in his thoughts as he had been—what, already five years ago? His wizened face thickened with age, charcoal hair slicked back against his head, blue eyes growing sharper, it seemed, each day since the passing of the Nuremburg Laws. Peter still remembered the way his father glanced over his shoulder at the two black-capped SS men seated in the café behind them, eating Sauerbraten and drinking coffee.

Behind them, along the *Brühlsche Terrasse,* the summer wind coaxed the fragrances of the cedars that sentried the Balcony of Europe. In the Elbe River beyond the green boulevard, boats listed against their moorings, others slipping under the *Carolabrücke*, the Carola Bridge. Men and women out for a Sunday stroll through the *Schlossplatz* seemed unaffected by the presence of the new police force, the *Schutzstaffel*, or perhaps simply chose to ignore the thumb of the *Waffen*-SS pressing their way through the city. Yes, they'd all shuddered at the brutality of the führer's decrees. But the baroque Zwinger Palace keep of the kingdom of Saxony, the burnt red roofs of the renaissance buildings that wound throughout the city, and the grandeur of the Semper Opera House beguiled them to believe that this city in the valley of the Elbe would survive the *Führerprinzip*, the rule of the führer.

Most simply wanted to expunge the horror of *Reichskristallnacht,* when the SS smashed the Jewish shopkeepers' windows and dragged to the street hundreds of able-bodied men, beating them to their deaths, or worse, sending them to the concentration camps.

The cobblestone still ran red, although the city had done its best to wash away the stains. Except his father, it seemed.

No, Dr. Hess had practically hung a sign over his physician's office, declaring it a safe house for refugee Jews in need of medical attention and/or safe passage to Israel. Peter couldn't count how many times he'd come home from class at the university to find his father's study door closed, only to hear the closet slide shut, the cellar door creaking open as someone escaped onto the shadow-hooded street.

Peter lowered her voice, leaning over his coffee. "Father, it's not that I disapprove, but I could clearly see Isaac Fischer leave out the back alley last night. And I suspect Herr Kempler is a member of the KPD. His window overlooks the alley. And his isn't the only one. What if any of the neighbors—"

His father held up his hand, met his gaze with eyes that silenced him. "In the face of evil, would you have me do nothing?"

Peter sat back, ran his finger along the lip of his coffee cup. Around him, school children kicked a football in the shadows of the *Frauenkirche,* the Lutheran Church of Our Lady. Pigeons strutted across the gray stones of the plaza, sparrows chirruped from the linden trees. No wonder Dresden had been the playground of Bach, Mendelssohn, and even Goethe.

"Perhaps I would be more discreet."

"Discreet. What does that mean anymore, when Jacob Reissler's son is hung from a government building, his body rotting from a lamppost? There is nothing discreet about what the SS is doing."

"Now you keep your voice down, Father," Peter hissed as the two SS men glanced his direction.

Still, his father had a point. He well remembered the day in November, only two years ago, when his classmates—two Jewish men studying medicine in the *Technische Universität* of Dresden—failed to show, a hushed breath falling over the city as the *Juden* population began to vanish.

He took a sip of coffee, forced it down, not able to stifle the choking cough.

Perhaps his father had a point. His version of discreet had been returning home that day to stare out his window, his chest on fire. Except, "*Germans* are being taken, Father. Disappearing. People like Herr Janssen, the organist. They say the SS took him, sent him to the camps with the Jews."

His father ran his fingers along the brim of his fedora, settled upon the table. "If we stare at our fears, we become paralyzed. Pursue faithfulness, son. One day at a time. This is all God asks."

Yes, well, sometimes God asks too much of a man. Sometimes a man has to wrangle his own deliverance.

Or, at least he hoped.

Peter rolled over to one side, swiping the images from his mind, but they came at him. Perhaps if he'd received a letter from Esther, or a visit, but her absence left him undefended from the voices.

"Herr Hess!"

Boots pummeled the narrow stairway as he threw on his pants, grabbed up his white oxford. The SS, like roaches, slammed open his bedroom door, his hand still at his waistband. They lunged at him, and he grabbed the stair rail before he tumbled down into his parents' parlor.

The SS officer behind him pushed him to his knees, jammed his Mauser into his skull. "Where is he?"

Peter glanced at his mother, glued to her antique Queen Anne chair, the one she'd stored in her parents' attic during their years in America, her face slicked with fear. But her eyes—they bored into him, resonating a strength he hadn't known she had. She tightened her jaw, and yes, he discerned the slightest shake of her head.

"I don't know," he ground out.

He wished then he had spent more time in the fields or fishing than in his textbooks, because he might have been able to stop them—given his father a moment to escape.

Instead, at the bottom of the stairs, the front door eased open. No!—his father stood in the outline of the hallway light. An expression flashed on his face—not exactly fear. More…expectation.

Or, determination.

Peter had cried out, and—

Peter!

Father!

"Peter!"

Heat splashed across his shoulder—someone slapped him. He jerked, opened his eyes. Arne crouched beside him. "You were yelling in your sleep."

Oh. He pushed himself up, scrubbed a hand down his face. Arne settled back on his cot, his hands on his knees, his eyes wide on him.

"You do that sometimes."

"I know. Sorry I woke you."

Arne shook his head, lay back down on his cot. "I can't sleep. I should be used to the quiet by now, but all I hear is my memories of home. I miss… Did you know that I have seven brothers and sisters? My sister Eva was three when I left. She's already in school by now."

If they even had a school to return to. Peter had his fears that with the Allies defeating Germany, they may have also decimated it.

He couldn't let that thought climb through him.

Yes, I've seen him. He's alive.

"I lived in Berlin, and the city was never quiet. Not really. Quiet, like this, I got from visiting my grandparents in Lauffen. We'd go fishing in the river, and Oma would make me latkes, and late at night we'd catch fireflies."

He could see Arne's life in his eyes, how the camp along the Baraboo River could conjure ghosts, despite its almost peaceful whispers.

"The fireflies remind me of home. I hope we return soon," Arne said quietly.

Peter stared down at the barracks of men, the silence pressing against him. Moonlight fragmented through the screen windows. The sweat of men and the odors of the camp kitchen stewed in the canvas tent despite the cool of the night.

He needed a drink. If he were careful, he might get to the washrooms unheard.

In fact, if he really wanted to, he might slide out into the night, beyond the rickety snow fencing that meant to detour escape, and lose himself between the buildings of Roosevelt.

Find Esther.

Five days. Five days since he'd seen her smile fade into the twilight.

Clearly, he'd been a desperate man, lying to himself. What a fool to think she might want him. No doubt she returned home and shook herself to her senses. What future did a woman like Esther have with a prisoner of war?

And what had he'd been thinking, anyway? That she'd wait for him? That he could return to her someday, start a life in America? He barely knew her.

Still, something about her letters made him feel alive. Even… respected. As if she saw past the POW uniform to the man who longed for honor.

Pursue faithfulness. He let the voice wind through him.

He got up, stealing to the door, creaked it open, then folded into the night.

The camp lay sleeping under the scatter of stars, the spill of the Milky Way above. The guard station located at the head of the camp lit up the far end, where, no doubt, Bert and his cronies hashed out a game of poker.

Or perhaps the guards had just finished off a case of beer donated from the local brewery. He'd seen some of the townsfolk bring it over, a contingent that he hoped Esther had joined.

No.

And nothing in mail call either.

He tried not to let it turn him inside out. Tried not to remember the taste of her lips against his.

Sometimes a man has to wrangle his own escape.

No. The guards had learned to trust him. And he'd earned it—which meant he'd earned the right to leave camp, to work on the local farms, to have a decent lunch and live like a free man. More, if he escaped, he'd be shipped to Fort McCoy, or even Fort Robinson in Nebraska, where he heard men lived like true prisoners.

With good behavior he hoped that maybe the United States would let him stay.

He'd wait. And hope that Esther might truly want *him*...

He crept around the edge of the tent, listened, then scurried across the open ground to the lavatory tent. The guards had drilled a well into the ground for the men to wash up. With the men moving from town to town, they'd learned how to make their prison portable.

He slipped into the darkness of the tent, tried not to alert—

"The Janzen girl will be waiting for us. She said she'd have her daddy's truck down by the Baraboo, at the bridge west of town."

Peter froze, recognizing Fritz's voice.

No.

He crept closer.

"We'll finish them off and be to the border by midnight. One last victory for the führer."

"What about the girl?"

No. Oh no—Ernst Merkel he'd known from his days in basic training. The fact the powers sent him to Fort McCoy told Peter that Ernst's Nazi affiliations slipped below the radar, right along with Fritz. Sure, the Nazis only comprised a handful of the 137 men in the camp, but they fed on each other, terrorized the younger prisoners.

"We'll get rid of her—"

The wound in Peter's side flared as he stepped out of the tent.

Fritz crouched next to Ernst and—oh no, Hans Vanderburger. They startled, glanced up at Peter, and everyone froze.

Perhaps this was what happened when men stood up to darkness.

Until darkness stood up too. Fritz found his feet. "What are you doing here?"

Peter said nothing for a beat, just to gather himself, just to confirm that he wanted this fight. But if Fritz and gang escaped, the Americans would batten down the hatches and, well, any hope of seeing—or even writing—to Esther might die with Fritz's scurry over the flimsy fence.

Not to mention what would happen to the pretty Janzen girl.

"Stopping you."

Fritz kept his voice low. "I'm giving you one chance to go back. No one has to get hurt here." His gaze went to Peter's ribs, and he let a smile slide over his face.

Peter ignored it. "I'm not letting you leave."

Fritz glanced at his comrades. Hans rose, Ernst edged up beside Peter.

Fritz laughed, a short, quiet huff that had nothing to do with humor. "Come with us." He stepped close, the cabbage from dinner sliding out on his breath. "You know you want to."

Yes. For a second, standing in the dark, the stars a witness, he wanted to. He could find Esther—he'd just track down the hospital. And he could blend in, look like any of the farm boys from Wisconsin.

Maybe—

"He won't. He loves these Americans." Ernst whispered in his ear. "Don't you? I saw that fraulein with the blond hair—"

Peter pushed him back, not hard, with his forearm. "Leave it."

"That's it, isn't it?" Fritz said softly, that smile still around his mouth. "You want to stay right here, with these Jew-loving Americans. Like father, like son."

Everything inside him stopped, as if a hand pressed its fingers through his chest. He tried for his breath, couldn't snag it even as Fritz stepped up to him, his voice dark and earthy. "And you'll die here, just like your father. I wonder if he cried out when they gassed him—"

Fritz didn't have a chance of seeing his right hook, the way it came out of the darkness. He jerked back, blood spurting from his nose, a guttural oomph of pain punching into the night. Just for a second, a strange, almost patriotic feeling surged through Peter.

Then Ernst jumped him.

He slammed to the ground, striking back, hitting flesh, hearing bones crunch—hoping they weren't his own.

He threw off someone—probably skinny Hans—but a boot landed in his kidney and white light strobed into his eyes.

Peter had Fritz around the throat, his leg around his waist, and he held on with everything inside him, even as more boots slammed into his spine, his ribs, his head.

Sirens, a spotlight, and his vision turned to red.

Fritz slid out of his arms, and then all Peter could do was curl tight and try not to howl.

Shouting raked over him, invaded his brain, melting into him, shaking through his body.

He hung onto consciousness until he heard English voices, Bert, calling out his name. Then darkness sucked him in, and he was, mercifully, lost.

*****

Even a week after Linus's return, Peter still walked into her dreams in the fragile light of dawn.

And when he did, she let him stay there, just for a moment. Let him smile at her, even lift his hand to her face. Let his thumb caress away a tear.

You're not lost.

She let herself hear that even if, now, she had no hope of believing it. She'd left herself so far behind, so long ago, she had no idea what she might have been.

But, in the dewy moments before she had to be the woman she didn't know, she tried to put her heart to rights. *"I could have loved you, Peter. But I made a mistake."*

And always, he put his hand again on her face, his thumb brushing her cheekbone. "No, you didn't. Have faith."

But she'd left that too, far behind.

Then, when she awoke, she lay there, breathing past the jagged edges of her heart.

How could she have begun to care so deeply for a man she barely knew? Whom she'd met twice, gotten a handful of letters from?

Maybe because in his letters she'd seen more than just his friendship. Something deeper behind his words had healed something inside. Like walking into sunlight after a long winter.

She simply couldn't break free—no, she didn't want to break free—from Peter. Letting him find her in the cold chill of her dreams to smile at her, to whisper in his low tones that he believed in her, that she could find herself again. No, despite the sweet pain that accompanied his visits, she couldn't sever him from her life. Not when he was the only one who saw her, and not the girl she'd become.

You're not lost, Esther.

"Get off me!"

The words jerked her awake, into the hazy darkness of the wee hours of the night. No, she wasn't at home, Sadie curled into the cradle of her embrace. The hospital.

Linus's room. The lamp on the grounds outside bled wan light through the window and over Linus, thrashing in his sleep. She wiped her mouth, her lipstick smudged. How could she have let exhaustion lure her into slumber.

And while on duty, no less.

"Get—no!"

Linus's face twisted, his body jittery as he fought through his nightmare.

"Linus—wake up."

She leaned over him, pressed her hand to his chest where his heartbeat banged against his ribs. "Linus!"

His eyes opened, but she saw only his nightmare in his eyes. "Get away from me!"

She should have expected it—especially after yesterday's violence, but maybe her own fatigue dulled her reflexes, because she didn't even put up a hand in defense.

She took the full brunt of his blow. His fist slammed into her jaw, exploded heat through her face. She flew back, hit the opposite bed, and crashed to the floor.

Her nose burned, and she touched it. Blood poured over her finger, down her face, splotched her uniform.

"Get out!" Linus, still in his sleep. He let out a string of cursing she knew he'd only learned through his suffering.

Footsteps slapped down the terrazzo hallways even as she pushed herself to her feet, grabbing at a towel to staunch the bleeding.

Caroline appeared at the door. Her eyes widened in horror then in the disgust at Linus that Esther couldn't let herself feel.

Wouldn't let herself feel. It had started with his kiss, and each day escalated into something darker. Something she simply couldn't admit.

"What happened?" She wet a cloth, handed it to Esther in exchange for the bloodied one. Esther sank onto the side of the bed, watching Linus's face twitch.

"He's having a nightmare. I think his medication might be keeping him from waking."

"This time. Yesterday he was fully awake when he hurt you. Wait—is that bruise from him?" Caroline took her arm, examined the imprint of his grip.

She hadn't known Linus when he'd lashed out at her yesterday, when she'd tried to leave after her shift, his eyes so wide, something of violence in them that shook her to her bones. *I told you—don't leave me!*

But she could argue that she never really knew him.

Still, he'd clamped her arm so hard, she winced. He saw it and jerked his hand away, turning to the wall, his eyes closing. "I'm sorry," he said, his voice thick. "I can't help it. I just don't want to be alone."

"It's okay," she'd said. It had to be okay.

"I'm getting restraints," Caroline said now, quietly. And, heaven help her, Esther didn't stop her. Even assisted Caroline as she strapped his wrists to the bedrails. Then, she stood back as Caroline rapped him on the chest, a slick veneer of sweat over his body, dribbling down his forehead.

"Linus. Wake up."

He lunged at her even as he blinked to consciousness. Stared at Caroline in the darkness, unseeing. "What—?" He looked at his hands, then searched the room, his eyes black. They landed on Esther. "Let me go."

His tone, more than his words, sent a shudder through her.

"Linus, you hit her." Caroline moved in front of Esther. "These are for your own good."

His expression slackened, and guilt shadowed his face. Esther was thankful she had stopped bleeding, her nose only throbbing.

"I'm sorry." His voice hitched. "Esther—I..." He shook his head.

Oh, see, he didn't mean… She moved to unbuckle his hands.

Caroline clamped her hand on Esther's arm. "No. We don't know what other dreams you'll have. We'll unbuckle you in the morning. Try to go back to sleep."

His eyes narrowed on Caroline. "I can't sleep like this."

Caroline ignored him. "I'm going to check on the patients in convalescent ward." She squeezed Esther's hand. "No."

Esther hated the way he looked at her, not unlike Sadie when she left her on the doorstep when she had to go to work, or worse, when she'd packed them up and moved them back to the Hahns'. *Why, Mama? I like Carowine's house.*

But Bertha had pulled her into her arms and fed her a rare rationed-sugar sandwich, and Esther found her tucked into their attic bed with the quilt up to her chin when she arrived home from her shift.

One more week until her notice came due. Dr. O'Grady had said nothing to her about her resignation.

"Please, Esther. I know I get violent—but I don't mean it. It's just… not easy." Linus shivered and she pulled the covers up to his chest.

"I know."

"It's like I'm trapped and…" He closed his eyes, swallowed. "It's better when you're here."

She knew all the screaming to break free.

"I have to go back to work."

His jaw tightened. "Of course you do." His chest rose, fell. His lips tightened into a grim line. "Of course you do."

She left his door open as she eased out into the hall. The phone at the nurses' desk jangled and she checked her watch as she sprinted for it.

Four a.m. She picked up the phone. "Roosevelt Hospital."

"We have a patient from the camp—he's been badly beaten."

She didn't recognize the voice. "What camp?"

The pause on the other end told her the truth.

"Bring him in. I'll get the doctor on call." She flipped open the book at the desk, ran her finger down the sheet. Dr. O'Grady.

O'Grady. She drew in a breath. But a wounded man was a wounded man. And O'Grady simply didn't know the prisoners like she did. Okay, one prisoner. But if the rest of the Germans were like Peter…

Of course she reeled Dr. O'Grady from a sound sleep. "We have a trauma on the way in, Doctor."

He might have said something, although she lost the coherency in the fumble of the phone as he hung up.

She opened the trauma ward, prepped the trauma room, checking the IV tray, stocking saline solution, antiseptic, prepared a suture tray.

The military burst in through the back door, carrying the victim on a wool blanket, four guards wearing T-shirts and cotton pants. Blood saturated the shirt of the biggest man.

"Put the patient on the table."

They lifted him and he groaned. She turned and held in a gasp. Blood dripped down his face from a gash on his eyebrow, his eyes swollen nearly shut. His arm hung at a cruel angle—his shoulder clearly dislocated, and his torso—they'd ripped his shirt from his body—mottled with bruises—the outline of boots. Worse, one of his ribs had cracked and clawed through his skin, blood running over his body and pooling onto the sheet.

Her gaze arrested, however, on the opened gash along his side.

Stitches hung like coils in his skin, the rip of the nearly healed wound jagged and raw.

No.

Please…

She made herself look at his face, trace out of it the high aristocratic cheekbones, those lips that could turn in a kind smile.

No. She clawed at her voice, found it webbed inside her. "What happened to this man?"

"We're not sure. He may have been trying to escape. His fellow Nazis found him—stopped him."

He's not a Nazi. The words pooled in her mouth, threatened to spill out.

"Patch him up, nurse."

She wasn't sure where to start—please, Dr. O'Grady, get here soon. So much blood—

"Soldier, can you hear me?"

His one eye opened, and something twitched on his face. *Yes, Peter, it's me.* She gritted her teeth when he coughed and red, frothy blood bubbled around his mouth.

Breathing—she listened for sounds, found them only on one side. The broken ribs may have perforated a lung. Then she removed her stethoscope from his chest and just listened to the rattle of blood in his airway. She checked his carotid pulse. Rapid and thready.

"Help me move him. I need to check for profuse bleeding." The bigger guard stepped up, helped turn him to check for a puncture—perhaps a stab wound?—in the back. Nothing but a purpling bruise along his lower back. She'd have to check for internal bleeding.

She checked his skin, found it clammy and cool.

Detaching the sphygmomanometer from the wall, she wrapped it around his upper arm. Peter's breathing seemed labored. Surely that lung was collapsed, the air building up pressure in his chest.

"What can I do?" Caroline appeared, moving in front of the burly guard.

"You have to call Dr. O'Grady again. This man has a pneumothorax and is going into shock." She knew from the look on the guard's face that he didn't understand. "His lung has collapsed!" Caroline's expression tightened. She glanced at the guards then back at Esther. "Dr. O'Grady's not coming."

Esther stilled, listening to the heart sounds.

She let the air drain, pulled off her stethoscope. "What?"

"He left."

For a second, the world seemed to narrow, a piercing wail from far away the only thing in her ears, then below her, blinking up at her, Peter's damaged eyes. "He left? But he's on call."

Caroline cut her voice lower. "He's a POW. Remember what I said about—"

"So he's going to let him die?" She probably raised her voice a little too high. Still, in the glaring light of the trauma room, the tone seemed appropriate.

Caroline shrugged. "I can call someone else."

No. God—she couldn't. "Please. Call Dr. Sullivan."

In the meantime, she'd have to do what she could to keep Peter alive.

Because no, she couldn't say good-bye, not yet.

Not to him.

Not to herself.

"Let's get him on oxygen…"

CHAPTER 11

They'd strapped him to the bed.

Peter wasn't going to escape. Oh, how Esther wanted to scream that—the man could barely move. A sling strapped his right arm to his body—his shoulder had been dislocated, the three ribs beneath it fractured. And a truth embedded deep inside her told her that something about the report from the guards—and the other prisoners—didn't sit quite right. Peter, escape?

And, even as the accusation gnawed at her, she'd told herself it had nothing to do with her. He wouldn't escape for her, would he?

She ignored the sweet, forbidden swirl of emotions churned by that thought.

Still, as Esther buckled on the leather straps, securing Peter's left wrist to the bed—per Dr. O'Grady's terse orders when he'd shown up for his shift—the truth chewed at her insides, brittle and sharp.

Peter was a prisoner. Of war. The *enemy.*

However, watching him sleep the last two nights, his dark blond hair soft and catching the barest hint of dawn as it fell over the bandage around his head, his face stripped of expression, his bare chest rising and falling under the bandages around his torso—no, he didn't bear any resemblance to an enemy.

In fact, she had this insane, terrible urge to curl up beside him.

Not that anyone would know. Dr. O'Grady sequestered him in

a private room, although the guards had talked him out of demanding an armed man at the door. After all, they only had a flimsy snow fence penning in the remaining able-bodied 136 prisoners down at the marsh. And with Peter strapped to the bed, he wasn't going anywhere.

Even if he had—*supposedly*—tried to escape.

She glanced at the clock as she sat up in the chair, rubbing her hands down her arms, humming softly. Three-fifty-five. Five more stolen moments—then she'd return to her desk, do another walk through the wards, then sit by Linus's bed until he awoke.

She hoped Linus wouldn't have another nightmare. She'd begun to fear his sleep. And in the daytime, well, the demons that ran through his mind in the dark roamed his face in the haunted wells under his eyes. He sometimes—too often—stared at her without seeing her. And not once had he asked for Sadie.

Not that she'd bring Sadie in to him. After all, it was a hospital, and she was too young to visit the infirm. Still, the lack of Sadie in Linus's thoughts nagged at Esther.

If he wanted Esther, surely that meant he wanted his daughter too?

Peter stirred, a groan, then a breath that drew deep, caught. A wince crossed his face.

"Shh… Don't move. Go back to sleep." She said it so softly, he couldn't possibly have heard it, yet his eyes opened.

She stilled, struck with the urge to run. Instead she allowed herself a smile, one that she didn't have to fabricate.

He blinked at her, as if shifting her image from his dreams to reality. Then he, too, smiled. And something about it heated her clear through. Oh, he had devastation in his smile. And his voice, low and caressing her bones. "I knew an angel was camped by my bed at night."

She wanted to roll her eyes, but, well, the line charmed her.

"Is that a blush, nurse?"

"I think you need to go back to sleep, soldier."

"I am sleeping. This is my dream, and I'm in charge." But he said it with a smile. "You are so beautiful, you know that?" Then he reached out to her, his wrist jangling against the bed frame. His smile fell. "Oops, I forgot."

"I'm sorry. The doctor said—"

"I know what he said. That other nurse told me I nearly died. If it hadn't been for you, I might have. How did you know how to apply an occlusive dressing? My lung would have collapsed if it weren't for you."

What nurse told him? Caroline, probably, who checked in on him while Esther sat with Linus. She couldn't scrub from her memory Caroline's expression as they wheeled Peter out of surgery to repair his damaged lung, and into the recovery room. She'd met Esther at the door, grabbed her by the exhausted arms, stared her down, and said, "This is him, isn't it?"

Rosemary had brushed past them, on duty as a scrub nurse, and had shot her a look that turned Esther's response to bile. She swallowed it down and nodded.

But the horror of having both Linus and Peter in the same hospital, separated by about ten steps in the corridor, followed her home even as she curled up to Sadie, drawing her petite body into the well of her embrace.

She had to let Peter go. Had to tell him about Linus and Sadie. Had to tell him good-bye.

She had breathed into Sadie's soft skin, the fragrance of her hot sleep like perfume. It would be best this way.

But no words came. Even as she sat next to him in the hollow moments of the night, nothing came.

Nothing but the urge to uncuff him and run with him somewhere, anywhere, Sadie skipping between them.

"Who did this to you, Peter?" She watched him work circulation back into his fingers—the ones half-hidden by his bandage, the others in the cuffs.

Peter shook his head. "It doesn't matter."

"It matters—they beat you nearly within an inch of your life. They should be punished."

"And then what? They clamp down on the camp? They move us away from Roosevelt, maybe to Fort McCoy?"

His words scraped away any last vestiges of fantasy she harbored. Yes, they could move them, and she might never see him again.

Worse, he might be beaten again, and this time left to die on the trauma room table. She didn't even know how to begin thanking Dr. Sullivan for tromping in, sleep in the creases around his eyes, willing to save Peter's life.

She wanted to be able to save lives. To do surgery, close damaged lungs, stitch up lacerations of the kidneys, removed damaged spleens. She wanted to be the one to decide whether to show up in the middle of the night, and to command the respect of nurses—instead of being silenced to stand on the sidelines, forbidden to speak unless spoken to.

"I nearly died seeing you so hurt," she said, her voice so shallow she might not have spoken. But oh, despite the ache in saying that, it felt like the lancing of a wound. She breathed out, put her hand to her mouth, blinking back the prick of her eyes.

"Sort of how I feel watching you sit there, so much pain in your eyes, it hurts worse than breathing in and out." His face softened, something so kind she had to look away. "What is it, Esther? What is it that kept you from writing to me, kept you from coming to see me, but that drives you to my bedside in the darkness of the past two nights?"

She closed her eyes. *I'm engaged. I have a daughter. I shouldn't be here.* The words clogged in her throat. She shook her head.

The chain on his bed rattled, and she opened her eyes to see him reaching for her through the shackles.

Oh, she shouldn't... But, almost without her permission, her hand found his. He wrapped his around hers, folded his fingers between hers, held on.

They fit well. And warmth shot up her arm into her body. He tightened his hold even as she cupped her hand over her forehead, bent her head, and wept.

* * * * *

Hold on, Esther. Hold onto me. He held the words inside, longing to deliver them to her, longing to rip off the cursed buckle and draw her into his arms. But something about the way she curled into herself, the way she cupped her hand over her eyes, as if holding on to his hand was the furthest she could extend herself—

It hit him like a brick—harder than anything Fritz had dealt out.

She felt guilty.

Yes—her posture, bent over, protecting herself as if waiting for some assault—he recognized the posture of shame.

Oh, he knew it too well. *I think I brought them here.*

His mother had stared at Peter with a look of coiled horror, her voice so slim it cut through him like a knife. *Who did you bring?*

The SS. I recognize them from the café where father and I were arguing.

Then he'd curled into just that ball.

"I did this, didn't I?" he said now, on a thin slice of despair.

She shook her head.

"I did—only I don't know what it is. Please, Esther. I want to help."

"You can't help me, Peter. For a while, I thought…." Her breath emerged so serrated, the shards of it made him wince.

She made to tug her hand away, but he held on. "No. Esther. Whatever it is—I want to know."

She looked up at him then, a look so terrible, her eyes reddened, her cheeks glistening, that the ache in it swiped his breath from his chest. "No, you don't."

"I do—is it me? Is it the kiss—I'm so sorry. I shouldn't have let it happen. But I meant everything I said. The war's over, and we'll be let out soon—"

A knot of desperation had gripped his chest ever since she'd taken his hand, the kind of desperation that could see the future and told him that if he let go, she might just flee from the room. And, prisoner that he was, he couldn't run after her.

Nor, maybe, should he, if he was going to cause her this much pain.

Oh, what had he done, dreaming up a future for them? Like she might be some sort of reward—

"It's not the war." She wiped her cheeks with the meat of her hand, first one, then the other. "I need to get back to the nurses' station."

"Please! Esther—"

"I'm getting married!"

He stopped moving. Stopped thinking. Just went numb, his entire body stripped. "Married?"

She yanked her hand away from his—he'd relaxed his grip just enough to let her.

"Yes. The man you saved in Germany is my fiancé."

"Linus?"

She was blinking now, looking past him, out the window to the dawn. "Yes. Linus Hahn. He wasn't my friend. He's my fiancé."

Something about the way… Is. *He's my fiancé.* "He's not dead." The words tasted like char coming out of his mouth. "He lived."

She nodded, but the way her eyes died made him want to weep. "There is something you're not telling me."

Her beautiful face crumpled, just for a moment, and she cupped her hand to her mouth.

"Do you love him?"

She closed her eyes.

Then, shook her head.

A fist released in his chest, and he hated that he wanted to cry out from it. She didn't love him. She didn't love him. "I—don't understand."

"We have a daughter."

She said it while looking away from him, down at his shackled hand, still open for hers. "You have a…daughter?"

She nodded. Then cupped her hand over her eyes, as if unable to look at the past. "We had a night together—a stupid, mistaken night before Linus left for the war. I don't know what I was thinking. Just… I probably thought it wouldn't matter. I didn't love him, even then. I knew it. But I let him talk me into the back seat of his car—"

"His car?" Oh, he didn't mean the tone, except anger boiled through him, and he almost welcomed the screws of pain his quick intake of breath coiled through his chest. "He made love to you in the back of his car?"

"Stop, please. I can hardly think it myself. I… And no, he didn't make love to me. He—he didn't love me either."

This was why God had shackled him to the bed. So he couldn't rise up and wrap his hands around this man's dishonorable neck.

But—wait. He'd been writing—courting, even, a betrothed woman. He swiped that thought aside, unable to face it. Or the truth that things might not have been different if he'd known.

So much for being faithful to God's principles.

"You got pregnant."

She nodded, finally lifting her face to his. Oh, she was so beautiful, her silky blond hair rolled up around her nightingale hat, those curved lips, the way her eyes, blue, or even green in the early light—reached out to him. He held out his hand again. Please.

She slid hers into it, staring at his grip in hers. "I was dismissed from the Red Cross. I didn't have a job or money, and when I wrote to my parents…" She turned his hand over, traced the swell of his veins in his hands. "So, I wrote to Linus, and he told me to come here, to live with his parents."

"They don't like you."

She looked up, blinking her beautiful blue eyes again. "Not much. But, see, I've disgraced them. So, yes. I'm marrying their son, who has returned from war."

She sighed, a shudder of breath through her. Outside, the birds had begun to chirrup, morning drifting into his room. He had imagined such a moment like this—seeing Esther in the morning light, her hand in his. Perhaps not exactly this moment, but—

No. She was engaged. He let her go.

"What am I missing, Esther? You have a man who loves you,

a child, and while you don't love him…" Although, wasn't that enough? She shouldn't be shackled to marry a man she didn't love. Or perhaps, well, she had acted as if she loved him, made a child with him… He stared at the buckle holding him to the bed.

She looked up, apparently misunderstanding, because she nodded. "I know—I should be thrilled—but, see…the letter."

The letter. "The one I sent?"

She nodded then shook her head, and her expression came back to him, stripped.

"What was in the letter, Esther?"

She rubbed her hands together in her lap. "Linus told me that he wanted nothing to do with me, or Sadie."

Oh.

"And then you wrote to me." He wasn't sure why those words burned coming out, but they did, searing through him.

"No. I wrote to you before I knew what he wrote in the letter. Because I suspected the truth, that he didn't love me, and I had to know." She drew a breath. "I had to know if he talked about me…" It seemed she forced her smile. "The way a man talks about someone he loves."

Someone he loves. Peter saw Linus in the mud, then, listened to him talk of home, of his friends, playing football, of a redheaded girl back home. Yes, he had talked of someone as if he loved her. But it hadn't been Esther. Not once had he mentioned her as his fiancé.

He looked at her hands, the way they wrung together in her lap.

"He didn't talk about you that way."

She nodded, a sort of sadness on her face. "I know. And, heaven help me, I was relieved." She blew out a long breath. "Relieved, Peter. I was sort of set free. And by then, I had started to…"

"To write to me."

She looked up, her smile quick, like lightning. "To care for you."

Oh. Now he had to look away, into the rose gold of the morning. But... "I don't understand then. Why does he want you now?" He turned back to her, and she was watching him, something tender on her face.

"I don't know. He was so wounded. I'm thinking that he feels trapped. Maybe even like his life is over. I think he came back a different person, even wrecked, and maybe he thinks I'm the only one who might understand."

Wrecked. "You do, don't you?"

"I do understand looking in the mirror and not recognizing the person there. I understand losing yourself inside your sins. I understand needing to hold on to someone because they see you as you want to be seen."

Her eyes flickered over to his. Again, that flash of smile.

Yes, he understood that too. Especially the part about being seen beyond the man in the POW uniform, under gunpoint. Perhaps this, more than anything, had filled his long nights with hope.

"You don't have to marry him, Esther."

She shook her head. "Yes, I do. And you know it."

Oh. He did know it. And that's what hurt, probably the most. He knew it and hated it. And that part of him—the desperate, wounded man inside—that was the man that spoke. "Why? So you can work off your sins?"

"I'm trying to make it right!" She cut her voice to low.

This, too, he understood. Understood facing the wretched truth and the scrawling of one's name on a dotted line in order to atone for one's mistakes.

Understood that sometimes the choices weren't about love or happiness. Sometimes they were about life. His father's life.

Sadie's life.

May the God whom you continually serve deliver you. His father's words as Peter stepped on the military transport rang through him.

But it seemed, suddenly, as if God had delivered Peter right into prison.

He tasted the bitterness of those words even as they scraped through him.

No. God had kept him alive as he'd stumbled into the smoke and chaos of battle, faithful to his Hippocratic oath. God had brought him back to the land he'd loved, given him a glimpse of safety. And, for some reason, God had helped him save Linus Hahn.

He swallowed down, again, the bitter taste of betrayal. No.

Still, it burned inside him. "Please, Esther. Don't… Wait. See, the war will end, and I'll come back, and…"

She shook her head, a stiffness in her expression. "No. I don't have a choice. Linus is my fate—"

"Linus is your atonement!"

She flinched, but he didn't care.

"You're marrying him because you are trying to erase what happened! You're trying to find forgiveness. But don't you see—you already have it."

"I don't have it!" Her tone slapped him, but he didn't recoil. Just bled for her, watching her unravel as she stood up, whirled away from him, clamped her hands around her waist. "Maybe you don't understand what it feels like to walk around always bleeding inside. To see the shape of your sins tucked beside you so desperately sweet, and yet know what this incredible love cost you? I haven't felt whole since that night. Well, until…" She turned, then, sharp. "I wasn't in love with you, Peter, I just thought I was. I was in love with the thought that someone might not see me the way I did. But—that's not going to happen."

It could happen. It did happen. "Esther, you don't solve the problem of your sins by trying to forgive yourself. You have to let God forgive—"

"I have to marry Linus. I have no other choice. I made my mistakes, and now I have to live with them. It doesn't matter what I want—it's the right thing to do." She cut her voice low. "And don't talk to me about God. He doesn't love a woman like me."

Her small words severed from him the desperate man trying to hold on to what he'd wanted.

He suddenly realized, this conversation wasn't about his heart… but Esther's soul. Perhaps, in fact, God had delivered him into prison for just this moment.

His voice softened, and he put a caress in it. "Esther, He loves you more than you can imagine."

She flinched again, and he wanted to cry out.

"Listen to me. Don't despise the grace given to you by staring at your sin. You must turn around and keep your eyes on the face of love. The face of grace. This is where you'll find forgiveness."

She closed her eyes as if his words pained her.

Please, God, I'm sorry I despised my imprisonment. It's Yours for Your glory.

"Esther, you're not lost. God knows exactly where you are. You just have to stop and let Him find you."

"I thought He had, with you."

He caught her eyes, those beautiful eyes that softened with a smile.

He held his hand up, spread his fingers open. She debated for a moment then slipped her hand into his. He closed his fingers around hers. "Maybe… Maybe we could just hold on to that, for one more moment."

She sat down in the chair, and her face softened even as a tear dripped off her chin.

"I'm sorry, I didn't mean—of course I care for you, Peter."

"Shh… It doesn't matter. I can't matter." But he took her words in, captured them.

They sat there in the silence of the morning, the gold sliding over the speckled gray and red terrazzo floor.

Finally, she got up, adjusted his covers, then leaned over and pressed a gentle kiss on his cheekbone, right below his eye. She smelled of a floral perfume, something he might remember, later.

He smiled into her touch, glad, for at least this moment, that he couldn't sweep her into his arms.

"Be safe, Peter," she said quietly. "I'll never be sorry I met you."

Then she turned, and her intake of breath stopped Peter, made him cut his gaze to the door.

In the outline of the morning stood a nurse, her red hair caught back in a snood, her hands fisted into boulders in her apron pockets. And she wore an expression not far from the one Fritz had given him in the yard.

Changing his world with a look.

CHAPTER 12

"If you try and escape, so help me, I'll come after you myself and make sure you don't walk for a week."

Peter grinned at the nurse—Caroline, was it?—and eased himself into the chair in the solarium. An upright piano on one end of the room begged to be played. "I'm just here to listen to the hymns."

"If you can hear over the Ping-Pong. Some of the boys have quite a match going. Apparently there's some high stakes. One of my guys bet all his pudding for a week." She winked at him. "I'd stay away from that action."

He would have compared her to Esther, but that wasn't fair. Caroline had a peasant beauty about her—chestnut-brown hair, freckles across her nose, a spare frame with a no-nonsense way about her mannerisms. Still, she'd gone from stone-cold, brusque treatments to finally giving him a gentle smile. Especially when he'd told her how he'd grown up in Iowa. It helped, too, that she'd caught him humming a hymn.

"The preacher from the Methodist church is due in today. He should be here in about an hour or so—after their service is over. But I'm going off my shift, and I don't think the other nurses will take the time to—well, they're a bit afraid of you." She gave him a wry smile. "Promise you'll walk back to your room when he's finished?"

"I wasn't trying to escape." It felt good to say this—not like he hadn't had the chance, but he feared for Arne and some of the other men who would suffer at Fritz's hand if Peter brought trouble for the Nazis in camp. They had a long, very long memory.

"I believe you." She smiled at him. "Esther isn't in today, by the way."

He nodded, ignoring the pinch inside. Four days without seeing her felt a little like someone had reached in and torn his heart from its moorings, but like his other wounds, he'd have to breathe through the pain. She didn't belong to him.

Never really had.

"I'm going to bring Charlie in too. He needs to hear some hymns, I think."

Bells rang through the blue-skied day, the ring announcing the early services, probably over at Sacred Heart Catholic Church. Through the solarium windows he could make out the red spires of the church rising above the elms and red maples in lush bloom.

A mighty fortress is our God,
A bulwark never failing;

He let the hymn fill his mind, breathed it in even as two patients wheeled into the room. Both were missing legs, their blue hospital pajamas tucked under them, their robes cinched tight around their waists. One seemed vaguely familiar—dark hair, a stocky build. He—

"I hope you brought your dough, Linus."

Linus.

"Please. Please try, Tommy," Linus said, rolling over to the Ping-Pong table. He picked up the paddle.

Help. The moment in the darkness, when he'd checked on the two German soldiers he'd come to rescue, rushed back to him. *Help.*

Linus sprawled in the dirt, his blood puddling beneath him. He clutched his leg, writhing.

Peter crawled over to him and dug out his English. *Stay still, pal, and I'll do what I can.*

At the Ping-Pong table, Linus served the ball. Tommy sent it back. Like the ticks on the clock, the ball dinged the table, back and forth over the net. Linus slammed it hard, and Tommy lunged for it, missed it.

"My point." Linus held up the paddle, twirled it, a grin on his shaven face.

Am I going to die?

Peter had no choice but to tie off the leg in a tourniquet. *Not if I can help it.*

I have a girl back home, you know. Someone. I can't leave her behind.

Peter had leaned close to his ear, tugging off the man's helmet. Sure enough, there was a picture inside. *This her?*

Yeah. If she'll still have me.

More patients had roamed in, taken seats around the solarium. A couple nodded to him, as if he belonged here, one of them, a soldier. He found a grin, nodded back, the question searing inside him. Did Linus really love her?

Tommy and Linus battled it out. Linus missed, and the crowd groaned. "C'mon, Linus! Don't let him take you!"

Linus spun the ball on the table then slammed it over the net. Tommy swished the air.

"Point."

Please, send this for me. To Esther. He pulled the grimy letter from his pocket, his trembling hands shoving it into Peter's. *She'll understand, I know she will.*

Who's Esther?

Linus looked at him, shook his head.

See, he should have seen it then. Oh—

No. I don't have a choice. Linus is my fate—

Linus is your atonement!

Linus laughed as Tommy lunged for another, a harsh laugh that grated through Peter.

C'mon, Tommy. Peter willed Tommy's next point. And his next. Linus's grin vanished.

"Lost your magic, huh, champ?" One of the men in the crowd—a tall, lanky guy missing one arm—stood up. "Number-one Ping-Pong player in the school, and now look at this. Beaten by a kid. Turn it in, old man. It's time for the ball and chain."

Laughter rippled through the crowd. Linus grabbed up the ball. "Shut up. I'm not getting married."

"What do you mean, you're not getting married? Your mamma's practically got the church reserved. And your old lady is here just about every day—"

"I'm not getting *married*!" Linus slammed his serve over the table. It nicked the edge of the table.

"Out." Tommy tossed the ball back.

Linus caught the ball in his grip. "In. My point."

Tommy shook his head. "Out. It nicked the table."

"I said it was in. Don't be a cheater."

The room died to a crisp silence.

"I'm not cheating, Linus. I—"

"Shut *up*!" I said it was in." His voice ground down to a nub.

Tommy eyed him for a long moment. "Fine, old man, it was in." He glanced at his audience, lifted his shoulder.

Linus threw the paddle at Tommy's head. Tommy dodged and it crashed into the wall behind him, splintering.

"What the—"

But Linus had already cleared the table, faster in his wheelchair than Peter would have given him credit for—or any of his fellow patients, for that matter, for no one moved as he launched himself at Tommy.

"Linus! Stop!"

"Hey!"

Linus had Tommy on the floor, and they rolled like helpless, angry men, Linus slamming his fists into Tommy's head, his nose. He wrestled atop him, pinning him, his hands on his throat.

"Linus!" Hands grabbed at him, pulled him off, and he thrashed out, kicking, taking down Tommy's two-legged protector, rage twisting his face.

Linus jumped on his new assailant, fisted his pajamas, slammed his fist into his face. But Tommy had pulled himself over, yanked his arm around Linus. Pulled him off even as the other man shoved him away.

Then three other soldiers landed on Linus, pinning him.

Linus lay on the floor thrashing, his face hot, crying, swearing. "Help! Help! Rosie! They're killing me, Rosie!" His voice tore through the room, pitiful with the tone of it, wrenching through Peter—and probably every man there—so reminiscent of their own battle-wounded cries. "Rosie!"

And then she appeared, and Peter should have known it all along. The woman in the picture. The woman in the doorway to his room watching Esther kiss him, the woman in Linus's heart.

The woman Linus had wanted to come home to.

Rosie. With the red hair caught in a snood, wearing a white apron over her blue nurse's dress. Rosie, who had probably loved him since first grade, definitely hoped to marry him when he returned from war. Rosie, the nightingale who parted the chaos, dropped to her knees, and gathered Linus into her arms.

Linus clung to her, coming back to the wreck of himself, and sobbed.

Rosie, the woman Linus loved.

Am I going to die, man?

Peter sat in the chair, staring out at the blue-skied morning, listening to the hymns filter through the window, and wished the answer had been yes.

*****

"O Lord, how shall I meet Thee, How welcome Thee aright?"
Thy people long to greet Thee, My Hope, my heart's Delight!"

The words twined out of Esther like old bones creaking, driven from cobwebbed corners in her soul, the tune of the old hymn stirring to breath inside her.

"O kindle, Lord, most holy, Thy lamp within my breast."

Sadie hung on to her hip, her arms around her, pretty in her pink sundress and curls. Esther had pin-rolled her own hair, found a dress for herself that didn't bag on her and turn her into a refugee.

Although, she felt like one, tiptoeing behind the Hahns into St. Peter's Lutheran Church. Eyes tracked her, and she silently begged the judge to stop near the back. But no, their pew sat three rows from the front to the left side of the altar. Within reach of the fire and brimstone.

The sun through the stained glass windows gilded the polished wood pews, and at the side of the altar, the pipe organ gleamed gold as it rang out the hymn.

"To do in spirit lowly All that may please Thee best."

The judge loomed beside her, taller than she remembered—or perhaps she'd just never stood this close to him. In his black suit, the wide red-and-yellow-patterned tie, the way he held his fedora in his hands, with Mrs. Hahn in her black pillbox hat, her long-sleeved navy suit, the voices raised in precision and harmony, all of it peeled back time.

"Don't fidget, Esther. It's not proper." Her mother cast a look on her, her blue eyes lighting on Esther's wayward foot. Esther tucked it back in line with the other, wrapped her hands around the curled wood of the pew as her mother returned to the hymn.

My heart shall bloom forever, For Thee with praises new
And from Thy name shall never, Withhold the honor due.

Next to her, Hedy made eyes with Francis across the aisle, and as Esther looked up at her beautiful sister, Hedy winked.

Esther followed her gaze to Francis, saw him overdramatize his singing.

I lay in fetters, groaning, Thou com'st to set me free;

"What are fetters, anyway?" Hedy said into her ear. Mama shot them both a sing-or-else look.

Hedy straightened, held out her songbook, lifting her glorious voice. Oh, to sing like Hedy. She could probably be a singer someday, on a stage somewhere, with her golden-blond hair, her pretty smile. And someday, maybe Esther could be just like her. Beautiful and with a boy like Francis flirting with her across the aisle.

"'I stood, my shame bemoaning, Thou com'st to honor me.'" Esther glanced at the hymnal that Mrs. Hahn held, pushing away the rest of her memories.

Still—"

"Hedy, God doesn't suffer harlots!" Her mother's voice rising through the farmhouse, through the vent in the second-floor bedroom. If Esther pressed her eye to the curl in the grate, she could just make out her mother's expression, the eyes flaring with anger, the snarl of her mouth, her hat still pinned to her head. And Hedy, standing there, her weight on one skinny hip, staring out the window.

"I'm not a harlot, Mama."

"You will be, and then what? There's no coming back from your sins, then."

"Maybe I won't want to come back."

The crack of a palm against Hedy's face jerked Esther away, and she scooted back, her hand to her mouth.

Hedy didn't cry out. But moments later the house shuddered as the door slammed.

I'm not a harlot, Mama.

"Love caused Thy incarnation, Love brought Thee down to me;
Thy thirst for my salvation, Procured my liberty."

Sadie wiggled on her hip and Esther set her down on the pew. Mrs. Hahn looked over, raised an eyebrow, but Esther ignored her. How many verses did this hymn have?

She took count of the people she knew in the audience—there was Dr. Sullivan and his wife, and behind them, one of the younger nurses, who had married just weeks ago one of the soldiers from the ward.

Clearly, Esther wasn't the only nightingale to give her heart to a wounded man.

Maybe we could just hold on, for one more moment.

Peter's words clung to her like the heat of the sun on her skin. She curled them into herself, letting herself see his eyes, the way he listened to her confession without condemnation.

Even, after it all, still wanted her. Still…

"Rejoice, then, ye sad-hearted, Who sit in deepest gloom,
Who mourn o'er joys departed, And tremble at your doom."

She caught the words, let them tiptoe inside.

> *Do not despise the grace given to you by staring at your sin. You must turn around and keep your eyes on the face of love. The face of grace. This is where you'll find forgiveness.*

How she wanted to see the face of grace. But she kept hearing that slap. *I'm not a harlot, Mama.*

"Ye need not toil nor languish, Nor ponder day and night
How in the midst of anguish, Ye draw Him by your might.
He comes, He comes all willing, Moved by His love alone,
Your woes and troubles stilling; For all to Him are known."

She glanced at her daughter, her two fingers stuck in her mouth, sucking. Esther edged them out of her mouth, wiped her chin. The sun in her hair turned it nearly into a halo. Yes, perhaps God did know her troubles…and her joys.

"Sin's debt, that fearful burden, Let not your souls distress." She leaned into the hymn, drinking in the words. "Your guilt the Lord will pardon, And cover by His grace."

Cover by His grace.

"You're marrying him because you are trying to erase what happened! You're trying to find forgiveness. But don't you see—you already have it."

She closed her eyes against Peter's words, but they crashed over her again, their tone nearly turning her inside out. Yes. She was trying to erase her past. Make it right. But maybe she had been staring at her own sins so long, she hadn't looked up to see….grace.

Grace just seemed so….inappropriate. Why should God forgive those who intentionally sin?

She opened her eyes, lifted them to the altar, the communion wine and bread spread out on the table. Grace. She hungered for it.

Esther, He loves you more than you can imagine.

Tears burned her eyes. She blinked then reached around for her handbag to find a handkerchief.

Looked up.

There, three rows behind her, Rosemary caught her eye. Her red hair turned to fire in the sunlight, her painted lips a perfect knot of disapproval. She slowly shook her head as the final verse rose around them.

"He comes to judge the nations, A terror to His foes,
A Light of consolations, And blessed Hope to those
Who love the Lord's appearing.
O glorious Sun, now come, Send forth Thy beams so cheering,
And guide us safely home."

She clasped the purse shut, turned back. Safely home. Wherever that was.

Mrs. Hahn closed her hymnal, turned, and lifted Sadie off the pew. Settled her on her lap. Esther sat with her hands folded on her knees, stiff, as the congregation recited the Apostles' Creed and the pastor delivered the sermon about Jesus and Nicodemus.

"But whoever lives by the truth comes into the light, so that it may be seen plainly that what he has done has been done through God."

Rosemary's stare burned a hole in the back of her neck.

They rose for the communion prayer, and Esther gripped the pew, her legs weak, perspiration sliding down her back. She might faint with the heat in the church.

"Mrs. Hahn—" she started as the church began to file out to the altar for their communion. Mrs Hahn shot her a look, wide-eyed, as she shifted Sadie onto her hip.

They moved out of the pew and for a moment, Esther stopped. Bread and wine, the propitiation of Christ's death and life in her.

A harlot.

She turned, bumping against the man behind her. "Excuse me," she barely mumbled as she quick-walked to the back of the church. She felt eyes scrape over her as she fled.

Tripping down the steps, her heart in her mouth, she crossed the vacant street and headed straight for the park. Found a bench under an elm.

Listened to the organ's mourning trail after her.

Overhead the swallows chirped. The July sun syruped through her, touching her bones. Her heartbeat settled back to itself.

See, it had simply been the heat inside the church. She pulled off her hat, let the wind loosen her hair, cool the moisture from her body. And she hadn't been sleeping well, not since her job at the hospital ended two weeks ago.

And Linus—Linus had been even more distant, almost angry whenever she went to see him. And yet, he begged her to stay with him, last time throwing a pudding dish at her when she got up to leave.

"Sadie needs me—"

"I need you!"

She wrapped her hands around her waist, closed her eyes, raised them to the sun.

He just needed more time. Hadn't he said that he didn't want to get married until he could stand at the altar? That might be months—even a year. Surely he'd see, by then, that he didn't love her.

He didn't love her. She knew it in her bones. Saw right through his need to the truth.

Linus feared being unloved. Just like she'd feared it as war loomed closer, just like Hedy feared it and gave herself away in a desperate thirst for it. They all simply wanted that taste of something that could nourish their empty places, make them feel whole. For that, she couldn't fault him.

The bells rang, and she looked up to see the ushers opening the doors. She got up—at the very least, she should relieve Mrs. Hahn of Sadie so she could greet her friends. And perhaps, with Sadie as a buffer—

Oh, she'd turned pitiful along with everything else.

Esther stood back from the bottom of the steps, spotted Mrs. Hahn, and lifted her face in a smile.

Mrs. Hahn could bring a woman to her knees with a look. No wonder Bertha said little and served much.

The woman came down the stairs, Sadie's hand clutched in hers, then all but dumped the girl into her mother's care. "I never..." She shook her head, turned away.

Yes, well, she probably hadn't.

Esther crouched down next to her daughter. "Sorry that Mama left, sweetie."

Sadie looked past her. "Mama! A black squirrel!"

Esther took her daughter's hand. "That's right, honey. Only in Roosevelt. They ran away from the circus and came to live here, where they'd be safe."

"And why are they black and not brown, like the other squirrels?"

"I guess that's just the way God made them. To be black." Or maybe they'd turned black when they ran away from their home. To Roosevelt.

She lifted Sadie to her hip, listening to the chatter of women, watching the men lighting cigarettes, children skipping into the park. The bells had stopped chiming.

Behind her, one voice spliced the conversation.

She tightened her jaw, even as she parted out the other sounds to listen.

"And then I saw her kiss him. That *Nazi*. I just don't know why the Hahns put up with her. Linus deserves better. But maybe they'll never get married. Linus doesn't want to, you know."

She turned, and Rosemary didn't even bother to hide herself, just flicked a gaze at her, past the huddle of women, and smiled.

Mrs. Hahn, however, standing with her own group of women, stilled—in fact, it seemed to Esther that even the wind stopped in the trees, the birds ceasing their songs. Then, she pasted a smile on her face, one that turned the day to January.

"Linus will marry Esther, Rosemary. Friday evening, in fact. At the hospital." She lifted her voice, still that smile. "And you're all invited to the joyous event."

CHAPTER 13

"According to the rules of the Geneva Convention, you should be in solitary confinement."

Bert Siefert's dark words clawed into Peter, sharp and tenacious. "But something just doesn't sit right with me. So, you stay out of trouble, and you'll be home before you know it. You make more trouble, we'll ship you off to Fort Robinson, and you can wait it out with your Nazi pals."

I'm not a Nazi. But Peter didn't argue—better to keep his mouth shut and do his time by driving the tractor on the Janzen pea farm, mowing the peas into windrows for Arne and Fritz to fork onto the flatbed trailer.

With the slain peas fermenting under the early August sun, the sky a limitless blue, the sun a haze of gold, Peter felt nearly healed. Who knew that the smell of home—of sauerkraut in its brine—might be scoured up by wet pea silage? His cotton pants reeked of it, his T-shirt soiled with green stain, but somehow it soothed his corrosive ache for Esther.

Now, he sat atop the Flambeau Red JI Case V-series tractor that his uncle would have given his prize hog for. He glanced behind him, monitoring his speed as Arne and Fritz scooped the silage into the trailer. From there, they'd put it through the viner and separate the silage from the peas. Then, off to the cannery, a job he'd feared they'd assign to him after he returned from the hospital.

But Mrs. Janzen had requested him back, and apparently Bert Seifert hadn't bought into Fritz's accusation that he'd caught Peter escaping.

Even though the thought plagued Peter more than he wanted to admit. Since seeing Linus erupt, then collapse into the arms of Rosie, well, it only churned up the still-simmering desire to find Esther—and her beautiful daughter Sadie—and run for the hills.

Especially since he'd sat in the solarium the entire morning, finally returning to his room after the church service, and not a man there realized they'd been worshipping with the enemy.

Then again, when voices raised as one to the High King of Heaven, how could they be enemies?

"You going to ever let me drive, Peter?" Arne asked, leaning on his rake.

"Leave him alone," Bert said, finishing off an apple as he walked behind them. Peter had seen him nick it from the crib in the barn. "He can't rake."

"I can take a turn," Peter said, setting the brake. He stepped down, stole the rake from Arne. "Slow and steady on the gas."

Arne grinned, something raucous in it, and Peter shook his head. Every day, a morsel of Arne's youth returned to him, the haunted look dissolved by the rolling hills, the smell of the shaggy black spruce ringing the fields, the kindness of Mrs. Janzen. Yes, somehow, it helped him return to Germany and fishing with his grandfather.

And maybe someday he really would.

Arne fired up the tractor and Peter held in a wince as he scooped a forkful of silage onto the wagon. So, maybe he'd take it easy, just a bit. Two weeks out of the hospital, and his ribs still burned when he moved too fast.

However, the work took him away from his helplessness. What kind of man was he if he let Esther marry Linus—what if Linus's anger erupted at her?

He'd been forming a letter in his head for the better part of a week. One of these days—maybe after he left, so the temptation to find her, rescue her, redeem her, didn't run wild in his brain—he'd put the pen to paper.

I'm not getting married. Oh, Peter hoped not. Linus's words, more than anything, kept him sane.

The tractor jerked as Arne let the clutch out too quickly. The wagon rattled on the drawbar and Fritz put his hand on the end. "Go easy there, kid. We don't want this thing to mow us down."

Fritz didn't look at Peter, hadn't met his eyes but once since Peter returned to camp. But that one look bore enough for Peter to keep his distance.

Soon. Soon they'd leave—move to a different location or even be shipped home. All he had to do was stay alive. Faithful.

The tractor belched, and the gears ground, the machine lurching forward as Arne slammed the gas. The tractor shot off down the row, toward the rise in the hill.

"Arne!" Peter shouted. "Slow down!"

Arne turned, shooting a grin at him.

Then, Peter could only guess at what happened. Perhaps Arne had his hand on the steering wheel as he turned, cranking the two narrow wheels uphill. Or maybe the lilt of the hill and the weight of pea silage conspired to knock the trailer off balance.

Maybe both, indeed, because one moment Arne shot them a grin, the next he vanished behind the shudder of the pea trailer as the tractor slipped, tipping sideways. For a moment, the trailer held it fast, the tongue wrenching from the whining argument between the two, and in that moment, Peter yelled. "Arne! Jump!"

Then the trailer shook itself and ripped free, skidding into the back end of the tractor. The tractor rolled over and slammed into the soggy ground.

The right wheel spun in the air, still turning.

"Arne!" Peter dropped his rake, sprinted toward the flipped machine.

Bert reached him first. Arne lay pinned, the weight of the engine crushing one side of his body, pressing him into the earth, the other leg wrapped in the steering wheel.

"Help me, help me—" His tone dug a hole through Peter, yanked him back to the battlefield even as he assessed the situation. The boy's breath came out rapid and shallow, and Peter shucked off his gloves, put his finger to his carotid artery. Rapid and weak.

"Bert, go back to the farm, get the truck."

Bert stared at him as if he'd slapped him.

"Listen—I'm a doctor—and we're running out of time. We need to get this thing off of him—go, get the truck!"

Bert took off down the field.

"Fritz—don't just stand there—cut the power!"

Fritz had paled.

"Fritz!"

The man cut the power on the tractor. The engine died to only Arne's wails.

"Shh. Save your breath—shh." Peter put his hand on the boy's chest, cupped his forehead. Cool and clammy. He rounded the tractor, found Arne's leg shattered beneath the weight of the engine. If he ever walked again—

No. First, they had to get him free.

If he lived that long. He returned to Arne. His face had paled, his breath reedy. "Stay with me, Arne. Think of home—of fishing with your grandfather. C'mon—"

Fritz hovered above him, unmoving.

"Let's see if we can pull him out."

"We can't lift this thing." Fritz's voice tunneled out from someplace far away.

"We can try!"

Peter climbed to his feet, braced himself as he grabbed the front of the tractor. Glanced at Fritz. He shook his head but bent beside Peter, shoving his work-worn hands. "I'll hold it, you wrench him free."

"On three."

Arne howled. Fritz roared. "Get him out!"

Peter grabbed Arne under the armpits. But his leg, wedged deep beneath the tractor, trapped him.

"Help me, please." Arne's voice shrank into the cry of a crow above.

Fritz sat back in the muddy, rank silage and hung his face in his hands.

"It's your leg, Arne. It's wedged under the frame, and frankly, I think you're already close to losing it. We may need to take it off to get you out." Peter tried to say it as gently as he could, but Arne still pressed his hand over his face and his shoulders began to shake.

Behind them, the army truck slogged over the field, pea silage clogged into its wheels. Peter hoped Bert had also brought the axe. Sure, they should be able to hoist the tractor off him, but how long would that take?

He stripped off his belt, rounded the tractor, then wedged himself as close as he could to the kid's leg, feeling through the muck as he cinched the belt around his knee and cut off the circulation.

Arne came alive on the other side. "No! Don't do it, please! Oh no—please, Peter, don't—"

Peter came back around to Arne. Crouched behind him. Found his battlefield voice. "We'll try, Arne, I promise. But your chest is crushed, I have no doubt you're bleeding internally, and in a moment, your lung might collapse. We may have no choice."

"Let me die—please, Peter, let me die."

"You don't mean that, kid."

He didn't, his expression so raw the fear reached out and grabbed Peter too. How he hated this part of his job.

Peter's voice gentled. "Think of what you have to go back to. Your family. Your kid sister. They want you, even without a leg."

Arne's jaw clenched and oh, Peter wanted to find the courage for him.

Deliver him, O God. Deliver us all.

The truck skidded past them. Bert left the motor running and jumped out. He dragged a chain from the back end out to the tractor.

Fritz got up, and they looped it through the high, back wheel.

Peter leaned close. "We're going to pull the tractor upright. The minute the pressure is off your chest, you are going to lose consciousness with the loss of blood and possibly the air rushing into your lungs. I promise, I'm going to do everything I can to help you keep that leg. Your part is staying alive."

Arne's eyes nearly climbed out of his skinny face.

"Ready?"

Arne shook his head, but Peter nodded at Fritz.

Fritz shot a look at Bert.

The truck growled as Bert worked the gears, and the tractor shuddered.

Arne's breathing quickened.

Peter grabbed him under the shoulders. Wiggled him through the pudding of earth—not enough. "More, Fritz!"

The tractor shuddered again. "Its stuck in the silage—it's too slippery! We can't move it."

Peter looked at Arne's face, saw the fear even as he slipped into darkness.

Yes, he hated this part of his job.

* * * * *

"Are you hurt? You're covered in blood."

Peter looked up from where he sat in a wooden chair in the hallway outside the trauma room. Inside, Dr. Sullivan was trying to save Arne—not to mention what remained of his leg.

He was thankful the kid hadn't been awake for when they'd rocked the tractor off him with the truck, enough to dislodge his leg. Yet, if Arne lived, he'd at least have both legs, even if it would be a miracle if he ever walked again.

Caroline sat next to Peter in the wooden chair of the reception room and reached for his bloody shirt. He flinched, and she gave him a look that made him release his grip on his torso.

On his re-cracked ribs. Probably. The burning suggested that he'd done some damage, but perhaps he'd only strained them.

"This is Arne's blood. Mostly."

"Let's get you into a room." She helped him up, guided him across the hall to an examination room, then led him to a table. "Who's Arne?"

"A kid. A fellow prisoner. A tractor rolled over on him today." He winced as she pulled up his shirt. She reached for scissors and cut it off him.

"Is that who Dr. Sullivan is operating on? I saw Rosemary follow him into the surgical suite."

"Yes—only..." He made a face. "I wanted to go in there too. I should be in there. I did my share of battlefield operations—"

"You have a tear in your wound under your arm. Otherwise, you seemed to have survived this round." She tore off a piece of surgical tape, closed his wound with it. "Stay here."

He sat on the table, drawing in the smells of the hospital—the acrid snap of Betadine, the sickly sweet odor of ether, the chlorine in the cleaning solutions, the bite of old coffee drifting from the kitchen. Nurses jockeyed a noisy cart of supplies down the hall. He ran his hands over the nubby, stiff cotton on the table and watched as, outside, the lamps flicked on, splashing light onto the ground, although the twilight hadn't yet descended.

He liked farming. Better, however, was the chance to save someone's leg.

Their life.

Someday he'd return home, to his life, join his father's practice. Drs. Hess and Son. And then he'd dive into saving lives, forget the ones he'd lost.

Caroline returned, a white hospital surgical shirt in her hand. "Put this on. You can't walk around bare-chested."

He took it then closed one eye as he lifted his arm over his head.

She pulled it over him. "She's getting married on Friday."

He didn't have to have a name. Still, her words swiped his away. He opened his mouth to nothing.

"Esther. She's marrying Linus on Friday night. Here at the hospital." Caroline stuck her hands into her pockets, walked to the window.

"I knew who you meant. And—why? I thought—" No, he'd *hoped* that Linus had spoken—or rather shouted—the truth. That no, they weren't getting married.

Probably he'd held on to that too much.

"Mrs. Hahn wants to silence the rumors that her future daughter-in-law is in love with a prisoner of war."

Oh. He stared at his hands. Arne's blood embedded the wrinkles, the pores.

"So?" She rounded on him. "And?"

"And what?"

"You're going to let her marry another man?" Caroline raised an eyebrow.

"What choice do I have?"

She gave him a look that suggested he might want to drag back out to the pea silage where he belonged. "Listen, what do you want me to do? Escape? Storm in here, steal her away? She doesn't want to marry me—and frankly, she probably shouldn't. I'm headed back to Germany any day—and who knows when—or if—I'll get back here, and..."

She still wore the fairytales-do-come-true sort of disappointment on her face. "Okay, fine." He took a breath. "I don't want her to marry him either." He slid off the table. "He scares me, okay? He's wounded—and not just physically, but he's broken inside too. I've seen it over and over with the guys I dragged off the battlefield. They die, not because of their wounds but because of what they've seen. Linus has carried the war back home, and—" He clenched his teeth, backing away from the image that flashed into his brain. "Yes, I'm afraid she's going to be a casualty."

The dark fear of it had tunneled inside, turned him inside out on his bunk, and now settled in his gut, churning. "Worse, I think he's in love with someone else."

Caroline's eyes hadn't left his. "I know."

"You *know*?"

"Rosemary Mueller. His high school sweetheart. She's in his room every day, during her shift, and sometimes at night—whenever Esther's not here."

"Did you tell her?"

"I'm not sure the wedding can be stopped. The Hahns have it all figured out."

"I'm going to talk to him—"

Caroline grabbed his arm. "Are you kidding me? You want to turn this into some sideshow? Listen. I'm sorry I told you. I don't know what I was thinking. I just…"

She wore a sadness in her expression. "I know what it's like to lose someone you love. I hate that, for anyone. No matter what side of this war they were on."

He slid her hand from his arm. "You have to tell her about Linus. I can't write to her—there is nowhere I can send a letter. Please, Caroline. Tell her."

"I'll tell her, Peter, but I can promise you that it won't matter. She's getting married on Friday to Linus Hahn. And unless you do something about it, there's no stopping that."

* * * * *

"It's a beautiful dress." Bertha laid the powder-blue silk and wool crepe two-piece suit on the bed, smoothing it. "I think Linus will love it."

Esther picked up the dress and hung it on the attic door. "Thank you, Bertha. We'll be ready to go in a moment." She turned to Sadie, picking her up and setting her on the bed while she buckled the straps to her white patent shoes. "Don't kick, Sadie."

"Me can't help it. Am I really going to see my papa?"

"Yes, sweetie, you are. But you have to be on your best behavior. There are sick people in the hospital and they need little girls to be quiet."

Please, Linus, be in a good mood.

She pressed a kiss on her daughter's nose, taking a whiff of her powdery softness, and then scooped her off the bed. How could he not love his cherub daughter?

She took Sadie's hand, led her down the stairs, then the next flight. Bertha waited by the door, bearing a package of zucchini bread.

"That smells good."

"It's Linus's favorite. I'll just drop it off and go."

"Please, stay as long as you'd like." Esther opened the door, shooed Sadie outside into the August heat. Mrs. Hahn was out tonight at a pie social, or she would have been accompanying them. No one had offered to throw her any wedding showers, but Mrs. Hahn had spent the week preparing for what seemed the social event of the season. She had even hired a pianist to play in the solarium after the ceremony. And bought a fancy cake.

The entire shebang seemed surreal, as if someone else were getting married to this man she didn't know.

Didn't, in fact, want to know. And that truth could turn her cold in the high heat of the August nights.

The late afternoon sun dipped behind the shaggy black spruce, behind the Baraboo River. The pungent, briny odor of the cultivated peas from the far-off fields saturated the town. It reminded her of an old sock left out in the rain, moldy and seasoned with gutter water. Across the street, in the park, a pack of kids had picked up a game of kick-the-can. Sadie grabbed her hand, began to skip. "Ima gonna see my papa."

Bertha glanced at Esther and smiled.

At least someone wanted to be around him.

Please, Linus, be in a good mood.

Twilight had tiptoed into the fragrances of the evening by the time they reached the hospital. Esther led them through the front entrance—so strange to use this entrance and not the nurses' corridor—across the rounded front entry, past the waiting room into the hallway.

Usually they asked visitors to stop at the reception desk to inform a patient when they had visitors, but, well, she'd practically lived here for three years, not to mention the past two weeks since resigning her job.

She did, however, stop to knock on his door—just in case he might be sleeping, but Sadie couldn't wait. She shoved it open, crashing it against the bathroom door, barreling in. "Papa!"

Esther froze. No, Linus wasn't napping. Not with Rosemary seated on the bed beside him.

And, from the looks of it, they hadn't been playing cards.

She untangled herself from his arms as Linus looked up, a murderous expression on his face. "What are you doing here?"

Sadie stopped. Turned around, her face crumpling. Esther held out her arms, and Sadie fled into them, wrapping her pudgy legs around Esther's body.

"Linus." She smoothed her daughter's hair. "We—uh…"

Rosemary stood up, adjusted her dress—Esther noted she hadn't the excuse of a uniform to hide behind. No, Rosemary appeared right dolled up, with her red hair in victory rolls and a pretty floral green dress on that made her appear fresh and young and in love.

"I brought you zucchini bread," Bertha said quietly from behind her.

Oh, yes. Bertha.

She turned and Bertha held out the bread. "Give me Sadie."

They made a trade, Sadie's eyes filling. "Mama will be along soon," she said, kissing her puffy cheek. Sadie's big, wounded eyes tracked past her to Linus as Bertha took her from the room.

Then, holding the zucchini bread as a sort of…offering? Shield? Esther turned.

The anger had washed from Linus's expression—well, most of it, at least. "Why did you bring her?"

"She's your daughter. Don't you think it's time you met her? Especially since we're supposed to be married in three days?" She let her gaze land on Rosemary when she said it. The brazen hussy she was, Rosemary didn't even blink.

Linus's jaw tightened.

"Or had you forgotten that part?"

"I'd like to. Thanks to you, my mother is forcing us—"

"Thanks to me! How about thanks to your—your…"

"I'm not the one who was seen kissing a Nazi, thank you." Rosemary folded her arms. "He's the enemy."

"He's a human being who, by the way, saved Linus's life, so you might want to remember that."

Rosemary frowned, glanced at Linus, who simply stared at Esther. "It's—wait a second. You've been with that medic? The one who—"

"Yes, saved your life. He sent me your letter, Linus. Like you asked him to."

Linus glanced at Rosemary. "I think Esther and I have to talk. Alone, Rosie."

"Linus—what does she mean he saved your life?"

"Please?"

She tightened her jaw but traced her eyes over Esther as she brushed past her.

Esther stared at the zucchini bread. The cinnamon scent drifted out of the oily spots in the brown packaging. She set it on the bedside table and sat on the opposite bed.

Her hands shook as she pressed them together. "Yes, I got your letter. Which is why this entire thing has baffled me." She got up, went to fill a glass of water for him. "You don't want to marry me, do you, Linus?"

He closed his eyes.

"Why are we trying to resurrect something we never had? We made a mistake. We were stupid and we didn't think." She returned, sat across from him. Set the glass next to the zucchini bread.

"Because we have to. Because we…" He reached for the glass, drank the water. "Because it's the right thing to do."

She stared at her hands. "What if I took Sadie and left? Moved away."

"With him?"

She glanced up, met his eyes, surprised by the anger in them, his voice. "No. Maybe. What does it matter? He saved your life, Linus. He could have left you there to die. And he kept his promise—he mailed your letter."

"That was swell of him, especially since he also tried to see my girl."

She stared at him. "You asked him to. You wanted all memory of me dead—gone! You told me you wanted to put that night in a box and bury it. That seemed like a coffin to me. He didn't steal anything from you."

"Don't you want that night gone?"

She got up, walked to the window, where the light splashed onto the grounds. "I do. I want it gone. But I love Sadie, so if I had to live through this again to get her, I would. She's worth this for me."

"Then you should know that if you leave, my father will track you down and bring you back."

She stiffened. "He hates me."

"But Sadie is his grandchild. He's not going to let her go. For my mother's sake, if nothing else."

"But they threw me out. Your mother hates me." She watched as a couple of teenagers rode their bicycles through the circle of lights.

"That's when they thought Sadie wasn't mine. It's different now. She knows Sadie's my daughter. And don't think my father won't find you—he's done it before."

She took a breath, looked at him. He picked up the zucchini bread. Smelled it. "I love the smell of this bread. Bertha sent me a couple packages overseas. It's amazing how long zucchini bread lasts."

"That's because Bertha is your mother. Of course she sends you bread." *And cherishes your daughter.*

He drew in a long breath. "When I was nine years old, my mother caught my father philandering, again. She told him that she wasn't going to take another of his children under her roof. It wasn't hard for me to figure out who my real mother was. A real mother would do anything for her child. Including stay behind and take care of him, pretending he belonged to someone else."

He set the package on the table. "I figure he got her pregnant when she worked for his family. Probably he and his father had a similar conversation. Only, he possessed the courage I don't. He married the woman he loved."

"I don't think a man loves a woman when he cheats on her."

Linus's face tightened. "Rosemary was the girl I was supposed to marry. Until..." He shrugged.

"You are *not* blaming this on me, are you?"

"You are very pretty."

"You make me sick. You were the one that showed up in that borrowed car, took me out. I remember at least three drinks that you ordered. And I also remember saying no. A couple times."

His considered her a long moment. Then his expression dissolved. "I'm sorry, Esther." He looked up at her again, met her eyes, his dark eyes a texture she didn't recognize. But, finally. "I'm sorry. It *was* my fault. I showed up that night with one thing on my mind. And it wasn't about your honor."

She nodded but turned away before he might see how those words tunneled deep, loosened a tightness inside her. "And now?"

"And now we get married."

"And Rosemary?"

His silence made her look at him, and she saw it in his eyes. "You—you don't plan to leave her, do you?"

He swallowed, and for a moment she saw in his eyes herself, the woman who had longed for someone she couldn't—shouldn't have.

"I love her, Esther."

"Then tell your father the truth. Tell him you don't want Sadie. Tell him to leave me alone. I'll go away; you never have to see me again."

"No. Sadie's a Hahn. She stays."

"That's your father talking. But,"—she folded her arms against the shaking deep inside—"what should I expect, you're just like him."

His eyes widened, and for a moment she thought he might throw something, again. She sucked in a breath, willing herself to press him to the truth.

When she did, it took her breath away.

"I could marry Rosemary. And keep Sadie."

His words dug the strength from her. She hated that they made her reach out, balance herself against the marble trim. "And what? I'd become your housekeeper?"

His silence made her hate him.

"I won't be your prisoner."

"I think, either way, you already are." He opened his zucchini bread, smelled it again.

She took the water left in his glass, considered it for a moment, then in a move she never expected, she threw it in his face. "See you at the altar."

CHAPTER 14

Esther's words on paper haunted Peter the most. The private places she'd hint at in her letters, the nuances of hope in a future he couldn't quite surrender.

Could you tell me, please, how he died?

Linus was a good man who loved his town and his family. I will miss him.

I lived, like you, on a farm in Iowa, although I regret that my family didn't share the ties of yours. We too lived on dust and the taste of despair for too many dry years, but my father kept us in bacon and bread. It seemed, however, the dust parched him of any affection.

Yes, I had a sister, Hedy. We would lie in bed at night, the one we shared in the sweltering attic of our home, and roll our fingers over my father's discarded globe. We'd land on such countries as Italy or France or even Peru and conjure stories of places we longed to visit. Hedy and I traveled the world, around and back, before she left home at age seventeen. She died when I was ten years old.

I love being a nurse. I thought it would unlock the world for me. Instead, it has been my salvation these past three years, in a prison I alone created. I hope, someday, to learn more, even to pursue a medical degree, become a surgeon. But sometimes that dream feels like trying to catch a star, hold it in my pocket.

The day I received your first letter, we had a man who jumped from the roof of the hospital. He climbed to the edge and I followed him, in an attempt to lure him from danger. As I did, the night swept through me, and for a moment, I feared I too would jump. It passed, thank the Lord, it passed.

Do I believe in love? I fear how much I long for it. It makes me taste my own hunger, and I can't help but despise it. But yes, I do. I do.

"God doesn't love a woman like me."

"God loves you more than you can imagine." He spoke the words aloud, into the darkness, bringing back the shape of her fingers in his, the texture of hope in her eyes.

He pressed his hand to his chest, counting the healing bumps of his ribs, remembering her tones as she'd saved his life in the trauma room. He understood wanting to save lives. That impulse, perhaps, they shared. And knowing he had someone who cherished his words, his life, his dreams—someone he could write to in the hollow of the night, or after work stripped him down to exhaustion—it eased the loneliness inside. Perhaps he'd just needed someone to look into his life and tell him to hold on.

And maybe he didn't love her, either, but for the first time since he'd stepped aboard that train in Dresden, he recognized part of the man he'd left behind. The man he wanted to be.

The man he hoped to go home to.

He sat up, swung his legs over his cot. Stared at Arne's empty bed.

"I'm sorry, he didn't make it," Dr. Sullivan had said as he'd emerged from the surgical theater. Arne's blood smearing his white surgical shirt dredged up too many demons.

Peter would have to write to Arne's parents. And his kid sister, what was her name? Eva?

He got up, tiptoed out of the tent. Let the night scour the grief from him. He edged along the shadows, listening to the gurgle of the Baraboo River, the sway of the night through the reeds. Crickets buzzed against the pane of darkness.

He squatted against the corner of the tent, running his hand through his hair, now longer than he'd ever let it grow.

Faithfulness had fatigued him, stripped him, turned him brittle.

And what if, after everything, he returned home to nothing?

And you'll die here, just like your father. I wonder if he cried out when they gassed him....

Fritz's taunt wore through him. Peter pressed the heels of his hands into his eyes. *God, please.*

He'd made a deal. His conscription, his service for his father's freedom. Signed his name. Handed over his freedom to the SS.

"*Why, Father?*" Even now he could hear his voice from the past, so much anger coiled tight even as he'd thrown into his duffel the debris of his decision—his picture of his parents, taken at the Iowa County Fair in 1932. His medical graduation ring and, of course, his Bible. He'd crammed it all into the leather duffel bag that he'd dragged to America and back then sat on his narrow bed in the room that overlooked the red-tiled roof all the way to the Frauenkirche, the sun winking off the cathedral like some sort of ethereal fare-thee-well. He'd certainly departed from the life he'd spent the last three years scrabbling for. "We should have left, gone back to America. Why didn't we do that?"

"God called us back to Germany for a reason, Peter. Who knows but it was for this very season that we are here—"

"To do what?" His voice exploded out of him. His father stood in the doorway, his hands in his pockets, and he didn't even have the decency to flinch. Just stared at his son.

"To act justly and love mercy and be servants of God."

Peter just stared at him, even now remembered his father's quiet tone, the way he said it so simply, as if, of course, this answer should be evident.

"This is all God requires of us, Peter. This is our faithfulness in a world gone mad. How could I live with myself if I didn't help?"

Peter dragged a hand over his face. Hung his head.

He didn't expect his father's hands on his shoulders, the peace that stole through him, hot and solid in his touch. "May the God whom you continually serve deliver you."

And you, Father.

Please, God.

He looked up now, remembering the words, staring at Esther's stars. May the God whom you continually serve deliver you. *God, where are You?*

The stars did seem closer here in Roosevelt, as if he could pluck them, pocket them, and take them home with him.

No. He wanted to take Esther home with him.

She's marrying Linus on Friday night. Caroline's tight words rounded on him.

What was he supposed to do about that?

"You're going to let her?"

What could he do—jump the snow fence?

The idea seemed to have fingers, to seize him.

Yes.

He could jump the fence. Find Esther.

He looked like an American. Acted like an American.

Was an American. He didn't belong here, a prisoner of war.

And Esther didn't belong with Linus. The thought pressed into his sternum, tightened his chest. How could he stay here, let her walk into the arms of a man who cared nothing for her?

She couldn't marry Linus. Not a man like Linus. *Any* other man but Linus.

He stood, measuring the distance to the fence, a crazy swirl in his chest, buzzing through his body. Yes—

You make more trouble, we'll ship you off to Fort Robinson, and you can wait it out with your Nazi pals.

He watched the fence sway as if pushed by the balmy summer wind.

And, as he did, he felt it again. The hands. The presence of peace, flushing through him, turning him hot.

No, not hot. Warm.

Unafraid.

God loves you more than you can imagine. He saw himself then, holding her hand, seeing past her eyes to the broken Esther that thirsted for love.

But not his love.

He stared at the sky, drawing a breath, deep and full, without spiking pain in his chest for the first time in weeks.

A star lost its pinnings and he watched it arc across the sky, wink out into the night. *With you, I don't feel so lost.*

Oh, Esther… She wasn't lost. She just wasn't yet found.

Let her be found in Me.

The words pulsed through him. *Let her be found in Me.*

"What does that mean?" His voice rasped out, soft in the swell of night.

He traced her face in his memory, her soft smile upon him as he woke in the ward, the way she checked his wounds. Why would a woman like Esther marry Linus?

You're trying to earn your atonement.

He heard his own harsh tone and flinched. Saw her face, void of emotion, as she said, *God can't love a woman like me.*

Oh. *Oh.*

Esther was marrying Linus because she was trying to fit herself into God's love.

The truth rushed through him, full, fast, and took his breath away. And in the bitter silence behind it, he heard the words, again.

Let her be found in Me.

How, God?

Act justly and love mercy and be servants of God.

His father's voice seemed to embed the wind, the swirl of the stars. The smells of the silage rose to prick his nose.

It is our faithfulness in a world gone mad.

Act justly.

Love mercy.

He stared again at the snow fence, watched it wobble.

Stop her.

The sense of it pulsed inside him. Stop her. The thought rushed, hot, full through him, a surge of truth that nearly made him cry out. Stop her.

Except…

Well, they just couldn't catch him, could they? He'd find her, keep going, to Chicago. Yes. He could get them to Chicago, then he and Esther could vanish. He and Esther and Sadie.

He pressed his hand to his chest, solid against his racing heart.

Maybe this was why he'd bartered his freedom. Why God had sent him back to the land he loved.

The wind picked up again, and this time brushed against his skin, raising gooseflesh.

And certainly, then, God would set him free, right?

* * * * *

"Why didn't you leave? Just take Linus and run?" Esther stared at herself in the mirror—or what she thought might be herself—her blond hair in victory rolls, a blue pillbox hat, a netted veil over her face. The powder-blue suit with the skirting around the hem of the jacket, a pair of black pumps, the ones she'd worn on the train from New Jersey. Except for the scuffed shoes, she didn't recognize the woman with the sallow face and wouldn't look at the eyes that stared back.

Behind her, the sun had already set, the candles for the ceremony probably already flickering in the solarium. She stopped by on her way into the dressing room—aka, the nursing lounge—and saw that someone had engineered a pair of candelabras beside a small altar. Chairs lined up in rows, allowing for a small, almost ten-foot aisle for her to traverse. And a spray of hydrangeas, roses, verbena, all picked, probably, from the Hahns' garden, made the display seem homemade. Simple. Nothing special.

Nothing special.

"Why did you allow him to take Linus and turn you into the maid?"

Bertha sat on the chair, ignoring her, brushing Sadie's golden brown locks. Sadie played with her basket of white rose petals, cut from Mrs. Hahn's garden. She picked one up, let it drift to the ground. Another.

"Leave them in the basket, Sadie," Esther said, crouching to pick them up. Bertha didn't look at her, even when Esther tried to meet her eyes.

"There you go," she said to Sadie, turning her. "You'll be the prettiest one there."

"No, Mama is the prettiest." Sadie grinned up at her mother.

She didn't feel like the prettiest, but then again, she'd never been Hedy, had she?

Bertha stood up, straightened Esther's collar, fiddled with her netting. "I never had anywhere to go. And no one stood up to stop me. Besides, the judge was his father. A boy needs his father."

Esther touched her wrist, met her eyes. "Thank you for standing up with me today."

Bertha's eyes filled. "Linus was a good boy. He'll be a good man."

Esther turned away, checked her appearance one more time in

the mirror. Held out her hand for Sadie. "It's time we get married, sweetums."

"We getting married."

Sadie skipped out of the room, holding her mother's hand. "We getting mar-*ried*."

They walked down the corridor. When they reached Charlie's room, Esther handed Sadie to Bertha. "I'll be right there. I have one last stop to make."

Bertha took Sadie while she ducked into Charlie's room.

He lay in darkness, disappearing, it seemed, more every day. She flipped on the light. Oh, someone hadn't shaved him for two days at least, a dark grizzle swathing his chin. But she didn't have time to do it now. Still, she adjusted his covers then sat on the side of his bed. His external wounds had healed, but something still trapped him in the shadowlands.

"Charlie. I won't be able to beat you at cards anymore. Not that you don't deserve it—I saw you cheating that last time, hiding the ace of diamonds up your sleeve." She brushed his brown hair back. He needed a haircut too.

"But see, I'm getting married today, and I won't be coming in anymore—"

"Esther!"

She stilled, her hand on Charlie's face. No, it couldn't be—

"Esther."

She turned. Peter, dressed in white surgical shirt, a pair of brown trousers, his blond hair slicked back, clean shaven, as if he'd recently scrubbed in.

"Peter?" Standing before her, something sweet and urgent in his eyes? He even smelled good. "What are you doing here?"

"I saw you duck in here—I'm hoping I'm not too late."

"Too late for—" She caught her breath, hating the rush of hope. "Oh, Peter—you can't. We can't."

But she stared up at him, and with everything inside her she wanted to leap into those arms—and how thirsty had she become, that on the day of her wedding she longed for this other man? This honorable and kind man. This man who saw her and cared enough for her to—

"You broke out of camp. You escaped!"

"It was hardly a big event—the guards are playing poker at the guardhouse. I only had to wait until Bert did his rounds and then hop the fence."

"Are you—what were you planning?"

Something twitched on his face with her question. "I… You're not marrying Linus."

His words shook her. So bold, so sure—nothing of the desperation of the previous argument. He nearly decreed it, like a command.

One she wanted to obey.

"Listen—I know you think you're supposed to do this—but—he's not a good man, Esther. He doesn't love you."

"I know that."

"He loves Rosie."

How—oh. Linus had told him the night he'd nearly died. "You knew this?"

"I knew he loved someone he left behind, at home. I thought she was you. I didn't figure out it was Rosie until Linus got into a fight in the solarium. Rosie calmed him down."

"Linus got into a fight?"

"I have a feeling there are a lot of fights in front of Linus." He ran his hands down her arms, clasped her hands. "Just because you made this mistake—"

"It's more than a mistake. Linus is Sadie's father."

"I can be her father."

She blinked at that. Rebelled at how much, suddenly, she wanted it.

"We'll go to Chicago—or even Minneapolis. I went there, once, with my father—we can get lost there, I know it.

She could see it in his eyes—their life together. A house, children. He spoke without an accent—who would know?

She put her hand to her mouth. "What if they catch you?"

"They won't." He gripped her arms, now the urgency. "We can do this—together. All I know is that you're not supposed to marry Linus and I'm here to stop you…"

She stared at him and expected a wildness around his eyes to accompany his words. But instead his hands slipped down to hers again, clutched them in his. "Jesus came to set you free from your mistakes, Esther. This is *not* how you earn His love—because you already have it. You don't have to keep living in the destruction of your sins. Come with me—"

"And Sadie?"

"Yes, of course—I saw her, with the golden curls? She's adorable, Esther." His eyes searched hers.

And for a moment, she nearly said yes. Nearly gave in to his words.

Until she looked—really looked into his eyes. "You don't want to do this."

"I do…" His face screwed up. "I do—of course I do. I—"

"You came here to stop me. But you don't really want to run away with me. You just wanted to stop me."

His jaw tightened and he winced. "I think I love you, Esther—I want to love you. And I know I could spend the rest of my life trying to make you happy. You put the next breath inside me, and it's because of that—it's because I could feel what tomorrow might be that I want to stop you. But more than that—I think God wants me to stop you."

"Why would He want that?"

"Because you are precious to Him!"

She blinked at that, the words rolling over her, through her. Precious—

She dropped his hand, backed away from him. "I don't—I, uh—"

"Esther! What will it take for you to see how beautiful you are to Him? How much He loves you? You don't have to prove anything to Him."

This. Right here. Staring at this man—he even wore white, and the way he held her with his eyes, so much truth in them.

Precious.

Beautiful.

"You don't need to become a woman who you think God wants, because you already are the woman He wants, the woman He loves. And you're not lost, because God has found you. And He wants you to discover the woman you can be—in His grace. In His forgiveness. In His love."

He stepped closer to her, cupped his hand against her cheek. "You are not found by fitting yourself into what you think is the right place, but by letting God forgive you, letting Him mold you into the life He wants for you."

Even as he said this, his voice changed, and the smallest of smiles tilted up his handsome face.

"You are only found when you have surrendered yourself into

God's hands and let His love transform you."

She wanted that. She heard it in Peter's words, saw it on his face—that transformation, the woman she might be…someday.

Oh, she wanted it. Thirsted for it.

God, I want You—I don't want to thirst anymore. The prayer—if was it a prayer, because it felt more like a cry—ripped through her. *No more thirsting!*

"Yes." She wasn't sure she actually said it—wasn't sure how, even, she'd manage to say no to the roomful of guests, to Mrs. Hahn. She'd have to move in with Caroline maybe, and— "But only if you go back to camp. Tonight. Go back before they catch you out."

Peter blinked at her—caught his breath. Then, a smile poured over him. "You'll write?"

"Every single day."

Peter caught her chin in his hand, and even as she smiled, he kissed her. Something sweet and urgent, and she wrapped her arms around him, holding on.

Holding on.

She kissed him because she longed for the future she saw, because he made her feel whole and wanted. Because being in his arms, for the first time, possibly ever, she knew what grace might feel like.

He slid his arms around her waist and pulled her close, his body strong against hers, smelling of cotton and summer heat and strength.

She kissed him for the day when she would truly, fully, love him.

He let her go, backed away. "Is that a blush, Mr. Hess?"

He gave her a sheepish smile.

A shot sounded someplace below on the first floor of the building. Crisp and sharp, it echoed through the hospital.

"What was that?"

His eyes widened. "I don't—"

And then, a rumble shook their feet as something moved the building off its moorings. Peter grabbed her—his arms enclosing her tight against him, cocooning her in his embrace. The hospital floor rocked again.

"Get down!"

Then, even as she hit the floor, as Peter protected her body with his own, the hospital convulsed and…exploded.

CHAPTER 15

War had found Roosevelt, Wisconsin.

The rumble, the eruption of sound that burrowed into his bones, swept Peter back to Germany. To huddling in the muddy troughs meant to protect them from Patton's attacks.

He heard the echo of men wailing as they held their shattered bodies together, staring into the smoky sky, begging for life. He tasted the memory of his own fear as he gathered his courage behind his teeth and found his feet, slogging through the fire, the churned dirt, searching for the living.

"What's going on?" Esther's scream brought him back to himself, to Roosevelt.

Another explosion shook the building. Behind him, the windows shattered, the building twisting on its foundation, the cement falling in fist-sized chunks into the room.

He clasped his hands over hers as the windows' glass shattered on the floor.

Esther curled into a ball beneath him, gasping in deep breaths. "What's happening?"

"I don't know." The lights remained on in the hallway—probably a good sign—although smoke already burned the air. Faint, but the reek of it scoured the hallways.

"They did it—oh, no, they did it." He could barely hear his own voice above the thunder of his heart.

Even as Peter had tucked Esther in close, held her against himself, heard her scream echo through him, the memory raced back at him.

"We'll finish them off and be to the border by midnight. One last victory for the führer."

Esther rolled in his arms, her eyes wide. "Who—did what?"

"Fritz—I overheard him planning something. I thought he was just talking about his escape, but—" He sat up, ran his hands over her arms. "Are you okay?"

"Sadie. I have to find Sadie!"

She pushed away from him, scrambled to get her feet under her, wobbled, then grabbed the bed. He coiled his arm around her waist, steadied her. "We'll find her." He took her hand.

Smoke already filled the hallway, a haze that blanketed the doorways, the nurses' desk. "Stay low and don't let go of me!"

He closed doors as he ran down the hall—the patients had a better chance of staying alive if they stayed in their rooms, waited for help. Around him the halls filled with people, coughing, frantic, shoving past him, elbows in his gut. A few wore suits, dresses—clearly Esther's wedding guests. He pulled Esther close to him, curled his arm around her, made her bend over. "Hold your breath."

"Sadie!" Esther screamed above the crowd's chaos. "Bertha took her to the solarium!"

The smoke tore at his eyes, turned his vision to water. "Close your eyes. I'll get us there."

From the distance, sirens blared.

"Sadie!" Esther screamed.

"Over here, over here!"

Peter pulled them toward the voice and cut into a small room—

a bathroom. The room seemed clearer, and through the veil he made out the little girl—the one he'd seen in the hall, with her burnished golden hair in curls.

She launched toward her mother, who caught her, clutched her to herself. "Shh… It's going to be okay. We're going to be okay."

Peter shut the door behind them. A women's bathroom. He grabbed a towel and shoved it into the gap under the door.

Across from them, a dark-haired woman crouched in the shower, her hands pressed to her mouth. "Are they bombing us?"

He stared at her. *Are they bombing us?* In *German*.

"Nein," he said softly. Held out his hand. "We're going to be okay."

She stared at his hand like it might be a grenade. Her gaze found Esther. "Linus. Linus is in the solarium. We were in here when…"

"The hospital was attacked," Peter said, getting up, grabbing a towel, wetting it.

"So much for the war being over," the woman snapped, something harsh in her voice. She pushed herself to her feet. "We have to get Linus."

He turned to her. "You're not going anywhere. I'm sure the fire department is on its way." He shoved the washcloth into Esther's hand, turned, and grabbed a towel, saturating it also.

Then he pressed his hand to her cheek. "Stay here. I'll be right back."

She clutched Sadie to her, her makeup channeling down her face. "Where are you going?"

"I'm going for Linus."

She nodded.

He cupped the washcloth over his mouth and edged back out into the smoke.

A thick smoke-blanketed silence, back-dropped by the growl of the fire, filled the hallway. Screams ricocheted through the stairwells. He dropped to his knees, blinded by the smoke, and ran his hand along the wall toward the solarium.

The room's windows lay jagged in their panes, the floor erupted as if it had been punched with a fist from below. "Linus!" He coughed, lay on the floor. "Linus!"

"Here!"

He heard the voice, and it jolted inside him—of course he'd heard it before, but the darkness, the press of death in the room—he expected to find Linus lying sprawled on some rubble, his hand clutched to his torn leg, begging for morphine.

Instead, Linus lay behind the Ping-Pong table, his hand pressed to the neck of a lifeless friend—smoothly dressed in his army uniform. Blood saturated his shirt, his clothes.

Linus looked up at him, his eyes almost unseeing. "They found us. Don't you see? They found us."

"They haven't found us yet. Are you hurt?"

Linus just stared at him. Peter did a cursory search in the wan light. "I think you're going to be okay, Linus. You can let him go." He moved to pry Linus's hand from the dead man. Linus pushed him back. "No—get away from me. Just. . . ." Then he stared at Peter.

Something sparked in Linus's eyes, a sort of snap as something released.

"Linus—?"

Linus took his hand away, stared at it, then at Peter. Then his face crumpled. "I don't want to die."

"You're not going to die. Come with me, Linus." He grabbed Linus's arm, but Linus shook him off. "Get away—"

"Linus—listen to me. You're going to be fine. But you have to come with me. Esther is waiting for you."

Nothing registered. Linus shook his head.

"Rosie is waiting."

That shook him. "Rosie? Where—" Linus moved toward him. "Do I—do I know you?"

Peter ignored him, draped his arm over him. "Hang on." Peter pushed the cloth over Linus's face as they entered the hall.

He couldn't feel heat, but he kept his face low, holding his breath as they scrabbled toward the bathroom. Linus coughed, his body racking. "Don't breathe in—" But of course, then the smoke raked into Peter's lungs.

He opened the door, spilled into the room.

Bertha grabbed up Linus. "I thought you'd died." She clawed him to herself, her breath in quick, hard gulps.

Peter shut the door behind them. He turned to Esther, noticed how her gaze poured over him first, then shot to Linus.

Then, mercifully, back. He took her hand.

"I don't know where the fire is, or what we should do. If we stay here, there just might be another explosion."

"What happened?" Linus disentangled himself from the woman.

"I think a couple prisoners escaped from the POW camp—maybe managed to steal some ordnance from Fort McCoy—and used it on the hospital." *One more victory for the führer.*

Esther wore huge eyes. "What are you talking about?"

"I think Fritz and Ernst and Hans attacked the hospital." He stared at her. "I—I—"

"The Fritz who beat you up and accused you of trying to escape?"

She glanced at Bertha, back to Peter. "They're going to think you did it. They're going to think—oh, Peter, you have to run. You have to get out of here. They won't send you to another camp. They'll *execute* you."

Her words shook him. Yes, they would. He drew in a breath. "Let's get you all out of here."

Linus was staring at him, tears running down his face—more from the smoke, probably, than any flush of emotion. "I know you. I—your voice. I know it."

"Yes," Peter said quietly. "You do."

Linus seemed to want more, but Peter didn't have the time. He turned back to Esther. "Let's go." He positioned the towel over Sadie's head. "Stay under there, honey," he said. Then he pressed the end of the towel to Esther's mouth. "Hold on to me. Don't let go."

"Never."

He gave her a smile.

Then he motioned to Linus. "There's a fire escape at the end of the hall. We get there, we'll be okay."

"Maybe we should stay until we're rescued."

"We won't be rescued. And if the fire roars through here, we'll be trapped. We have to go. Now."

He reached over to Linus, who surrendered his arm. Peter draped it over his shoulder, muscled Linus to standing. Bertha pressed another cloth to her mouth.

"It's dark and hard to see. Hold on to Esther. Don't let Esther drop Sadie."

Bertha nodded.

Oh, God, please deliver…

*****

He came for her.

Peter came for her.

He came to stop her from marrying Linus. Linus—who Peter now shouldered as they scrabbled down the murky, smoke-filled hallway. She clutched Sadie to her breast, Bertha's hand fisted into her jacket.

He came for her.

But if he didn't run, he'd be caught.

And, if people like Dr. O'Grady had their way…

The lights had cut out. She blinked against the smoky blackness, making out little. From the open windows at the front, she made out the press of wan light, heard voices shouting.

Still, as she passed rooms, she called out, listening for patients' cries. The doors stood ajar, the wards seemingly evacuated. She'd outlined a plan for evacuation months ago, for use during a bombing drill. *Please, please let it have worked.*

She counted doors as they crawled—only five between the nurses' station and the fire escape. Except—

She tugged at Peter. He turned, his face so close to hers she felt his breath on her. "Charlie. His door is closed. I'll bet they forgot him!"

Peter touched her face. "I'll come back! Keep moving forward."

Keep moving. She'd spent her entire life moving forward. Not stopping to inspect the casualties, to heal. Just kept moving, bleeding every step of the way. *"You don't have to keep living in the destruction of your sins."* Well, it seemed she hadn't known how to escape them. Or perhaps had no reason to…until today.

She tightened her hold on Peter, let him lead her past Charlie's room.

They came to the end of the hall, the door already ajar that led to the iron fire escape. She gulped in the cool summer air, sweet in her lungs.

A spotlight shone across the front lawn, sprinkled across patients lying in the yard, nurses trying to calm them.

Linus had already started down the stairs, hopping, hanging on to the rail.

Peter pressed her toward the door. "Go. I'll go back for Charlie."

"Let someone else go back for Charlie!" She couldn't believe the words left her mouth, but they did, a sort of wrenching cry that made her wince. She shoved Sadie into Bertha's arms. "Go!"

Bertha gave her a dark look but pushed past her.

"Mama!"

"I'll be right behind you." She pressed a quick kiss to Sadie's forehead. She rounded, planning to help Peter, but he stopped her.

"No—you go. I'll get Charlie."

The expression on his face rocked her back—the kind a doctor gave to a nurse when he had to deliver bad news.

"You won't make it out."

He caught her face in his hands. "Then my life is in God's hands. But how could I live with myself if I didn't help?"

See, this was why she could love him. Why she'd wait for him. Why she'd even let his word about God settle inside, nourish her to healing.

Because he'd come for her.

"I don't want to leave you."

"You're not. I can't protect you and save Charlie. For him, for me—go."

Oh, she wanted to believe him—the hunger inside gulped at his words. "You'll make it?"

"I'll make it."

He pressed a kiss to her forehead then pushed her toward the escape.

But she turned at the door. "Then... Promise me you'll run, Peter."

He gave her a hard look then pressed the now dry cloth to his face and tunneled back into the smoky hallway.

Please... Oh, please... She thundered down the stairs, her feet slamming against the metal, turning the corner, tripping down to the soft, moist grass.

Fire engines lined the streets, a spray of water arcing from the main truck, snakes of hoses from the other. She caught up to Bertha, found her staring at the building, fire reflected in her eyes.

"Mama!" Sadie leaped into her arms. Esther cocooned her, turning to survey the destruction, her heart a boulder in her chest.

Fire clawed out the windows on the east side of the building, the windows in the solarium now spitting out flames. Glass shattered, showered the shrubbery to the gasps of the onlookers, most of them gathered across the street in the parking lot of the St. John's Lutheran Church. Nurses and able-bodied men—many of them wearing suits—oh, yes, her wedding!—carried patients across the lawn on sheets. Others hobbled toward safety on crutches or the shoulders of others. She spied Mrs. Hahn, with her hand to her face, locked inside her husband's embrace. She looked up, saw Linus, and broke away toward him.

Water hung in a high, soggy mist, layered Esther's skin, her dress. Sadie clung to her, legs in a vise around her waist.

She should do a head-count of the patients on her floor—except, well, she hadn't worked in over two weeks, and she didn't have any idea how many patients they might have.

"Esther!" The voice lifted over the chaos, and Esther turned as Caroline threw her arms around her. "I was so afraid—Teddy picked me up late, and we were parking the car when the building blew—people are in there—what happened?"

"Peter thinks it was prisoners—escaped prisoners from the camp."

She hissed it, wanting to clue Caroline in, but she stared at her. "Peter is here?"

And that's when Linus, who had collapsed on the lawn, staring at the building, his expression lost, came back to himself.

"Peter." He said the namewithout emotion. He looked up at Esther. "Peter?"

She swallowed.

"That was his name. The man in Germany who…" He blinked at Esther. "He's the prisoner of war. He's the one who saved my life."

"Twice," she said quietly.

"He's an escaped prisoner."

Esther looked back, toward the hospital. Hurry, Peter.

Then, as if by the force of her conjuring, he appeared, standing like a hero at the top of the fire escape, Charlie tossed fireman-style over his shoulder.

He muscled Charlie down the stairs. Hurry.

"Are you okay, Esther?"

She turned then, and her voice left her. Just simply vanished beneath the gaze of Dr. O'Grady. He wore a suit, as if he'd been—attending her wedding? He crouched next to Linus. "Are you okay, soldier?"

But Linus just stared past him, past her, his gaze on the man hitting the grass, moving toward them, Charlie over his shoulder.

Peter tumbled Charlie in the grass. Leaned over him, pressing his fingers to his neck. Checking his breathing.

"It's him," O'Grady said, a strange tone in his voice. "It's—that prisoner."

At his words, Peter looked up.

Met the doctor's gaze.

Run. She wanted to leap up and, with everything inside her, throw herself at O'Grady. Cover his eyes with her hands.

Please.

Peter stood up. Drew a breath. Glanced at her with a wan smile.

And then, as Esther's breath left her, Dr. O'Grady slammed his fist against Peter's jaw. Peter sprawled to the ground, and she screamed.

"No!" Get up, Peter. Get up and run!

But Peter stayed down. Just pressed his hand against his jaw.

"You'd better stay down, or I swear, I'll make sure the police shoot you on sight!" O'Grady turned toward the fire engines, the patrol of officers. "Help! Help! Over here! I've caught him!"

Run, Peter, *run.*

But he stayed down, even as the police came, even as they shoved him face first into the soggy grass, the burning hospital like eyes winking at his destruction. They cuffed him, none too gently, and dragged him away.

Then Linus's gaze turned to her, something in it that stripped her of every thought save one.

Run.

CHAPTER 16

"He coerced you to get into the hospital. He used your friendship to sneak in, to sever the propane line, to let the gas fill the boiler room." The judge spoke without emotion, his back to her, as if he might be reading the titles of the cloth-bound books lining his study.

"No."

"He wanted to kill Linus, because he was in love with you."

"He went into the fire to save him. He was trying to keep me from making a mistake."

The judge's jaw tightened as he turned and pressed his hands into his smooth mahogany desk. "I'm just trying to keep you out of prison. But if you want to continue to defend him, go ahead. Of course, there's no way we'll let you marry Linus. But maybe we'll let you visit Sadie now and again."

She closed her eyes. Let herself hear Peter. *God loves you more than you can imagine.* Oh, she hung on to that now, had to. Her voice came to her with more strength than she'd supposed. "Peter is innocent. He came there to ask me not to marry Linus. Not to blow up the hospital. He was going to go back to camp."

"Sure he was. Why didn't he want you to marry Linus?"

The judge's gaze shot to his son, seated in the chair behind her. He'd said nothing since they'd returned to the house, since he'd brushed off Dr. O'Grady's private examination then settled himself in the judge's cigar chair. Not one word in her defense, even as the night bled out into morning and she'd fought to defend herself.

She gripped the arms of the chair. "Why didn't he want me to marry Linus? Because Linus doesn't want—"

"Did you sleep with him too?"

Her mouth opened. She swallowed. Closed her eyes. "Of course not."

"Then why?"

She didn't recognize her voice, something about it so foreign to her. So rife with hope. "He loves me. He wanted me to wait for him."

The judge let out a huff of air that resembled the noise her father's hogs made.

"Why would he love you?"

Now that question she didn't have an answer for. She shook her head. "I don't know."

The judge had no more words. Just sat there, drumming his hands.

She ran her hands across the leather arms of the chair, watching the rain through the window spit upon the grass, drag debris from summer down the street, spill into the drains. The bells rang from St. Peter's, a mournful cry that dragged out the hours.

You don't need to become a woman who you think God wants—you already are the woman He wants, the woman He loves. And you're not lost—because God has found you.

God had found her. He'd stood up for her. He'd...forgiven her. She knew it, even as she watched the judge stand, take out a pack of Luckys, light one up. He came around to the front, sat at the edge of the desk, letting the smoke spiral out.

"This won't do. Not at all." He drew in his cigarette, blew it out. Looked at her. "I guess you only have two choices. Either you conspired with this Nazi, or you let yourself be seduced by him. Which I would guess that no sane woman would allow of herself—I mean, to fall for an enemy of her country. Yes, I believe you must have been out of your mind." He drew in another breath. "Probably they'd be able to treat you at Reedmont."

Reedmont Psychiatric Hospital. She met his eyes. "I'm not crazy."

"Then you're guilty."

"You're an evil man."

He sifted the ash off his cigarette. "All you have to do is tell us what he did to you. How he coerced you. How he used you." He bent close to her. "Five people died, Esther. They're already lining up the firing squad."

"I swear to you, he didn't do it. He's a good man. He saved your son. Twice. That should tell you something."

"This, from his harlot."

Harlot. Yesterday the word would have found the soft places inside, burrowed deep, branded her. It would have silenced her, turned her against herself. Loosened her from any moorings… Made her feel lost.

Now, it only illuminated Peter's words.

You are not found by fitting yourself into what you think is the right place, but by letting God forgive you, letting Him mold you into the life He wants for you.

"I'm not a harlot. I am a woman who made a mistake. Just like your son did."

You are only found when you have surrendered yourself into God's hands and let His love transform you.

"Peter is innocent. I am innocent." She drew in a breath, found a voice she didn't ever remember having. "And I'm done paying for my crimes."

"I agree."

The voice jolted her, slicked the saliva from her mouth.

"That's enough, Father."

Linus sat up, looked at his father, then at Esther. "I'm sorry." He closed his eyes, then something ranged around his face. His jaw tightened, and he drew a breath. When he opened his eyes, something about the look seemed so familiar—

Yes. She saw it then. The carefree, almost buoyant chap who'd bandied her around the dance floor. Strong and confident and Linus—back to himself.

The Linus she had, ever so briefly, fallen for.

"Linus."

"I'm sorry, Esther. I'm sorry for the way my family's treated you. And for the things my father—for the things *I* called you. I'm sorry I didn't want Sadie—that I still don't want Sadie."

"Linus—don't be rash," the judge started, but Linus held up his hand.

"Don't, Father. You never wanted me either. Let's just be truthful here."

She saw the sadness in his eyes, void of bitterness.

Out of her periphery, she watched the judge's mouth tighten.

Linus's voice hardened. "I have a feeling my grandfather had a similar conversation with my mother, perhaps with you sitting in this very chair."

The Judge's face twitched, he gazed out the window. "We need to pay for our mistakes."

"The only people paying for 'our' mistakes, father, are the poor women we've made them with."

Linus turned to Esther, who still hadn't caught up, her heart whooshing about her chest, untethered. "I'm sorry, most of all, that I behaved so poorly. That I did to you what my father did to my mother."

The judge crushed out his cigarette. "That's enough, Linus. I think you've done enough damage."

"No, Father. You have. And if you don't want our crimes spread around this town—although I have to believe that everyone already knows—then you'll leave us alone. Right now. Esther and I need to talk."

Talk? About what? But she had no bones to move, to protest.

Linus reached for his crutch. His father went to help him as he struggled to his feet, but Linus slapped his hand away. "I don't need any help."

The judge pulled back. Glanced at Esther, then back at Linus. "No, I guess you don't."

Linus bore a sweetness, almost, to his smile when his father closed the door behind him. He leaned against his father's desk, pushing the ashtray away. "I hate the smell of his cigarettes. Always have."

She let herself smile, but it fell away fast. Just in case.

Linus's eyes softened. "I *am* sorry, you know."

She wanted to know. To believe him, right down to her bones. And perhaps, yes, the way he started to reach out, then let his hand fall, perhaps yes.

"You don't love me." She tested the words more than declared them.

"No. I've always loved—"

"Rosemary."

He nodded. "But, to be honest, you don't love me either. We never did, really."

"No."

His chest rose and fell. "War. It turns everything over, makes it urgent, desperate. I was feeling invincible—and terrified that night. And you—" He met her eyes then. "You are so beautiful, Esther."

It made her forgive him, just a little. More forgiveness would take time. But she would find that inside too.

"Have I broken your heart?"

Still the arrogant Hahn inside him. However, she shook her head, a warmth in her eyes. "No. You've set me free."

He reached down, took her hand. "Good. Because I want you to be free. And I will help you. Whatever you want. Wherever you want to go."

"And Sadie?"

He ducked until he met her eyes. "I will learn to be a sort of father, if you let me. And pray that Sadie will someday have a proper father."

She caught a tear on her fingertips.

"I—I probably shouldn't ask, but... What about Peter?"

Linus tightened his grip on her hand. "Like you said, he saved my life. Twice. And I still have some pull with the local law."

Thank you. The words breached her lips, but she couldn't mouth them. Instead, she returned his touch, her hand tight in his, fast, and it was enough. However, "Linus, that night we were together, I—I lost a part of myself."

He let go of her hand. "Me too."

Outside the rain had died, the sun bearing through the gray dawn.

"Do you think it's possible to find that person you were again?"

She shook her head. "I think maybe, with God's love, we can find someone better."

* * * * *

Peter had expected to be shot at dawn, like the villain in a Ringo Kid comic of his youth. After all, the mob that carried him away—if it hadn't been for the Roosevelt police, he might have been drawn and quartered on the front lawn of the hotel—threatened all manner of execution by daybreak.

And the way Linus had looked at Esther… Peter lay on his cot all night, drawing her name into the ceiling with his prayers.

But the sun had found the morning, parting the night and drawing stripes through his cell by the time he heard footsteps down the hall, the jangle of keys against the leg of his guard.

The deputy appeared. "You have a visitor."

He hoped it might be Bert, ready to transport him back to camp.

"Linus."

The man appeared, clean shaven, his hair slicked back, wearing his uniform—gray-green jacket, insignias on the collar, leaning on his crutches.

Linus stopped before the cell, looked at the guard, and nodded.

"Are you sure?" the guard said. But Linus just brushed past him, down the hallway, and nudged open a door at the end. He had already found a seat across from the pine table when Peter followed him in.

The guard shut the door behind him. The bolt slid into the lock.

Peter stood before the table and couldn't help the mental comparison. He knew he appeared rough—he'd caught his reflection in the window and noted that he'd fared better in town than he had with his fellow Germans. Then again, he'd never call Fritz and Ernst and Hans his fellow Germans.

Also, he looked like a prisoner of war. Linus looked like a hero. A man worthy of Esther, if Peter didn't know the truth.

"Sit down, Peter."

Linus gestured to the seat and Peter pulled it out. Linus worked something out of his jacket pocket. "I brought you some of my mother's zucchini bread." He laid the waxed paper package in front of Peter.

Oh, how he wanted to inhale it, his stomach roaring to life, but he kept his hands knotted on his lap. "Why?"

Linus offered a smile—something quick, even apologetic? "I thought you might be hungry."

"How's Esther?"

Linus's smile dimmed, and in that moment Peter saw himself coming over the table, wrapping his hands around Linus's throat. "This wasn't her fault."

"Calm down. She's fine. She and Sadie have moved to her friend Caroline's house, for now." The way he said it, without a fragment of anger…

"I don't understand."

"I think you do." Linus nudged the bread toward him. "Have some breakfast. You must be hungry."

Peter considered Linus for a moment. Something…seemed different. Healed, or perhaps set free. And a sudden warmth in the texture of his eyes made Peter reach out for the bread.

He held it in his hand, broke off a piece, and willed himself not to turn into a fool.

"I should have known that you and Esther would find each other. That you'd see inside each other that compassion that makes you people who would race *into* a fire and rescue a coma patient."

"How is Charlie?"

"I don't know. But I was referring to me. I was stuck inside the chaos and heat of what I saw in battle, what I suffered. Most of all, the future looked gray to me. I came home to my shame and couldn't break free." He pulled out a picture, handed it across to Peter.

"I thought you'd like to have this."

Peter slid it toward him. Yes. A picture of Esther in her nightingale uniform, probably taken before the war.

"Where did you get this?"

"Esther gave it to me before I left. It was in my gear when it was sent back."

"You had another woman's picture in your helmet."

"Yes." Linus took off his hat, ran his fingers along the brim. "I love Rosemary. And, if she will still have me, I want to keep my promise to her." He closed his eyes for a moment, his shoulders rising and falling. "I hurt her pretty bad with my behavior."

And Esther? Linus still couldn't see—

"But I hurt Esther worse." Linus put his hat on the table. "I used her and called it love, but of course we as men know it was nothing of the sort."

His words weren't helping calm the rising simmer inside.

"You should know that I could have loved her. And, I think if I had my right mind overseas, I would have never written that letter. And yesterday I would have married her. Because, even when I couldn't see her, she was there, late at night, early in the morning. Deep down, I knew that she could help heal me, if I let her."

Yes. He knew exactly how Esther could do that. Give a man back the pieces of hope that have slipped from his grip.

"But we both know who really loves her here." Linus looked up at him. "Who would die for her."

Peter folded the bread up in the paper, his appetite gone. He set it on the table. "It doesn't matter. They'll probably have a trial. Shoot me or something."

Linus nodded. "They planned that."

Peter closed his eyes. *May your God whom you serve continually, deliver you.* He breathed in the words, swallowing back acid in his throat.

"But I told my father that you saved my life. Twice. That you deserved a second chance. Like you gave me." He put his hand on the table. "Like you gave Esther."

Peter closed his eyes.

"They caught two other escapees, by the way. With the Janzen girl, outside of town. She managed to get away from them, get help from a local farmer. He called the police."

Two? Oh, please don't let Fritz have gotten away. "Only two?"

"Only you three escaped."

Peter churned the words over. Maybe Fritz hadn't escaped... "I'm sorry I didn't tell anyone about what I overheard. I didn't believe them."

Linus shook his head. "No one would have believed you either."

Peter stared at his hands. He still reeked of smoke, his hands grimy from the sodden yard.

"I gave the army my testimony—told them you were innocent, and how you saved me on the battlefield. Then my father worked out a deal on your behalf, at my request. The army is sending you to Fort Robinson, in Nebraska. From there, you'll eventually be sent home."

Except, his home was here.

Linus stood up. "After that, what you do is, of course, up to you." He stood, held out his hand.

Peter stared at it. Reached out. Clasped it. Linus held it tight, and as Peter looked up, Linus's eyes glistened.

"*Tausend Dank*, Peter."

"You're welcome, Linus."

His guard let him wash, change clothes, fed him lunch. Then, as evening fell softly into his cell, Bert came into the prison.

"I'm just here on official business," he said. "But if I weren't, I'd say that I'll miss you."

Then he led him out into the summer night and down the street to the train station.

Bert left him on a wooden bench on the empty platform as he retrieved his ticket.

Stars tumbled across the murky sky, the moon an eye of fire, watching him in the blackness. He shivered as the wind scoured up the creosote and tar from the tracks. From far away, he heard the blow of the incoming train, searched down the tracks to find it.

That's when he saw her, standing below a streetlight, her hands hidden in her trench coat. Still beautiful, her hair down in waves over her face, her eyes shiny, her pretty red mouth in a sad smile. She lifted a hand.

He waved back, a small gesture with his shackled hands.

Then, while he watched, she turned and gestured to the sky. Reached up and plucked a star.

She turned, then she blew it to him.

Sometimes that dream feels like trying to catch a star, hold it in my pocket.

The train rolled in then. Exhaled black smoke, coughed.

When he looked back, she was gone.

PART 3

Good night my love,
You'll be dreaming soon,
And you'll never know
Where your dreams will take you.

Return to me
In your memory,
And know that I
Was your sweet, sweet lullaby.

CHAPTER 17

Peter had returned home to find hell.

Indeed, the soul had been stripped from Dresden.

The blackened rubble of the Zwinger palace, the Semper Opera House, and the charred skeletons of the city clawed the gunmetal sky, had possessed the power to reach deep, tear jagged swathes through him, and turn him, bleeding, outside of himself.

The wind moaned through the cardboard flaps over the open walls of his flat. The cement and stone wall had crumbled onto the street from the incendiary bombs, the heat of inferno during the Allied bombing of the city in February 1945. Peter had torn a flap into one of his makeshift walls where he remembered a window and draped over it a tablecloth he'd unearthed in the rubble, the cranberry roses sooty as it flapped with the wind, carrying in the stench of human waste, old ash that he feared might be human, the apparition of death seeking lost souls.

Sometimes, in the pitch dark of night, he didn't know whether he slept or simply relived that night through the crying of his neighbors huddled in their own pitiful rag beds, still grieving their own survival.

He'd heard so many stories that the heat of the blaze blistered his own skin, the smoke scorched his lungs.

He became the man in the cellar, fleeing the grip of carbon monoxide in the tunnels under the apartment buildings, running for air until he slammed into a dead end, clawing through brick and mortar to find air, any air—the air that rushed in and incinerated his lungs.

He was the woman who fought the tornado of flames sucking her into the furnace, losing hold of her baby, wailing as the fire gulped the child whole.

He saw himself in nine-year-old Heidi Maas, clutching to her young breast the shattered, deformed plastic of her doll, her six-year-old eyes glassy with the image of her mother turning to ash before her.

The firebombing of Dresden haunted the countenance of his patients, words sometimes buried too deep to crest, bubbling forth in nothing more than a moan.

Outside, a truck backfired, and in his bed made from the broken, seared wood of his parents' bed and the mattress stuffing and clothing he'd scavenged from the neighborhood, Peter flinched.

Please, God, don't let Mother have burned to death.

Honestly, he didn't know what to pray for, his words brittle in his parched throat. Had he wished, instead, that the Nazis rounded her up, sent to her a work camp?

To Terezin? Or Treblinka?

A dog barked, feral on the streets, fighting for the scraps with the rest of the desperate.

Footsteps. They scuffed against the hallway outside what might be called his living quarters, although what did one call the gutted remains of one's childhood home?

Peter stayed because in the deepest crannies of his faith, he believed they might return. Believed that if he stoked the tiny fire he'd crafted inside a dented metal canister, and bartered with the *hamsters* that ferreted the farmlands outside the city each day for food, and hung on to faith until the country might again find its footing, then his family might find their way back.

He might find his way back.

"Doctor?" The rap came on his door—the one he'd fashioned together, at least, and the quiet urgency of the voice drew him from the darkness of his restless slumber into the shadowy gray of early morning.

He hadn't slept, really, just longed to.

Hadn't really slept, perhaps, for two years. Since maybe that night, back in Wisconsin, after watching Esther leave camp.

That glance back over her shoulder. That smile.

Yes, he'd slept that night, letting her wander through his dreams.

Hold on, Peter.

He got up, brailled his way across the room, found the door latch. A woman, life shaken from her countenance leaving only the rivulets of suffering, illuminated her face with a candle on the other side. She wore a man's trench coat folded around her against the chill of the September night.

"Elise?" Peter asked.

"The baby. I think it's coming. She's hurting badly."

"Yes. I'm right behind you."

He was thankful Rachel had slipped him fresh supplies just yesterday—he'd need the antiseptic, the suture kit. The antibiotics. Ana was only fifteen. Too young to have an enemy soldier's baby.

Elise nodded, turned, and he followed her down the stairs, veering to the right and slowing at the fifth—or what remained of it.

The cellar, darkened, sooted, yawned at him as he scuttled by it through the alley. He always veered wide, fearing his mother's screams caught inside the cauldron. He swore he could hear them echo against his steps.

No. She hadn't been there. He'd interviewed neighbors—the few that ventured back to their crumbled homes. They hadn't seen her that night.

Perhaps she had left long ago.

Left. Not taken. Left.

Not taken.

Not like his father.

"When did she go into labor?" Peter asked, his voice low against the movement of the night.

"I heard her moaning this morning, but she didn't come to me. I was gone all day, clearing the streets, and came home to find her in her bed, her face pale." Elise turned, her hand reaching for his arm. "I believe she is afraid to have this child."

Why not? What kind of fate could this child hope for, a child of violence, of discard? Yes, some of the women had embraced their rape-conceived infants, stirred by the hope of life, regardless of its conception. Others...

"There is a home, outside the city. Run by the International Red Cross. For babies who—"

"Nein." Elise released him, her face broken in the flickering light of her flame. "We will bear it." She swallowed, her eyes flashing, sharp. Lightning against the pane of hollowed darkness. "We will bear it."

Of course. Against the fragmented landscape of Dresden, with the Church of Our Lady lain to waste, the people of Germany could do nothing but bear it.

The streets, even two and a half years after the bombing, bore the scars, the bouldered ruins of apartment buildings, mountains of charred furniture, walls, even human remains.

Too many human remains, even now.

Raucous singing lifted to his ears, pitched sour by the Russian syllables, the slur of their guttural tones. As with every other rule, the Russian conquerors raised a fist to the curfew, mocked it away with their vodka rations. The buzzards, they stripped the city of rations, even those dropped in by the British, the Americans, stealing hope from the dying.

Here and there, fires flickered in the open shells of apartments or down alleyways, the crude dwellings of the desperate.

Well, they were all desperate.

The memory of the terror still stenched the air.

Overhead, the early dawn had already swept the stars from the sky. Too late to pocket one for luck. Because if they were caught by the Russian soldiers, out past curfew…

"Hurry," Elise said, ducking through an archway, her steps sure, soft.

Elise and her daughter lived in the old grocery store. The building now sequestered families—twenty or so—into nooks, behind the shattered fish counters, the kiosks, the butcher's room-turned-ward, of sorts. On one end of the building, someone had built a communal stove, and it glowed like the eyes of a beast, smoke curling between its teeth.

Debris partitioned off Elise's "room," the walls made from wedged timbers, cardboard, and patched clothing. At least they had a bed, the remains of a settee, the tapestry mended with a burlap bag, the legs splintered off.

A bag of vegetables, hamstered from the fields outside Dresden, hung on a nail wedged into the chipped cement wall.

Ana writhed on the settee, her moans ghostly through the concrete building. In the wan candlelight, she seemed to almost turn in on herself, a ghoul with dark eyes, a scream on her face.

"Shh… It's going to be okay." Although he'd stopped believing his words long ago.

Or, nearly.

He gestured to Elise. "We'll need clean water to wash the baby."

She managed a stricken nod, slipped away with her candle. He heard her soft murmurs, waking her tenants with her need.

Ana wore a long skirt, a man's shirt over her stretched belly. Peter touched her leg, and she drew back, flinched. He wanted to howl at the wounds in her eyes.

"I need to check you." He gave her a smile that he hoped she believed kind. Still, she shivered under his touch, and he tried to be gentle.

She would have this child before dawn. Worse, the infant lay breeched.

"Lie back," he said and touched her forehead. A fever raked through her, judging by the simmer of sweat, yet still she shivered.

Influenza.

Elise returned, a dinged porcelain basin of water sloshing over her feet. "I'll stoke the fire."

"I need to get her to the hospital, or I fear we'll lose them both. If we cannot turn the baby, she'll need a cesarean delivery."

His words should have elicited a flare of panic, but Elise only closed her eyes.

Peter took a breath then knelt beside Ana.

He swept her up into his arms, ignored her howl of pain, swift, sharp.

Then she sank against his chest, her body a sack of bones.

"Bring my bag," he said to Elise and stepped out into the night.

The crash of glass shattering nearby, the guttural sounds of challenge between pie-eyed soldiers, fractured the lumpy darkness, thick with shadow. He ducked through alleyways, darted across streets, allowed for Ana to hunch into herself in his arms when a contraction took her.

Her baby moved in her womb, and he felt it against his chest. She hooked her arms around his neck, her mouth open in soundless pain.

The Red Cross had set up a center in the bones of the old university hospital, a makeshift surgery theater, trauma rooms, burn wards. Jack-o-lantern eyes surveyed the street from the three-story building where he'd dissected his first cadaver. Where he'd watched his Jewish friends vanish from class.

He hid in the alley across from the hospital, his eyes on the entrance, ears for the Russian patrols.

From down the street, an engine growled, choked, perhaps an ambulance trying to navigate through the carotid streets. Over the bones of the buildings, the sun began to sluice through the city, the rays molten between him and the entrance.

"Please… Oh, *bitte*…"

She vised his neck, arching against him. "Please!"

"Hang on, Ana," he said into her ear then trundled her close, glanced both ways, and dashed into the street.

A Russian patrol car rounded the corner as he tripped against the cobbled sidewalk on the opposite side, even as he spilled toward the yard of the hospital. He stumbled, caught them on a chipped stone column bracketing the door, rending the flesh from one hand but righting himself before he tossed Ana onto the front steps.

Whistles behind him, shouts—he edged the front door open, tracked into the tiled, mosaic entryway. A gurney lay empty in the entrance hall, and onto this he settled Ana.

Elise took her hand.

Ana opened her mouth and bore down.

"Not yet, Ana," he said, feeling her stomach. "The baby hasn't turned."

She let out a cry that turned his stomach onto itself.

"Doctor?"

Rachel. He knew her voice anywhere, the Midwestern accent, flat, calm tones. He turned, found her dressed in her blue uniform, the white apron, and for a moment, like always, the image of Esther, her hand in his as he awoke in the ward, took him. Even Rachel's blond hair, those eyes that followed him—she'd scourged up images he'd long ago eulogized. He'd had to, despite carrying Esther with him into the prison in Fort Robinson, then to England and the debris of the minefields, and finally home. In his memory, however, she'd become a specter, pale and gaunt, her voice reedy thin, hungry for the nourishment of her letters.

Except at night, sometimes. She found him in his bed, slid her hand into his… Hold on.

Still, after two years, without one letter, a telegram, even a scribbled postcard… How long, really, should a man hold on to the stars as they turned to ash in the light of day?

You'll write?

Every single day.

He shook the words, and their power to slay him, from his mind. "She's having a baby. It's breech."

Rachel nodded, glanced behind her to the flood of lights outside, the guards not stopping at the gate. "Follow me, and hurry."

He pushed Ana down the hallway, past patients lounged on the floor, sprawled on the priceless real estate of wooden benches. The wards, too overflowed with humanity. The stench of unwashed bodies, antiseptic, the chlorine in the cleaning supplies, smelling salts—they turned his hollow stomach as they wheeled Ana in to the operating theater.

Rachel turned to him. "I'll call the doctor."

"There's no time." He had already opened Ana's shirt, pulled the waistband of her skirt below her belly. The baby lay sideways under her skin. "Brace yourself, Ana," he said and laid his hands on her body.

Ana nearly lifted from the table. "*Halten*, oh, bitte, *stop*!"

Rachel met his eyes, shook her head.

"Prep her for a cesarean delivery." He stepped to the sink, grabbed the soap.

"You're not allowed."

He glanced at her. "Prep her, please. You can arrest me afterward."

Rachel took a breath, reached for the ether.

Ana gave violent, bloody birth to a little boy, red-faced, chubby, despite her fragility. Hardy Russian stock, and he placed him, squalling and miraculously perfect, in *Oma* Elise's arms, who looked upon him with an expression of redemption.

Yes, they would bear it.

He helped Rachel clean the theater in silence, dumping the bloodied clothes, sending the surgical instruments to sterilization. She hadn't spoken to him since he'd ordered her, in his physician's voice, to obey.

"I didn't know you were a doctor."

He picked up the needles, disassembled them. The points would be sterilized, sharpened. "I am. I served in a field hospital."

She dropped the bloodied surgical drapes into the laundry basket. "That's what you do with the supplies. You're—the one."

He picked up two vials of penicillin. Held them up to her.

She looked away as he pocketed them.

"What are you talking about?"

"I've heard them speak of you." She turned back to him, and in her sweet brown eyes, she wore a look that brought him back to that moment when Esther had finally heard his words. *God loves you more than you can imagine.* As if, for the first time, she'd seen morning.

Somehow he had to expunge her from his mind, or he might just lose it.

"You're the one they call the Nightingale."

*****

November 1945

Dear Peter,

I will admit that I stood at the rail, outside the halo of light, fearing its betrayal even as I watched the guard load you onto the train. You walked like a man with age in his bones—I'll never forget the way, too, that you turned and stared out at the light, the hope of one last glimpse on your expression.

How I wanted to press myself into the light then, to lay bare the things still cloaked inside me. How you rescued me, brought me back to myself, or at least the fragments of the girl I once knew, I once believed in. Not only that, but I saw in you a fate I longed for—to believe in a love that might not harden under the brutal glare of one's transgressions, but become, perhaps, more pliable, even sweeter. A love that pursues, even battles past the minefields of my insecurities.

But, perhaps you know all this—perhaps this was your intent when you scuttled your freedom to purchase mine. You may not know, however, how it is that you also set Linus free.

Linus has become the man I met, the one whose smile captured me across the dance floor, charming and gregarious. Somehow, that night in the burning solarium, the angry Linus died and a new man resurrected.

A man who has become a father to his daughter. And a husband to his wife, Rosemary.

They were married a month ago, a small ceremony in the Judge's quarters. I was not invited, to which I harbor no bitterness. I did, however, offer my blessing. Indeed, Linus came to me, and on bended knee, asked for it, right there in the middle of the front parlor of Hanson's boardinghouse. With the sun streaming through the stained glass transom, the scent of late season chrysanthemums, and so much apology in his eyes...

Of course I gave it. Because haven't we been held prisoner long enough?

Linus knew, probably, that I would free him. He belonged to me no more than I belonged to him, and I saw Rosemary in his eyes even as he embraced me, whispering gratitude in my ear.

You would probably like to know that Charlie too is showing signs of waking. Small movements of his hands, and his eyes following me across the room after I shave him. Perhaps your sacrifice for him will save his life also.

So, you see, Peter, you set us all free, and now I pray for your freedom.

The letter I sent to Fort Robinson returned to my post office box marked "POW liberated." I admit taking it down to the drugstore and tracing my own handwriting as I shared a phosphate with Sadie, wondering how to find you. Even, if I should. Perhaps I was clinging too much to the shadow of you, what I hoped you might be to me, instead of the truth.

Love has that power, sometimes. The hope of it can fill our mouths with the freshness of fruited tomorrows. I can taste the sweetness of your smile, see your blue eyes in mine, feel the heat of your hand upon my cheek. I hear your laughter, deep inside, still stirring my rusty soul. You have twined into the fabric of my life—there with me as I read to Charlie, your hands settled upon my shoulders, or when I finish my shift, walking home with me under the bushy elms. You sing with me as I lay Sadie to bed, and afterward, as I sit in the window seat of our room and consider the stars, you are there, counting them with me.

I pocket them for you, in hopes you are well.

And then, because you gave me the words, I pray, *May Your God, whom you serve continually, deliver you.*

I have to mention, by the way, that Dr. Sullivan has agreed to sponsor my education. I was accepted to a one-year program and am moving to Milwaukee at the first of the year to complete my management course in nursing.

Sadie will stay with Linus and Rosemary. Of course, Bertha is thrilled, and I suspect that Sadie, who spends the time I'm on my shift with her father, will thrive. I haven't told her yet, preferring to curl my body against hers in our tiny bed and breathe in her dove-softened innocence. In truth, the idea of not returning to her after my shift can render me hollow, as if a hand has severed my heart from my body.

But it is for a season, and only because she deserves Linus too.

I have decided to send this to the International Red Cross center in Dresden, Germany, in hopes that it will make its way to you.

I am nurturing the feeble hope that I have knitted myself into your days, and nights, as well. Thus, I'm holding on to you, Peter. Don't let go, and return to me.

Yours,

Esther

CHAPTER 18

"I could get into real trouble for this." Rachel's voice slipped from the shadows of the alley cutting onto Töpferstrasse, in the murky shadows of the square surrounding the Frauenkirche.

"I know." Peter let his voice tumble out low along the blackened cobblestones as she walked past him, sat in the chair opposite him in the courtyard of the market, where hamsters and others bartered clothing, medicine, and food for ration cards. A violinist—probably a former performer in the symphony—set up his case in the square, hoping the arias of Wagner's *Der Freischütz* might earn him dinner. The sun had wrung out over the river, dripping orange into the Elbe as it escaped behind the scarred skyline of the western banks.

"How long did she stand after the bombing?" As if God had pressed His almighty thumb upon the cupola of the Lutheran Church of Our Lady, the building lay in rubble, a debris pile of sandstone and metal spilling out across the square, the still-standing altar and the chancel like fingers beseeching grace from the heavens.

"Three days. The heat rose to over one thousand degrees, and the sandstone pillars simply melted. They couldn't support the rest of the structure. The dome crashed in, and the entire church crumbled."

He looked over at her. Rachel had a prettiness about her, with her blond hair, a grace in her green eyes that belied her profession. The kind of girl he might have met in a country church, wearing a floral dress, a cloche hat, a pair of white gloves. Instead, she wore a pair of army pants and a white shirt under her cloak. "What are you doing in Germany, Rachel? You should be at home with some returning soldier, walking down the aisle, making babies."

The wind, perhaps, made her press her arms over her chest, tighten them against herself. "I've been overseas since my husband died in the Battle of the Bulge. I just had to—be closer to him." She gave him a look that nudged the ache lying like a boulder deep inside his chest. "But I'm headed home next week."

He looked at her, silhouetted against the backdrop of the sunset. "Did you get caught?" He glanced at the burlap bundle she'd dropped behind him as she passed.

"No. The Red Cross just received a shipment of CARE packages. I slipped these out before they went into distribution." She lifted a shoulder, a smile tugging up her face. "I knew you'd need them."

"Thank you, Rachel."

She smiled at him. "I—I told Glennis who you were. She'll keep you supplied."

Glennis. "Red hair, sort of round face?"

"Canadian. She is sympathetic to what you're doing here, Peter. Or, should I say, Nightingale."

A pigeon waddled near, perhaps some latent impulse driving it back to the square in hopes of nourishment.

Peter had nothing to offer.

"Please don't call me that." He glanced at the packages. "I'm just trying to do what I'm supposed to, I think."

"Me too, Peter." She leaned over, and he nearly jumped when she slid her hand over his cold, bony fingers.

He stared at her hand, pale and clean against his. He stifled the impulse to yank his hand away, but his cold hunger compelled him to cling to the heat of her touch.

Hold on. But nearly two years seemed too long to wait with just a pocketful of dark stars.

"I can't figure you out, Peter. Are you American? Or German?"

"I'm German, but I grew up in Iowa. I was a prisoner of war in Wisconsin." Sometimes the smells could still gulp him whole, the marinating pea silage, the tangy pine that lingered at the edge of the fields, the antiseptic, chlorinated, cottony soup of the hospital, none of it hated.

The sweet, powdery scent of Esther's skin, the few times he'd gotten close enough.

"You were a POW? Why did you come back to Dresden? Everyone's left for the cities that weren't destroyed. You can't find food, shelter is horrid, at best. And influenza is sweeping the city." She glanced over at the miscellany of the Frauenkirche. "There's nothing here to come back to."

"My family lived here. I came back to find them."

She looked at him then, a sadness in her eyes. "Your family was in the firebombing?"

"I don't know. I—someone suggested that the Gestapo took my father away long before the attack. But I think my mother could have been here, that she went into hiding after my father's arrest—"

"Was he Jewish?"

"No. He just... He took in fleeing Jews, especially the ill. He..."

"Was a nightingale, like you. Comforting. Going into enemy territory to save the hurting."

Hmm. Perhaps. “I came back to find my mother. Then, I hoped to scrabble together passage to America.”

“America?”

“I—I grew up there. And I left behind—”

“A girl?”

His heart. He drew in a breath, with it the smell of dust, char.

She didn’t remove her hand, and for the moment, he needed it. “There’s a list, you know. Of the dead? The Red Cross adds to it every day as they identify victims.”

“I put her name in, but I’ve never heard back.”

“I’ll find out, Peter.” She gave his hand a squeeze, and for the first time since he’d left, since he’d made the journey from Roosevelt on the train to Fort Robinson, across the ocean to Great Britain, through the processing centers and finally back to Germany, something inside him eased. That terrible fist that tore into his chest, spearing him when he loved too fast, when he thought too long about his losses, loosened a fraction.

“Thank you, Rachel.”

She held his hand in silence, and he watched a woman hurry past them, holding a child in her arms. Merchants, with their feeble offerings of cigarettes, eggs, even the occasional *perogies* filled with unidentifiable meat, packed up their wares, surviving through, at least, this day.

He wanted to brush his thumb over the top of her hand, but his bones forgot how to move.

“How’s Ana?” He should have stopped by the hospital today, but— “Thank you for the penicillin —”

She held up her hand. “You need to know that there is a new duty nurse taking my place next week. She might be better at counting than I am.”

He drew in a breath.

"And Ana is very ill. She has no milk for the baby, and I can't find a wet nurse."

"You need milk."

"We need everything."

He glanced at the POW packages. "I can get you milk. These packages will trade on the black market. Or I'll find a hamster, have him find me some milk."

"If they find you trading on the black market—the Russians killed a man they found selling his luger, probably for food for his family." She tightened her jaw. "They don't want the Germans to have anything that might be spoils of war."

He'd seen that man. Hanging from a light post along the Elbe, a sign around his neck: Thief.

"I don't have weapons to trade. But I'm not going to let Ana's baby die."

"Maybe it's for the best, Peter. What kind of life would he have—belonging to no country? He'll be lost."

He'll be lost.

Peter reached for the burlap bag. "You're the nightingale, Rachel." He looked over at her, smiled. Wanted to love her.

Wanted to feel anything but the rubble in his chest.

He glanced at the church. "One-thousand-degree heat. That's… unimaginable." The kind of heat that could bubble a man's skin, turn him to ash, his blackened hands curled to his body. Still, he would have thought the church might have survived. He remembered the few times he'd stood in the cupola overlooking the city, the expanse of so much history—the cobbled streets where Bach strolled in search of a tune, or perhaps Goethe trolling for his muse. The church stood sentry over the city, pillared their faith. Yet the flames had loosened its foundations, crushed it to dust.

"I'll meet you here tomorrow night," he said, and she let him go, his hand colder with the loss of hers.

Peter picked up the burlap bag, carried it over his shoulder to his flat, climbing the stairs just as the light winked out from the city. He lit a stump of a candle, trying to decide whether to coax to life the tin can fire or simply abide the chill. Opening the burlap bag, he fished out the CARE boxes—three of them, filled with corned beef, bacon, margarine, lard. Honey, raisins, chocolate, coffee, and bless her, Rachel had found two cans of beer and a carton of cigarettes. Yes, he could barter these for fresh milk. The rest, he'd distribute.

As he put the supplies beneath his bed, he noticed a tiny package, wrapped in brown paper, set in the middle of his blanket. He picked it up, unwrapped it.

Held it to the light.

Creamy white, veins of lime green, and encased in the floppy folds of purple-veined leaves… Someone had left him a turnip.

* * * * *

March 1946

Peter,

I think of you too much when I'm studying late, when the night forces my nose into the crease of my textbook, and I release myself into the ethereal memories of your smile. I can smell you, sometimes, not the man in the hospital bed, but the one who came to me, the scent of rescue on his skin. I feel your arms enclosing me, the sweetness of your voice in my ear.

God loves you more than you can imagine.

Those words, more than your smell or touch, found the thirsty place inside. It feeds me when I am rising early for my shift, the absence of Sadie's body next to me turning me febrile.

I moved to Milwaukee, as planned, right after Christmas, leaving Sadie with her father and Rosemary, in whom I've discovered an ally.

Rosemary is pregnant with Linus's child, but she has made room in her heart for mine, which seems another miracle. Sadie writes to me daily in Rosemary's loopy scrawl, and sends me pictures. Every three weeks I take the train to Roosevelt and Sadie joins me in Caroline's room at the boardinghouse, although by summer, I will have to find other accommodations. Caroline is finally marrying Teddy. Indeed, we are slowly slipping free of the grip of war.

Our ward is full of evacuated soldiers, but so many more able-bodied GIs return home every week, triumph in their smiles, many bearing souvenirs and pictures of their "tour" in France or Italy. They disembark from the trains, a band greeting their first steps, and banners and speeches and glad scenes of women piling themselves into the arms of their husbands and brothers and sons.

I sometimes walk to the end of the block, watch the

returns, seeing myself in your arms, wishing you might have worn a different uniform.

But you should know, your uniform doesn't matter to me.

I wonder, however, when the lack of you finds its way inside me, if it is wise to linger inside the memory of you, to let your voice pull me from my life, launch me into a place where you and I are together, perhaps strolling along your beautiful Elbe or seated at a picnic on the shores of Lake Michigan. I see us hand in hand there, the lap of waves passing time as we find each other's smiles.

I am a foolish woman, I suspect, but the fool has wooed me, and I am still hoping that one day it will be you off the train, and I rushing to your arms.

Meanwhile, I will take my exams in May, and am considering my future. My old director of the Red Cross wrote to me, after Doctor Sullivan scripted a letter of recommendation. I couldn't believe his kindness, but he told me in confidence before I left for Chicago that he too had a son who was a POW in Germany. He hoped compassion might find him there, care for him as I did you those weeks after your beating. Red Cross Director Wynn invited me back into its ranks, and I am debating my application. Sadie, of course, needs me, especially with Rosemary and Linus beginning their family.

I am at Milwaukee County General Hospital, working a shift on the rehabilitation ward, not unlike convalescent ward in Roosevelt, and I'm living in the nurses' dormitory.

I have always feared the city, the specter of my older sister, Hedy, hovering over the stories of speakeasies and gin joints. Of course, she lived in Chicago, but any city whispers danger to me. I told you she died—but perhaps I failed to mention that Al Capone's men gunned her down in a basement swill called Tony's. I went there not long ago on the train and discovered it boarded up, the candy store above it blackened and gutted, the wind moaning out the sounds of whisky jazz, liquid blues. I will never return.

My roommate, Doris, loves the cinema—she is raving about a new film, *The Best Years of Our Lives.* I suppose—although I'm still wondering, if mine aren't ahead.

Which brings me, inevitably, back into your arms.

Holding on.

I am hoping this letter finds you, that the reason you haven't written has to do with the chaos of repatriation and not...

Well, holding on,

Esther

* * * * *

The Russian patrols—or brute squad, perhaps—Peter couldn't really assign military function to what he recognized as men gluttonous over the spoils of war—food, resources, women—came alive at night, fueled by too-ample shipments of vodka and the taste of dereliction in the air.

The patrols roamed the streets, two and three to a group, after curfew, sometimes finding prey, most of the time simply terrorizing the streets with the mean reality of occupation.

Peter pressed himself into the gated shadows behind the grammar school, his gaze on the grizzle-toothed remains of a cigar shop his father once frequented. He hoped that inside waited Spider, a man Peter had heard about after dropping the right tidbits around the city. Spider, Adolf Mueller said, could find anything.

Including milk.

Or penicillin.

Or even tickets to America.

But that would come later. After Peter found his mother.

Hopefully, however, Esther forgot him.

One letter. That's all he needed. Her words etched onto the page, something he could trace with his finger, see her bent over the paper, inking her thoughts.

Why hadn't she written? Even once. The absence of it had the power of a scalpel, separating his memories into pieces. Had she really stood beneath the light pole at the rail station or had his desperate heart only conjured her? Had she really agreed to wait for him? Or had she simply been appeasing him, afraid of his zeal?

One letter, Esther.

He tracked a Russian patrol cavorting its way down the street. Loud, vulgar. Then, as it rounded a corner and disappeared behind a pile of rubble, he slanted out across the road.

No shouts behind him, nothing to yank him around. He made it across the street, tucking himself inside an alcove. The cigar shop door hung off one hinge, barely open. He nudged it with his foot.

The building resembled a tomb rather than a place of business, with the blackened remains of cigar counters hunched in the middle of the room like coffins. "Hello?"

"Here." The voice emerged from beyond the main room, into the living quarters, and right behind it, a beam flickered in the recess.

He followed the beam, passed behind a curtain, and behind it found a man. The light in Peter's eyes obscured the man's appearance, except for U.S. Army issue boots and the slick gleam of a blade. From the body rose the tangy breath of cigarette smoke.

"Spider?"

"What did you bring?"

Peter untucked the bundle from his jacket. "Cigarettes. Beer." He held out the burlap bag. Spider swiped it from his grip. Shoved another into his grip.

"Goat's milk, like you asked. What do you need it for?"

"A baby."

Silence, probably as the swindler considered his words. Then, "Always trying to save the world, aren't you, Doc? Just like your old man."

Peter stiffened, the guttural chuckle finding his memories, rousing the taste of bile. His eyes adjusted then. "Fritz."

"Peter." Fritz lowered his light, something in his eyes that made Peter's gaze flicker to his knife.

Fritz saw it, perhaps, because he put the weapon away, tucking it into his boot. "You made it back. When?"

He hadn't expected the anger, how it suffused his veins, how he saw himself grabbing Fritz by the throat, squeezing. He swallowed it back down to his belly, shuddering against its power. Kept his voice cool. "About three months ago. I came through Saxony."

"They held me in France. I escaped." Fritz's face lifted up one side into a smile. "'Course, if the army had known it was me that night we bombed the hospital, I wouldn't have made it back at all. Why did you keep your mouth shut?"

"You—but they only caught Ernst and Hans. Did you go back to camp?"

"I figured that the best place to hide was inside their own stupidity. What kind of country keeps their POWs behind a chicken fence?"

Yes, he would wrap his fingers around Fritz's neck and—

No. He wasn't, couldn't be that man—

"Why didn't you betray me?" Fritz asked again, opening one of the cigarette boxes, opening a pack for himself, drawing out a cigarette.

Indeed, why hadn't he? Peter's silence had burned into his bones, and too often as he'd lain in his bunk in Fort Robinson, or on a ship across the Atlantic, or even in the camp in Sudbury, England, he'd seen himself rising from his chair, screaming out Fritz's name. Finally dousing the ever-present simmer of doubt—except… Well, he hadn't wanted to implicate himself.

Which meant he'd bartered cowardice for freedom. Perhaps he deserved to return home to destruction. "I didn't know for sure."

"You should have trusted your instincts." Fritz drew on his cigarette, the ash illuminating his eyes, just for a moment. Shiny black, like charred wood. "Besides, you're not German any more than I'm Greek. You have American blood inside you." His voice lowered, raking through Peter. "No wonder you saved that American soldier. Too bad he got your girl."

The cigarette burned in the darkness, a pinprick of hot light.

Of course Peter had known it all along. Of course Linus had healed, had come to his good senses, had realized the gift of Esther in his life.

Probably she married him and Peter became a memory, if that. No wonder she hadn't written.

Peter pushed through the hot band around his chest. "Thanks for the milk. Can you get more?"

"No so fast, Doc." Fritz edged up to him, the odor of the unwashed thick upon him. "Seems to me that a doctor should be able to get his hands on more of this. Seems as though the Red Cross considers you some sort of hero."

"I'm not a hero—"

"No. You're useful." Fritz drew again from the cigarette. "Always were. The minute I saw those Jews sneaking out the back door of your father's house, I knew it."

Everything inside Peter seized, hard, as if a rock had slammed through him. "What are you talking about?"

"I lived there, above you." He pinched his cigarette, two fingers to his mouth as he finished off the butt. "Watching you. And then, after you left..." He lifted a shoulder. "They were traitors, just like you. And stupid. Your father brought it on himself, you know. Brought it on your mother, too."

A roaring filled his head—"What did you do?"—and his voice didn't quite sound like his own.

"I did what any good German would do."

Peter's breath left him.

"I watched them. They took your mother out back, put her against the wall. Your father tried to stop them. Like you, he didn't go easy. They took him away afterward, left your mother's body in the alley. I hope they gassed him slowly."

Peter stood there, the roaring so loud now it consumed his lungs, squeezed until he had to reach out, palm the wall.

"I did them a favor. At least they didn't burn."

Peter saw himself pressing his thumbs into Fritz's trachea, watching the breath leak out of him, his eyes reddening. "You—"

Steps, outside. Glass breaking, sharp and crisp, a warning in the night. Fritz flicked off his light, pushed Peter with two fingers to his breastbone against the wall. "Shh."

Still, the metal door creaked open. *"Zdrastvooyta?"*

Fritz drew back, and in a second the blade gleamed. He put a finger to his mouth.

Peter stared at the blade, his hands shaking, still caught in Fritz's confession. Yet he should have moved faster, because Fritz grabbed his shirt, touched the point of his blade to his chin. Heat there suggested he'd nicked him. "Kill or be killed."

Kill or be killed. Peter sucked in his breath even as he listened to feet scrub against the cement floor, kick out pebbles. *"Perestan!"*

Fritz laid a finger to his mouth, moved in behind him as the soldier pressed his Mauser into the room, beyond the curtain.

Kill or be killed. Yes, well—

It happened so fast, Peter struggled to know who moved—Fritz or himself. Perhaps his own rabid fury made him grab the wrist of the soldier, shake the gun free, slam his fist into his face. Maybe he had also tackled the man—or it could have been that Fritz pushed him, but in a moment, Peter wrestled with the man on the floor, the soldier writhing, screaming—

Then silence. Wetness, sticky and hot, poured over Peter as the man's last breath gurgled out of his slit throat.

Fritz released his chin, let the head flop forward.

Outside, more voices punched into the room.

Blood saturated Peter's shirt, his pants, seeping into his pores.

"Better run, Doc." Fritz grabbed him up by the collar, half-dragging him away from the body, into the recesses of the shop. "Out the back, and don't turn around."

He slammed his palm in the back of Peter's spine, propelled him out into the street. Shouts from the main room made him stumble, but Fritz grabbed him up again, shoved him hard down an alley. *"Laufen!"*

Run. But Peter turned, grabbing his arm, tight, wanting to press his fingers right through him. "I have to go back—"

Fritz punched him, a ringing blow that exploded into his head. Peter fell away from him, slammed against a brick wall.

"I dropped the milk." He heard his words and couldn't believe they'd issued from his mouth. Milk?

"I'll bring you more. Tomorrow, before dawn. At the opera house. And bring me more cigarettes." Fritz tossed Peter away.

He ran, the blood sticky between his fingers, plastering his shirt to his chest, the sickly sweet odor raising his gorge.

He found an old fountain, moldy standing water reflecting the wash of moonlight. He broke the reflection, pressing his hands into the dank water, scouring the blood from his hands, his neck. He stripped off his shirt, doused it in the water, over and over, washing until, under a slice of moon, the water sluicing off it seemed clear.

But later, after he'd slunk home, after he'd pulled the sopping shirt off and hung it to dry, the carnage glowed red in the candlelight. Indeed, blood sheened on his skin, creased his pores.

He didn't bother to scrub it away as he lay on his bed and snuffed out the candle.

CHAPTER 19

October 1946

Dear Peter,

One hundred and forty-five letters. I did the math and figured out how many I have written to you over the past fourteen months since that night you left.

I fear they are simply being dumped in some waste bin on the far side of the ocean.

I have other fears too, but they are too terrible to voice. The greatest of these, of course, is that you were swept into the rage of influenza.

In yet another nightmare, you never made it back to Germany but died in a transport ship.

Perhaps you are languishing in a French labor camp, like so many other soldiers I read about of late. It seems the French are not quick to forgive the memory of Hitler marching down the Champs-Élysées and are anxious to repay the marks of their captivity on the backs of the returning POWs. The stories from my fellow Red Cross workers who'd attempted to administer aid to the returning

POWs, of escapees who dragged themselves across swamps and countryside, their bones razors through their skin by the time they reach refugee centers, can turn me inside out in my dormitory bunk.

Yes, I've joined the Red Cross, although for now I am stationed in Milwaukee, awaiting orders. I am living on the third floor of the nurses' residence of the Milwaukee County Hospital, working as a superintendent. We rise at five forty-five and by our seven a.m. shift, I must have my room in order, including dusting. Then we meet at the piano in the library before breakfast for our morning hymn. It's become a moment I cherish, because as I lift my voice with so many other women, I hear yours also. I haven't forgotten the tune I heard from you when I passed by your room after we'd said good-bye during your recuperation. I so often stopped beyond the door, longing to put a name to the music, finally discovering it at the piano in the library. "A Mighty Fortress Our God." The words have since embedded in me.

And though this world, with devils filled,
should threaten to undo us,
we will not fear, for God hath willed
his truth to triumph through us.

I am often threatened to be undone. Waiting for you, missing you with an ache that burns through me, razoring my throat, rends my heart if I let it. Sometimes it's the errant laughter of a patient following me down the hall. Rich like coffee, so that suddenly I must duck into the lavatory and press you away with a prayer for your safety lest the longing for you defeat me.

I wonder sometimes at the power of love, or perhaps the hope of it. For as the postman fails me, day after day, I am coming to believe that the hope of it is what I believe we had. Perhaps not the committed depth of love, but the sweet taste of desire, of belonging, of acceptance. The nourishment of it, so long forgotten, so sweet upon my parched heart, slacked my rabid thirst, and I fear it may have ruined me.

At least for a time.

Perhaps I will always be ruined, for too often I find myself thirsty for those brief moments where you smiled at me. Where, in your eyes, I saw the woman I wanted to be. Where I felt not lost. Even found.

But how long should I wait? I fear the answer, because it drives me back to my nightmares. To counting my letters.

I've met a man, a doctor here. Dr. Casey has asked me to marry him. He's a good man, a surgeon who saw the war and understands the wounded, who has walked in the dark of night of his own mistakes, his own loss. He loves Sadie, also, and can make her a solid home.

He is kind, and I do love him. Don't ask me to compare.

One hundred and forty five letters.

I pray that my nightmares have not crawled from my breast into daylight.

I am trusting in the triumph of the Lord to hold us both.

Yours,

Esther

*****

"What happened to you?"

He stood at his window, his gaze tracing over the scarred cityscape, the sky bloody as the sun surrendered to the claws of the blackened horizon. Across the street, firelight in the alleyways became specters in the encroaching darkness.

Perhaps they'd all become specters.

"We were supposed to meet— Peter?"

He didn't turn, didn't move at Rachel's voice. Just drew in his breath, tightened his jaw against her intrusion.

Although he flinched when her hand cupped his shoulder. A soft, gentle hand.

He closed his eyes. "Go away, Rachel."

The last thing he needed—wanted—right now was kindness. No, he needed something brutal, words that might match the violence inside him that clawed for release.

"No." But she did drop her hand from his shoulder even as she edged up beside him.

"How did you find me?"

"I looked for you when you didn't show up tonight. I found Elise. She told me how to find you."

"You shouldn't be out. It's not safe."

"I don't care about safe. I care about the fact that you're in danger. Someone said that a Russian soldier was killed by a black marketeer. The Russians have a reward out for his capture." She pitched her voice low. "Peter, the word on the street is that you were there. That you...did it." She glanced up at him, and he made the mistake of meeting her eyes ever so briefly. Reddened, glossy—she shook her head, her next words sharp. "I know you didn't."

"I might have." He looked away. On the street below, pack dogs ran into the shadowed alcoves, searching for crumbs. Occasionally one would snarl, snap at its mate. "I should have."

"You don't mean that."

He closed his eyes.

"You were there, though."

There, and again in the early morning, hoping he might unearth the bag of milk. In the dusty light of dawn he found it in the alleyway, dropped, perhaps as Fritz shoved him away from his crimes. He'd delivered it to the hospital, not sure how he returned to the flat, just remembering sitting in the weeds at the edge of their courtyard, tracing his mother's brutal murder in the shadows.

"My mother is dead. Shot in the courtyard of our home." He didn't know exactly where, of course, but he'd finally wandered the weedy, broken yard. He stopped at the wall, pressing his hand to it while the other covered his face. No wonder he couldn't drown the echo of her screams, and now the image of her body, ripped asunder with bullets.

He caught his breath, even now. Opened his eyes.

"I'm sorry. I looked for her—I didn't see her name. Probably that's why."

"She died while I was still training to fight for Hitler. She died as I was betraying myself." His voice emerged distant, almost apart from himself. "She died for nothing."

"Peter—"

"I'm tired, Rachel. I'm tired of faithfulness. I'm tired of being, of doing...of hoping. Of believing that someday God might deliver me. Us." His last words he may not have spoken aloud, just let them sear into him, because she stayed silent as the dogs barked and a baby from a nearby hovel cried.

Finally, her hand slid over his arm. "What happened, Peter?"

He shook his head.

She said nothing, but as she stood there, her clean scent, something of lavender and vanilla, spoke to him of softness. Of a moment where life didn't feel quite so brutal.

So he turned, and losing himself a little, he slid his hand around her neck, bent down, and kissed her.

She had soft, pliable lips, and instead of stiffening under his touch, they opened, kissing him back. She tasted of tea, and a hint of citrus, as if she'd eaten an orange, and he slid his arms around her shoulders and curled her into himself.

Kissing her more. Yes.

He slid his hand to cup her face, to trace her cheekbones with his fingertips, to balance her jaw between his fingers. *Esther.* He kissed her cheekbone, her soft eyelids, that place beneath her beautiful blue eyes, then back to her lips, so willing to give him everything he hungered for.

"Esther."

She stiffened beneath his touch. Pulled away.

He opened his eyes.

Oh.

No. Oh no.

"I mean…Rachel," he said, a lame apology that fell away from them into the sufferings of the night.

She pressed her hand to her cheek, where he'd pressed Esther's kiss. Her eyes glistened even as she forced—it had to be forced by the way it tumbled—a smile. "No, you didn't. You meant Esther."

He looked away, clenched his jaw.

"I'm a stupid girl."

He winced.

"I know you told me, but I thought… I thought you'd still see me."

"I do see you."

"No…not really. You may want to, but…" She touched his chin, turned his face. He cupped her hand in his. "I can see her in your eyes, you know. She's there, a distant flicker of longing. Of hope. She's the reward you're holding out for."

He pulled Rachel's hand from his face, held it a moment before giving it back to her. He couldn't meet her too-kind eyes. "I met her in America. In Wisconsin. She was a nurse, and I had no business falling in love with her. I'm not even sure it was love, now. Maybe just that thing that keeps the embers inside stirring. Maybe she simply believed in me, and that was enough."

He put his hand to his chest, pressing against his sternum.

No. He *had* loved her. Enough to taste the promise, enough to linger and nourish and hold him. Enough to wait.

"I haven't heard from her in more than two years—since I left

Wisconsin. I thought she would write, but… I've been so many places, how would she—"

"Oh! Peter, the International Red Cross catalogues the addresses of refugees, sends letters to the centers located around Germany." Rachel gave him another of those wavering smiles. "I—I found a box when I was searching for your mother." She turned away, toward his bed. His burlap bag of rations lay there. "POW packages and a bundle of letters I discovered with your name."

Letters.

He looked at the bag then to her. She held her hand to her mouth then swallowed, whisking a quick tear from her cheek. Tall and thin and regal, she could have been easy to love. Had he been a different man.

"I'm sorry, Rachel. I never meant to hurt you."

She touched his hand, one feather-light caress. "It's my guess that you would *never* want to hurt someone."

Oh… Well…

Then she pressed her hand to his cheek. "Ana's baby is surviving. Thank you for the milk." She stepped away from him. "I'm leaving in the morning. My replacement is already here. I told her to expect the Nightingale."

He barely felt his breath in his chest.

"Don't stay here, Peter. They'll find you. Come to the hospital. At least there we might be able to hide you."

She waited a moment—probably for his response. When he walked over to the bed and dumped out the burlap sack, he heard her slip away into the night.

* * * * *

February 1947

Dear Peter,

The New Year was met with a band and glorious speeches of endurance and bravery.

Of course, I thought of you.

Sadie turned four and has entered preschool, already learning, thanks to the tutelage of Rosemary, who has become, unexpectedly, a close friend. She has forgiven me, it seems, although I'm sure the presence of her own curly-haired daughter, Agnes, helps in the healing. Nevertheless, Linus has found the father inside him, and with Agnes's birth finally realized how to love his daughter. Sadie cherishes him, and we've both agreed, despite the ache in my breast, that she should attend Roosevelt Grammar.

Meanwhile...I can admit I long for another child, to be living my life like the nurses around me, caught finally in the arms of their beloved. I, like Annie in the musical I saw last weekend, might be able to stand alone, but it doesn't mean I wouldn't want someone beside me, reminding me of your words: God loves you more than you can imagine. Perhaps.

It's because you gave me this tender hope that I discovered how to take the steps toward the woman I am today. I once told you that I was lost. You told me to let God find me. To be found in Him. I've discovered that the finding is not to find myself—but to find Him. To discover, step by step, His grace, His forgiveness, His courage, His strength, His hope, His love, His peace, and finally His joy.

I have truly found myself...in Him. And finally can look in the mirror and see a woman I want to know.

It's because I am no longer lost, no longer thirsty that I am drawn to Dr. Casey's proposal of marriage. I have grown quite fond of him, and while his brilliance at surgery draws me, it is his kindness, the way he wraps me in his coat while we are catching a cab from the theater, or perhaps the way he addresses me as Nurse Lange, a flavor of respect in his voice that tells me that I will never want for compassion.

And, when I stand at the window, watching the wind as it stiffens the hedgerow outside the residence hall overlooking the hospital, the room I share with Maude Fisher, sterile despite the picture of Gary Cooper she has pasted to her wall, I know the truth.

You are not coming back to me. Either by will or by fate, our moment has passed, and while it nourished me, I cannot hold on to the hope that you will disembark on one of the troop trains, that I might find myself in your arms.

However, I do know our love was not a lie.

It lies in my pocket like a star, a treasure forever in my clasp.

Esther

Peter smoothed his hand over the letter, the indentations in the paper like creases in his palm. Six months ago she'd penned this. Six months…

He'd still been slogging his way home through Holland, then Germany, hitching rides on transports, counting the pinpricks in the sky.

Six months.

He closed the letter. His hand shook as he fought it back into the envelope. Then he brought the flap to his lips and ran it over his skin, a whisper against time.

His throat tightened as he gathered the letters together, stacked them into a pile. They made for a thick wad that he could barely grip in one hand.

He stood there then, scanning the room. His dirty bedroll, the tin pot that held his fire, the bag of hospital supplies, the box of food from desperate patients. The CARE packages.

May your God whom you serve continually deliver you.

He picked up his medical bag, dumped the contents out onto the bed. Then he opened the CARE package, took out the candy, the coffee, the corned beef, and the chocolate. He shoved these into his bag, on top of the letters.

Then he folded the bag under his arm, grabbed the other over his shoulder, and slipped out into the night, leaving the door ajar.

He didn't even bother to hide himself as he made his way to the grocery, didn't care that he passed at least three Russian patrols. Perhaps he'd already vanished—he'd certainly lost hold of himself, of even knowing how to describe the terrible whooshing in his chest.

He managed to steal his way to Elise's shabby quarters, dropping the remains of the CARE package into the room. He said nothing to

Ana as she lay in the bed, cast his gaze briefly over the baby kicking in a cotton blanket next to her.

She roused just as he left. He didn't look back even as she left her question in the darkness.

The hospital lay under guard—two brown uniforms, the scrubby faces of boys smoking cigarettes, their laughter, their language curdling the night.

He watched them, too long perhaps, but let himself linger in memory inside the corridors of the hospital, smell the sting of rubbing alcohol, the brisk iodine, hearing his father's voice resonate from his office, seeing his white coat, tasting the thick, deep satisfaction of saving a life.

Then, as the night turned thin, Peter fed himself into the shadows of the city.

The Elbe had turned to silver in the moonlight, and he found a spot beneath the bridge, enclosed in shadow. On the beach the spiny branches of a linden tree waved, as if beckoning him near. The wind shivered off the browning leaves, dropped them, glistening like monocles upon the water.

He stayed in the muddy shoreline, under the canopy of the Carolabrücke. It reeked of fish and the foulness of humanity, as if not too long ago it sheltered bodies.

Tonight it hid only Peter as he drew out the letters.

One by one, he dropped them into the river. Square airmail leaves, like the linden tree, littering the water. The moon turned them to stars as they floated away.

He stayed there, the wind lifting his collar, the breeze carrying the lick of the coming winter, until the darkness devoured the last of them. Then, leaving his bag behind, he crept out of the alcove and back to the boulevard.

It didn't take much effort to find a patrol. He gave them no fight as they wrestled him to the ground, pressed the cold muzzle of one of their Kalashnikovs to his ear.

"I know who killed your soldier," he said in German. Then in English, just in case. He tried Russian, the little he knew. "Ya zniaio...." I know...I *know.*

A thicker man, built like the Kremlin, pulled him from the dirt, shoved him against a building. "What do you know?"

German. Spittle edged the soldier's mouth, vodka washing into Peter's face—yes, he'd found the right patrol.

"I know who killed your countryman. That soldier—by the black marketeer. I know where you can find him."

He took a breath, let the rage nourish him. "But only if I get the reward."

CHAPTER 20

Peter always loved watching the night separate from the day. How the sun dented the darkness, piercing it, its rays bleeding color into the sky. How, as the sun rose, it carved out the horizon with fire, toppling night from its moorings until finally the light burned it away, leaving only the bruised sky to heal in the morning.

Peter often rose early when he lived in Iowa to watch the sunrise turn the cornfields to torchlight, and even in Wisconsin, lifting his face to the heat, letting it slide over him like a warm hand upon cool skin.

He waited for it today, huddled in the well of the bridge where he'd cast away Esther's letters, where he'd slunk back after his Russian interrogators tired of him. One eye pulsed, thickened by the Russian soldier's fist. He wiped a hand across his mouth. It burned, taking off a fresh scab.

At least nothing felt broken. Except, well…

He hadn't slept, not really, the images behind his eyes causing him to gasp, to open them in a sort of horror, to hear again his words.

You'll find him at the opera house. Early.

When they'd released him, he'd run the opposite direction. Because what kind of man betrayed his countryman?

Or his honor? He probably deserved to escape with only his life. Peter ran back to his barter bag he'd hidden, only—for what? He'd held on to the dream of passage back to America so long in the dead of night, he'd simply turned toward it out of habit.

But, really, what did he have waiting for him?

He watched the water, his reflection dark, warped.

He didn't recognize it either.

God loves you more than you can imagine.

He closed his eyes against the words, hating how they found him. Hating how, even now, he leaned into her memory, drew nourishment from it.

I know our love was not a lie.

No. He leaned his head back against the gritty, cold cement. No.

But she'd been wrong about the rest. *You are not coming back to me. Either by will or by fate, our moment has passed, and while it nourished me, I cannot hold on to the hope that you will return for me.*

He would have returned.

He touched his forehead to his knees, clasped them hard, and let the truth wring him out.

God didn't deliver. No matter his faithfulness, no matter his sacrifice. God didn't deliver.

The thought chilled him through and made him cup his hands over his eyes.

I'm lost, Peter. I'm lost.

He understood it then. Understood her expression, the unthreaded fabric of her voice.

Understood losing himself, the person that he'd always thought he'd been.

I'm lost, Esther. I'm lost.

O God, don't leave me alone in my disbelief.

He shuddered out the prayer, not even bothering to lift it to heaven. Because how could God hear the prayer of a traitor?

He got up, slung the bag over his shoulder. Crawled out from under the bridge. The sun had begun to touch the city, women already out, moving rubble for ten cents a day, or hamsters—young men scurrying to find transport out of the city to scavenge for food.

He made his way, almost by instinct, to the square of the Frauenkirche. Like a dog to his bone, maybe, searching for comfort. But his head spun from the halfhearted beating of his interrogators, and the tugging of a voice, deep inside…

"God called us back to Germany for a reason, Peter. Who knows but it was for this very season that we are here—"

His father's voice churned through him, scrubbing away the darkness, clearing his thoughts.

"To act justly and love mercy and be servants of God. This is our hope in a world gone mad. How could I live with myself if I didn't help?"

Yes, his father had been a nightingale.

The sun stumbled over the rubble of the Frauenkirche, turning every boulder into bullion. Only the altar and the chancel remained.

And though this world, with devils filled,
should threaten to undo us,
we will not fear, for God hath willed
his truth to triumph through us.

Her voice, light, soft, bled through him and vanished in the wind, captured in the voice of two schoolgirls standing behind him. "You okay, mister?"

No. Probably never.

He nodded to the girls, shooed them away. They backed up, their eyes reflecting a man he didn't know.

Pigeons cooed over the square, oblivious of the rubble, and the scent of a wood fire, something cooking, seasoned the air. How long might it take to rebuild such a fortress, such a magnificence as the Frauenkirche?

Or, maybe next time it might be built stronger, with bricks that might withstand the heat.

What if God stripped him of everything so that He might rebuild him, one day at time, one forged brick at a time…in Him?

I once told you that I was lost. You told me to let God find me. To be found in Him.

Maybe that was the key. Maybe a man had to lose himself, his pride, his honor, his strength in order to discover himself…in God. Maybe he'd just been serving God because…well, God delivered those who served Him, right?

No.

But what if God delivered, not because of duty fulfilled, but rather…grace.

I've discovered that the finding is not to find myself…but to find Him. To discover, step by step, His grace, His forgiveness, His strength, His hope, His love, His peace, and finally His joy.

Maybe he had lost himself, but he hadn't lost God.

Hold on.

Not to Esther. But to the One who gave him the love he saw reflected in her eyes. Maybe she was right—their love might not have been enough to build a life, but rather only to sustain with the sweet taste of desire, of belonging, of acceptance.

No. For him, it would have been enough.

Hold on.

He closed his eyes to the words, let them find the brittle tendons of his faith.

Hold on to grace.

Hold on to forgiveness.

O God, what have I done? The words shuddered through him as the cobblestone bit into his knees. What had he done?

It didn't matter that Fritz had committed crimes. He'd turned Fritz in not out of justice—but revenge. Peter's hands scraped the cobblestones as he found his feet, and he took off down *Augustusbrücke*, the streets so cluttered he had to wind his way through the narrow alleys that had made Dresden the perfect target for Allied bombing.

Around him, the city had come to life, of sorts. Women cleared the debris from the street brick by brick into green-gray wagons provided by the army. Dust churned into the air, the stew of oil and gasoline as Russian Kamaz trucks belched across the morning.

Russian soldiers, some directing traffic, others drinking coffee, eyed him as he tightened his coat around himself.

Most of the shops lay empty, although a few opened, with sallow-faced children standing in line, their ration cards in their grimy hands. A woman, well-painted, flirted with a cadre of soldiers seated in the shadow of a café, laughing as they drank tea. She glanced up at Peter, wear in the lines around her eyes, her body too thin for the comfort she peddled.

He looked away, cut down *Terrassenufer,* wanting to run, willing himself to steps that wouldn't alert. In the building overlooking the river, where the sun poured into the open faces of former dwellings, he saw women hoeing potatoes from dirt piled upon kitchen floors, the grim cultivation of desperation. Or perhaps innovation.

A soldier—the thin strap of his Kalashnikov cutting into his shoulder—eyed him as he sat on the back end of his Kamaz. Peter ducked into an alleyway, threading his way through the city.

Faster now in the shadows until he emerged on the Theaterplatz.

Only the statues of Goethe and Schiller remained to sentry the former grandeur of the home of Bach and Wagner, the Semper Opera House. The haunting strains of Richard Strauss's *Salome* echoed over the three stories of wreckage, former Corinthian columns, Baroque statues, Renaissance domes, and aediculae now spilling out across the blackened stones of the Theaterplatz.

Again, God had pushed His thumb against the pride of Dresden.

Women strolled by, one pushing a pram filled with rubble.

He stood at the edge, the wind sharp off the Elbe, lifting his collar as he rehearsed images in his head.

Fritz, beaten to death, pulpy and broken in some neighboring hovel.

Fritz, fighting back, his knife serrating another soldier's throat.

Fritz, cursing his name, sending the troops to the hospital in search…

Rachel. No, Fritz wouldn't know her, right? But that might not matter. The Russians bore no regard for nationality. For Geneva rules.

They might simply run every nurse onto the street. And then what?

He ducked back into the alleyway, his breath corroded with the refuse piled and rotting among the debris. The tinny smell of blood and—

"Peter."

He stilled at his name dragged over gravel, as if forced out on snaggle-toothed breath. "Peter?"

He turned, searched, saw nothing but rubbish—a broken chair, the curious form of a chandelier still intact on a pile.

"Over here. Please."

Yes. There. Under the cover of a splintered divan, a hand stretched out, its bloodied print on the orange upholstery.

He moved the sofa, and his breath splintered out of him.

Fritz. The man lay broken amidst the rubble, russet blood sopping his shirt, his face pasty as he stared up at Peter.

"You're late," he said, his voice so thin Peter had to hold his breath to hear it. He crouched next to him. "I must have run into a patrol—I..." His jaw tightened, his eyes waxy as he squeezed out a groan. "They shot me." He lifted his hand to reveal a thumb-size hole ripped through his gut. Peter pulled away his shirt, grimaced at the damage.

At best, he'd lacerated his liver.

Peter's expression must have betrayed him because Fritz released a harsh, bitter chuckle that sounded more like a cough. "Yeah. That's what I thought. I guess this is what I get, huh?"

"You need surgery. I need to get you to the hospital."

"Yeah. Sure. Like you're going to save my life."

Be found in grace.

"I might."

"Why would you do that for me, Doc?"

Be found in forgiveness.

He pressed his hand to Fritz's forehead. Cool, slick. Like the man might be going into shock.

"We're going to need a wheelbarrow or something. I'll be right back."

He edged back to the alleyway entrance. There—the woman with the pram. Perhaps—

Up close, she might have been twenty and, once upon a time, lovely, with her regal cheekbones, dark sable hair. Round hazel eyes. They looked at him with a fear, however, that reeled inside, unhinged him. "I won't hurt you. I just need your pram."

She narrowed her eyes. "I need it."

"I'll bring it back."

"And what will you give me for a day's work lost?"

What would he pay—wait. "Chocolate? Coffee? Canned beef?"

Her mouth opened. She glanced at the soldiers now lounging in the sun. "You'll return it?"

"By this evening. Right here."

She got up, nodded.

He strolled back to the alleyway, waited for her to follow.

They made the exchange as she dumped out the rubble from the carriage. She tucked the bag into her coat, buttoning it against what looked like a pregnancy bulge.

"Thank you."

"Don't lie to me, sir." Her eyes searched his and he couldn't help but reach out, touch her cheek.

"I'm a doctor. I promise, I'll keep my word."

He received a ghost of a smile, and for a pause, she leaned into his hand.

He left it there until she slipped away, cradling her bundle.

Then, moving the divan, he hoisted Fritz into the pram. "Try to keep your mouth shut," he said, checking the wound again then positioning Fritz's hand over it. "I'd like to stay alive."

Be found in courage.

"God, we could really use Your deliverance right now."

Fritz's eyes flickered over him, stayed one long moment before closing, his jaw tight for the journey.

* * * * *

"How did you get in here?" Nurse Glennis, her red hair in a snood, cut away Fritz's shirt, dropping the sodden cloth into a tray. She'd known

Peter immediately, helped him wheel Fritz down the corridor and into an exam room. Now, with the blinds closed, the smells of antiseptic righting him back to himself, a stethoscope around his neck, he let his heartbeat slow, paced out his examination.

He palpated Fritz's abdomen. A general rigidness, which probably meant internal bleeding. Fritz didn't have long if Peter didn't get inside him, close off the bleeders, repair his liver.

Even then, probably not, thanks to the staph infections rampant in the hospital.

"I came in the ambulance entrance, in the back."

"Is that where you got the jacket too?" She indicated the white lab coat, the one he'd buttoned over his bloody clothes. Unfortunately, the blood seeped through, staining it. He snapped on gloves, began to probe the injury.

Fritz had passed out halfway to the hospital, which had made the journey that much easier.

"He's lost a lot of blood. We'll need a transfusion before we can operate. And in the meantime, we'll need to pack his wound."

"You're not going to operate, are you?"

He looked up at her. She seemed younger than Rachel, with a round face, freckles. "Where's Rachel?"

"She left this morning."

"And the doctor on call?"

"He's here, in the hospital. I can find him—but you need to go. Now, before they find you." She had hazel eyes, flecked with green, and knew too much.

"I didn't kill that Russian."

"Of course not. But we have to report a gunshot wound." She raised an eyebrow. "It's going to look like you were involved. You need to leave." She handed him hot, moist gauze, and he used it to pack Fritz's wound as she inserted the IV line for the transfusion.

Fritz's waxy color suggested he might be too late. Peter shoved a rolled towel under his legs, bending them to lessen the pressure on his abdomen.

"We don't have time to track down the doctor. I need to get in there and see what the damage is, try and stop the bleeding."

She checked the blood flow then glanced at him. "You might be right, but we have a new nurse in charge. She's not going to let you operate. I know you're a doctor, Nightingale—the entire nursing staff does, but we've had Russians patrolling our halls all night, looking for you."

"Why me?"

"They interrogated Elise. She told them about you, about the milk—and there were others." She took Fritz's pulse, not looking at him. "People are hungry. You can't blame them."

No, maybe not.

Be found in strength.

"Listen, Glennis. I'm going to roll him down the corridor and into the surgical theater. And you're going to carry the IV. And should the Russians see us… Well, I'll put myself in God's hands."

"I hope that's enough." She opened the door, glanced out into the hall, then nodded and returned for the IV bag. He wheeled Fritz out.

This early in the morning, patients overflowing into the corridors slept on cots, on gurneys. A woman in a grimy housecoat cradled a child, a graying bandage encasing his hand. The wheels rattled as Peter pushed Fritz over rivulets in the marble. Fritz jerked, groaning.

They passed the nurses' station, and he didn't look up to meet eyes with the new duty nurse. Hopefully she'd believe he was a doctor—an American doctor.

He let himself breathe when he saw the station was empty.

Glennis opened the double doors into the surgery theater. Flicked on the overhead lights. They bathed the table, the ceramic basins, the saline solutions, the scrub sinks. "We'll need help. A scrub nurse and an anesthetist—"

"Stay here. Prep the catgut, drape him, and prepare the tray. I'll scrub in." Yes, he needed an anesthetist….

"Doctor—"

Shouting at the end of the hall made him grab up a mask, press it to his face. Glennis's eyes widened as the doors slammed open.

"Shto eta znachet?"

Peter didn't need the translation to understand; what's going on in here? The tone of the solider—ruddy-faced, dark hair, yes, he recognized him as one of the guards standing sentry this morning, his beefy hand on the door, the other on the butt of a revolver at his belt.

Peter's gaze flicked back to Glennis. She placed a hand on Fritz's leg.

He spoke in English. "What you are doing here, in my theater?"

The soldier left the door ajar, pressed into the room, right up to Glennis. Peter wanted to embrace her when she stood her ground.

The Russian pressed two fingers into her sternum, and she winced as she stepped back.

He pulled the sheet away from Fritz, considered his wound.

Lifted his gun from his holster and pressed it to Fritz's head.

"Stop! Perestan!" Oh…what… "Please. Don't. *Nyet*!" Peter slapped the soldier's arm, the shot detonating onto the stone floor, spearing the silence, reverberating down the hall.

Glennis screamed.

The Russian turned on Peter, yanking his mask from his grip.

A smile pressed up his face, probably at the beating betrayed on Peter's. Or perhaps the guilt.

Peter swallowed.

The soldier raised the gun, grabbing Peter up by the collar. He pressed the gun to Peter's temple. Peter closed his eyes.

Be found in hope.

"Don't. Please." The voice, small as it was, slid right over him, inside him, catching his breath. Two footsteps into the room. He held still, opened his eyes.

"We need all the doctors we can get. And I know you don't want to kill an American."

"Nyet *Americanitz.*"

"Yes, yes, he is. American doctor." The nurse came over to Peter, stepped in front of him, faced the soldier. "Yes, he's one of ours."

The soldier's gaze could have burned right through her into Peter, but she stood there while the man narrowed his eyes. Then, even as Peter's heart bled through his ribs, the soldier pointed his gun at Fritz.

The shot shook Peter clear through, his knees buckling.

The nurse turned, held him up as the Russian left.

Glennis stood in the corner, her hands pressed to her mouth, shaking. "Oh…oh…oh…"

"Shh. It'll be okay. I promise. It'll be okay." The duty nurse crossed over to her, pulled her to herself, held her. Then she looked at Peter.

Blue eyes, sweet and kind, just as he'd remembered, and that pretty, cherry-red half smile that could put the stars into his world.

Esther.

CHAPTER 21

Dear Peter,

Did I ever tell you about the night I met you? No, not at the camp, or even later, when you appeared at the hospital, but that night I returned home to find your letter.

I'd just finished patching up a soldier—you remember him, Charlie. He flung himself from the top floor of the hospital and lay in a coma the night of the fire. You dragged him to safety.

Of course you remember him.

And, you might be heartened to know that Charlie found his way back to us.

But you need to know our conversation that night, between Charlie and me. As he stood on the roof, contemplating his ability and need to fly, to end his anguish with life, he said to me, "I can't live like this. I ain't got nobody."

His words stung me because I terribly understood. I had no one.

Then out of my mouth came these words.

"I do know that we all gotta believe that there's something bigger ahead of us. Something better. That God isn't laughing at the way our lives turned out. Maybe He's even crying."

You walked into my life that night.

And I believe that God smiled.

I cannot return to the woman I was before you. I'd rather hold on to the hope of something brilliant than reach for something that will never shine. And Dr. Casey knows this too. Compassion, and even pity, does not a marriage make.

No, it must be built on the amazing gift God delivers to us through each other.

I realized that I cannot be in his arms and think of you. It's not fair to him. Or you. Or even me.

I am blessed to be a woman who has the peace to say no, to thirst no more.

You may never be in my arms. But it is enough that you were in my life.

Esther

Esther finished speaking, not looking up from the letter. Behind them dusk fell over the city, the blackening Frauenkirche, the Opera House, the steel bones of the city. As if God had taken the sky and pinched it, spilling blood, crimson spilled out across the sky, the cumulus bruised. But behind it, into the waste of the night, stars tumbled like debris, diamonds for the gleaners.

She could still take his breath clean from his chest. If anything, she'd only turned more beautiful, the gentle curve of her smile, those eyes that flicked up now at him, the curl of her hair. She had a way of sighing that could undo him, and she wielded it now as she tucked the note into her apron.

"I never sent it."

"Why not?"

She glanced up. "Maybe the letter was more for me than you."

"No. Believe me, it was for me." Oh, he wanted her in his arms. But since she'd taken Glennis away from the carnage, ordered him to wash, to shave, to hide himself in the call room, she hadn't returned.

For most of the day, he'd considered her an apparition.

Until she appeared in the doorway, gestured for him to follow.

He would have followed her anyway, she should know that. Or—

"You never wrote to me. I—I thought you might have died."

"I got your letters yesterday." Yesterday. Had it really only been last night that he'd littered them, one by one, into the Elbe?

"Yesterday." She said the word as if testing it. "Yesterday."

"Yes. Rachel found them. At the Red Cross center. I would have written, I—"

"Yesterday."

He lifted a shoulder.

She ran her fingers under her eyes. "So—if you'd gotten them sooner—"

"I would have written. I would have told you that—that I—" He closed his eyes. "Nothing's changed for me, Esther. I still love you, probably more, although I know that's not reasonable. I think—well, maybe one can fall in love with the hope of love, and that might be enough."

"It's reasonable." She pressed her fingers to her mouth, looked over at him with eyes that he couldn't bear. "I came here...because I'm a foolish girl. Because although I no longer thirsted, I did hope. I…" Her voice broke, turned high, soft. "Hoped that you missed me."

"I missed you. I promise I missed you."

Her mouth curved then, sliding through him, over the raw places, healing. His mouth dried with the power of it.

Be found in love.

"Esther—" But she was already in his embrace. Already curling her arms under his, around his shoulders, pulling herself close.

Already lifting her face to his.

Already kissing him.

Oh, she tasted like…like she belonged to him. Sweet, and rich, and surrendering to his touch in a way that made him want to weep.

But he didn't. He held on, kissed her back. Molded her body to his.

His.

Be found in peace.

When he pulled away, he simply held her, smelling the lavender of her hair, feeling her curves settled against him, her soft sigh as the sky winked over them.

"The stars here are the same as home." She leaned back, and he brushed his lips on her cheekbone.

"What stars?" he murmured.

She giggled, healing him through as he kissed her again, softly, sweetly.

Be found in joy.

AUTHOR'S NOTE

Did you know that, in 1945, Wisconsin and Minnesota hosted German POWs in over 140 POW camps throughout the state? In fact, America held over 200,000 German POWs from 1942-1946. What's most interesting is that these POWs worked on farms and in canneries throughout Wisconsin, Minnesota, and other states, right next to first-generation German immigrants who, ten years earlier, might have been their neighbors. Indeed, some of the German immigrants had family fighting for Germany, and relatives in the very POW camps nearby. I read a newspaper account about a woman who was moved because she heard hymn, sung in German (her native language) coming from inside the camp, which was housed just across the street from her home. It made me realize that beneath the stamp of enemy just might be a fellow Christian, pressed into serving their country. An even bigger theme in Nightingale was, just because someone made a mistake once, did he or she deserve to be imprisoned inside that mistake forever? I applied this theme broadly to both Peter and Esther. Esther might be healer, but she's trapped inside her sins, unable to see God's grace setting her free. And I wanted Peter to see that his service in the war might be to fight the demons that held her captive. His story is a Daniel story, of sorts--a prisoner sent into a forgiven land to do good and hold onto faith. Esther's story is that of the woman caught in sin—and set free to sin no more. Both of them have to surrender themselves into God's hands, to let Him set them free and mold them into who He wants them to be.

If you have made a mistake, don't let it mold your life. Let God set you free with His grace, His forgiveness, and discover who you are when you let God take over. Be found in Him.

Thank you for reading Esther and Peter's story.
In His Grace,
Susan May Warren

Soul-stirring romance...set against a historical backdrop readers will love!

Summerside Press™ is pleased to present our fresh new line of historical romance fiction—including stories set amid the action-packed eras of the twentieth century.

Watch for a number of new Summerside Press™ historical romance titles to release in 2011.

Now Available in Stores

Sons of Thunder
by Susan May Warren
ISBN 978-1-935416-67-8

The Crimson Cipher
by Susan Page Davis
ISBN 978-1-60936-012-2

Songbird Under a German Moon
by Tricia Goyer
ISBN 978-1-935416-68-5

Stars in the Night
by Cara Putman
ISBN 978-1-60936-011-5

The Silent Order
by Melanie Dobson
ISBN 978-1-60936-019-1

Coming Soon

Exciting New Historical Romance Stories by These Great Authors—

Margaret Daley...DiAnn Mills...Lisa Harris...and MORE!

ZION DIARIES

BODIE & BROCK THOENE

Explore the romance, passion, and danger experienced by those who lived through Adolf Hitler's rise to power and the Second World War.

NOW AVAILABLE

THE GATHERING STORM

A desperate escape.
A love ignited.
An ancient secret revealed.

As Nazi forces tighten the noose, Loralei Kepler's harrowing flight from Germany leads her toward a mysterious figure who closely guards an age-old secret.

COMING SOON

AGAINST THE WIND

A perilous journey.
A race against time.
A dawning hope.

Famous violinist Elisa Lindheim Murphy faces the greatest trial of her life on seas made treacherous by Nazi U-boats as she and Jewish refugee children seek asylum.

THEIR FINEST HOUR

A fiery struggle.
A fervent pledge.
A heroic last stand.

While the clashes in the skies over Britain increase in ferocity, American flying ace David Meyer also battles for the heart of the feisty Annie Galway.